NATIVE

A Novel

by

E. Compton Lee

BLUE FORTUNE ENTERPRISES LLC

Lavender Press
an imprint of Blue Fortune Enterprises, LLC

For information contact :
Blue Fortune Enterprises, LLC
Lavender Press
P.O. Box 554
Yorktown, VA 23690
http://blue-fortune.com

Cover design by BFELLC

ISBN: 978-1-961548-21-3
Second edition: March 2025

Other Titles by E. Compton Lee:

The Native Trilogy:
Native
My Name is Sloan
2026

The Heartbreak of Josie Whitt

CHAPTER ONE

Allegheny Mountains
Coleton, Pennsylvania

ANNIE
Summer 2002

We were just girls when Clare and I first met, and until I moved to California hardly a day passed that we didn't see each other. By all rights we shouldn't have been friends. Town girls never spoke to kids from the Holler. We were teenagers before seeing her outside the classroom and then only at dances. At first she came alone, wearing gaudy dresses out of thrift shops or Walmart, and her hair hung down her back in snarls. She stayed on her feet all night, asking boys to dance, and when she wasn't dancing, she stood in a corner and glared at the crowd, drinking a Coke we were sure was spiked. Rumor had it that she ended up in the back seat of a car on every date. Even Ronnie Black, the football star, brought her to a dance once. He held her hand in the crook of his arm and walked into the gym, smiling defiantly at anyone who looked his way. And we all did, of course. But we never spoke to Clare. Or at least I didn't until the year I turned fourteen.

It was a summer as hot as this one was turning out to be, only that year the rains came. Nearly every afternoon, clouds, low and heavy, moved in and the rain lashed down, pelted the ground for a furious fifteen minutes before the sun came back out and the world steamed with swampy heat.

No surprise we discovered Crab's Eddy. Cat Creek flowed down the hills and through the Holler, eddied and widened, forming a swimming hole next to the Norwood farm. The teenagers from Coleton spent afternoons there. It was the gathering place—unless you were a Raymond or a Blanchard or anyone else from the Holler. They might live next to the creek but some unwritten rule kept them away while we were there. Except once. Three boys with dark hair and eyes stepped out of the woods and stood at the water's edge. Caught by surprise, our group stopped its chatter long enough to take in their rangy bodies and uncertain stillness. We turned our heads and refused to look at them. Even so, we knew the instant they gave it up and slipped back into the trees. One of the bolder girls licked her lips and sighed. "I heard none of those boys are virgins past the age of twelve."

"Like a little of that, would you, Shawna?" said Ronnie Black, moving his hand closer to her leg. She stared at him hard and said, "Piss off."

Piss off? No one told Ronnie Black to piss off. Not Ronnie Black, the football star with the blond hair and blue eyes. Yet he seemed neither surprised nor angered by Shawna's behavior. He reached out and took hold of her ankle. She jerked her foot away, grabbed her towel, jumped on her bike and pedaled off, her tires spinning dirt and rocks while we watched in stunned silence.

"What the hell did you do to her?"

Ronnie rolled over on his stomach. "Beats the hell out of me."

At fourteen, I was one of the youngest. Unlike Shawna, I was what grown-ups politely referred to as a late bloomer. I didn't fit in with this crowd of sixteen-and-seventeen-year-olds, yet nothing would have kept me away. Spending the summer in the house alone with Mom was unthinkable and inviting friends over was a risk. But there were always kids at the eddy, stretched out on towels, a boom box playing. You didn't have to wonder or wait for a phone call; you could count on company, lots of it. I rode my bike along the twisting nine miles to it every afternoon, the sun beating on my back.

Until one afternoon when I swung my bicycle off the macadam road onto the grass path leading through the trees and there were no voices floating toward me. No deep male laughter, no giggles from the girls, no boom box, nothing. I hopped off my bike and went in on foot. It was hot as ever and sweat rolled off the small of my back into my jeans and bikini bottom. I came into the clearing and there were three boys standing to their waists in the eddy. No girls. Just three boys: Donnie Lepley, Jim Starkey, and Ronnie Black. All football players, all good looking. I thought about leaving, but they'd seen me so instead, I shook my towel onto the beach and settled on it, poised and tense as a rabbit. I slipped off my jeans and busied myself with sun tan lotion. As I rubbed, the boys came to the edge of the bank, pushing through the water with their strides. I found it hard to keep my eyes from the muscled legs, the hair that clung wet and soft along their thighs. I lowered my eyes and concentrated on the lotion.

Ronnie Black shook his towel and stretched out beside me so close I could feel the air stir when he moved.

"Let me do that," he said.

"Do what?"

"I'll put some lotion on your back."

"No, that's okay."

Ronnie laughed. "What are you afraid of?"

"Nothing."

"Yes, you are." Donnie and Jim splashed out of the water and stood dripping in front of us. Donnie shook himself, flicked the cool water on me. They settled onto their sides, didn't even bother with towels. Next to me, Jim propped his head in his hand, and I could see the indentations the rocks made on his arm. Ronnie put his foot against his chest and shoved. "I was here first."

Jim grabbed his foot and twisted. "Pecker head," he said, but it was without feeling. The three boys stretched out on their backs, their hands behind their heads, staring at the sky. I rolled onto my stomach and laid my head on my folded arms, pretending to concentrate on my tan. I could feel the bottom of my bathing suit where it crept up on the left side, Ronnie's side. I held still, willing myself not to reach back and pull it into place and draw attention to that part of me.

It was Ronnie who suggested the walk into the Holler. We'd never been, of course. It was an impossible idea; no one from town ever went there. Yet as soon as the words were spoken, I knew we would go, that we had to go, to have stayed at the eddy then would have meant defeat.

I soon regretted not changing into my jeans. The under growth was thick, scratched my legs and sawed at my ankles. As we continued walking, a car with the grass growing up through the floor appeared in front of a trailer. In another patch there was a truck with the windows shot out and in another two buses faced the road. The houses became closer together and were smaller; sometimes no more than a box covered with tarpaper and a stovepipe coming out of the roof. Suddenly cars and trucks lined both sides of the road, bumper to bumper. Many had weeds growing out the windows. There were no yards now. Bedsprings, bed frames, molding, blown furniture, sinks, cans, broken bicycles, rusted out wash tubs, toilets, car parts; anything that might one day be needed and could be stolen and brought here filled every available space. Wild, resilient brush, high as my shoulder, grew between the cracks. Here the homes slid into the ground on one side and had become shapeless, their endings and the beginnings of tacked-on vans and wrecked buses indistinct. Worn paths to the doors and smoke rising slowly from the stovepipes, even in this heat, made it clear that people lived here. Ragged curtains flapped at a few windows and hopeless, bony dogs stood watching us, their chains ending who knew where. All the doors and windows were locked. To her surprise, the only smell Annie could detect was the acrid odor of smoke.

On one of the porches, someone rocked in a chair. His skin and clothes, the same washed-out gray as the building, receded into the shadows. Next to the house, heavy carcasses hung in the trees. We gazed at the blue marbled meat hanging rock still. Jim touched my arm, and without speaking, we all turned and went back down the road.

"What was that?" he whispered, when we were out of sight of the house.

"Venison," said Donnie.

"Are you sure that was deer meat?" said Jim. "It looked awfully big to be deer. More like beef to me."

"Could be beef," said Donnie.

"I didn't know people in the Holler raised beef."

"They don't. But some of the farmers in the valley do."

"And they buy it and butcher it themselves?"

"Well, they butcher it. But I wouldn't say they bother buying it."

We walked in silence for a while. Even Ronnie Black didn't know what to say until he pointed to the rise of Cat Mountain. "If we hike up there, we might be able to look down and see the whole Holler." As we climbed, I thought about those dark-haired boys that had emerged at the edge of the eddy. Did they have beds? Running water? Did they stay warm in the winter? I tried to picture their mothers preparing food, what the kitchens looked like, and couldn't. I wanted to peer in the windows and watch those who would steal other people's cows and butcher and eat them go about their daily lives. There was no pity to my curiosity. People who lived like this were capable of anything.

As we headed up the mountain, we entered another woods. The going was rocky and steep, and as we climbed, the trees became bigger and the air cooled. The climb made my legs ache. I toyed with the idea of going back but thought of the old man on the porch and the hanging, still meat.

Ronnie looked at me and said, "Just a little farther, Annie."

I steadied my breathing and leaned into the mountain to gain purchase. Grabbing onto low limbs, I pulled myself along. We climbed another half mile.

"There," said Ronnie. He pointed to an overhang made by a huge rock. Under it the ground was level and thick with leaves blown in from last fall. It was much darker even than the surrounding woods and the air was damp from the wet floor. I rested on one foot then the other, glad not to be climbing. I rubbed my arms against the chill.

"Look at that sky," said Ronnie. "We'd better stay here until after the rain." He watched me as he said this. Jim and Donnie hunkered down.

"I don't think it's going to rain," I said, even though heavy clouds were moving right into the mountain.

"Sure it is," Ronnie said. He sat down next to where I stood. "Have a seat,

Annie." He patted the ground at my feet.

"The ground is wet."

Ronnie took my wrist. "Sit here." He tugged me with a jerk onto his lap. The warmth of his skin and arms around me was suddenly, strangely comforting. Nonetheless, I pushed away, plopped onto the ground. He looked amused.

"Boy, the ground is damp," he said. "My suit is getting wet. Maybe I'll just take it off."

Three sets of eyes swung towards him yet Ronnie looked only at me. "You've got goose bumps," he said. He put his hand on my shoulder. "You're shivering." Very deliberately, he pulled down the strap of my bikini top.

I tugged it from his grasp. "Quit it!" I said. I started to rise, but Ronnie took hold of the bikini bottom, and I dropped onto the ground again.

"Cut it out," said Donnie.

"It's okay," answered Ronnie, and before I could move, before I even knew his intention, he took my hand and shoved it inside his suit.

"You like that?" With the deftness of the natural athlete, he grabbed the front of my bathing suit and yanked it down. The air against my bare skin made my nipples hard.

The other two boys' faces went rigid. I looked at them, one and then the other. I looked as long as it took to see which way my future lay and when their eyes dropped from mine, I knew.

I struggled to my feet. But I was too slow, hampered as I was by the straps of my suit. Ronnie only had to reach up, to grab the seat of my pants. We were poised this way when Clare, on a painted pony, rode into the little clearing.

"What's going on?" she said, all innocence.

"Grab her."

Jim reached for the pony's bridle.

Ronnie jumped up, abandoning me and lunging at Clare. He grabbed her wrist and ankle, meaning to pull her from the horse. Her face never lost its bland, curious expression, only her eyes deepened as, quick and supple as a snake, she leaned over and bit his hand. She must have bit him hard for he bellowed like a bull, let go of her instantly. When he leapt back, blood bubbled along his fingers. Clare reached toward me. I had managed to get my bits of bathing suit back in place. I grabbed onto her hand and she pulled me behind her. Jim still held the bridle. Clare flicked the reins, a polite reminder. Obedient, he let go.

I was shaking hard and held on to her waist as the pony walked sedately through the woods. She didn't even bother to hurry. Following no path, she wound her way through the trees. We ducked as we went under low branches, my forehead sometimes touching her shoulder. I focused my mind on the pony's haunches as he stepped under himself, his back legs straining. A dusty, sharp aroma lifted from his sides, and I felt the hair, sticky with sweat, against my bare legs. I couldn't bring myself to speak and we rode in silence.

I didn't go back to Crab's Eddy that summer. Even so, I heard when Ronnie Black went to the hospital. In a few days, the Band-Aids he used couldn't hide the spreading redness, didn't begin to contain the swelling. When the chills and fever started, he carried his ballooned and darkening hand to his mother.

She promptly put him in the car and drove him to the hospital where Dr. Ismail told the family it was doubtful the boy would keep his hand.

"It looks like a human bite. Nothing filthier."

Mr. and Mrs. Black watched Ronnie become delirious, toss and turn and vomit on hospital sheets just a shade paler than he. He kept his hand as it turned out, but he never grabbed a girl again. For the rest of his life his fingers were frozen in the shape of a claw, the hand and wrist withered where the infection had eaten away the tissue.

Shortly after Ronnie was released from the hospital, his father drove his new Buick into the Holler, went as far as the road, left the car, and walked to Clare's house. No one knows what happened there, but when Mr. Black returned to the Buick it was stripped clean as a whistle: tires, battery, even the side windows were gone. The man couldn't prove a thing. Not about his car, not about his boy.

As for me, instead of swimming, I spent the afternoons farther up the mountains riding horses through the woods with Clare.

CHAPTER TWO

Allegheny Mountains

Spring 2014

Standing on my front porch, I looked across the valley to the mountain where my friend once lived. I wondered if what I saw was smoke lifting from her grandfather's chimney or just part of the floating mist that hung over everything. It was the first morning of my return. A taxi had dropped me off at two a.m., and I'd fallen asleep in my clothes, wrapped in a comforter. All my husband had said when I left was, "If you change your mind, Annie, let me know." My mother told me if I left Stewart Walker and took up with Clare Raffienne once more, I would never darken her door again. Never darken her door again. She loved phrases like that.

I pulled my jacket tighter around myself and noted the light frost on the ground. It was still too dark to check the fence lines so I walked to the barn and gave Lonesome his breakfast. While he munched his hay, I sat on the worn steps and waited. I listened to the rhythmic chewing and the birds as they woke and, when the light outside the barn went from gray to pearl, I set out to walk the sixty acres that had once been my pastures. It was the Norwood farm. My husband's parents had given it to him as a graduation present. In two years, the weeds had grown high as my shoulder. As wet with dew as though it had rained, the brush soaked my pant legs, and by the time I made the circle and headed back to the barn, the fabric clung cold and wet as high as my knee.

I stood in the entry a moment, my hands on my hips. When Stewart and I had moved to Los Angeles, we'd rented the farm to a young couple, assuming they would love it as much as we had. Before leaving, I cleaned the barn for them: stripped all the stalls, swept and dusted, even washed the windows. They'd had a wonderful time, filling it with horses and inviting friends by the carload out to ride. Looking at it now, anger gave me energy. I started through the stalls and feed room gathering up bailing twine, empty cartons, beer bottles, fast food wrappers, feed sacks and dirty syringes. I threw everything into large black trash bags and loaded them into the manure cart and drove them to the ravine at the back edge of the farthest field. When all the junk was gone, I started with the pitchfork, heaving out the rotting manure and bedding piled knee deep in the stalls. The sharp sting of ammonia made my eyes tear and despite the damp cold, my undershirt was wet with sweat. I threw my coat over a stall door.

It was late afternoon when I put away my equipment and drove the last load across the road to the manure pile. My back and shoulders stung with the effort of breaking up the mass and pulling it out of the cart. When every bit of wet, heavy straw was on the ground, I returned to the barn and put Lonesome in the cross ties. He was a gray, possibly a thoroughbred/quarter horse mix. Unable to bring myself to sell him, I had turned him over to Clare's care. He accepted the change with his usual tolerance. Throughout my acquaintance with him, he maintained a polite disdain for the ways of man. He refused to become ruffled by their various idiosyncrasies, but went stoically wherever asked, stood patiently when necessary and often babysat those more excitable beasts who were unable to achieve his brand of calm.

I brushed him, combed his mane and tail, picked out his hooves and put dressing on them. As I worked, I thought of Clare. Clare Raffienne. Clare from the Holler. Clare, who was now working at a fancy new barn even though the Raffiennes never worked for anyone.

I put my arms around my horse's neck and laid my head against him and felt fear ease out of me for the first time in two years. Eventually, I pulled away to mix his grain and clean and fill his water bucket. I put hay in the corner of his stall.

By now it was dark and getting colder. There were seven fireplaces in the house, and when Stewart and I had lived here, he carried wood upstairs to the bedroom whenever the nights were cold. Tonight I laid the fire in the room off the kitchen. I'd never built a fire before and used newspaper to get it started. Cheating, Stewart called it. There was smoke at first, and the paper caught with a roar. It burned fiercely for almost a minute before fizzling to smoke. I kept at it, rearranging the logs; poked at the tiny chips of flame, adding more paper. It went out again. And again. Finally, I stuffed the entire fireplace with paper and lit it. An inferno burst onto the hearth and up the chimney. I waved my arms, tried to blow it out, but needn't have bothered. The blaze vanished as quickly as the others. I kicked the logs as hard as I could and yelled, "Burn you son-of-a-bitch." A small flame started. Quickly I fed it bark, twigs, and finally small logs. They caught, created a fire that, though small, glowed with purpose.

I fixed macaroni and cheese from a box for supper and unlocked the gun cabinet and looked for a bottle of Scotch. It had been Stewart's idea to convert this piece so it would hold his liquor and wine. I found Johnny Walker Red hanging from a slot that had once cradled a rifle. I unscrewed the top and drank straight from the bottle. I ate in front of the fire and watched the flames' blue and gold lights. My gaze shifted to the near wall. We had replaced the crumbling plaster with drywall, paste spackled on unevenly and painted white. In the corner of that wall was the barely discernable figure of a kneeling woman, her hands raised above her head as she coiled her hair. She was naked. While working I had taken a few free form swipes and when I'd stepped back, we saw what I had created.

"Let's keep it," Stewart said.

The form was crude, primitive, but oddly graceful. We named her Godiva. She was still there, brought out by the fire light, head bent slightly forward. Our lady in the wall.

I put my cheek on my raised knees and curled around my legs. Christ. How would I get through the night? How would I get through the next day and all the days that followed? The only thing that kept me from calling my husband and begging him to take me back was the fact that my cell didn't work out here and the land line was disconnected.

CHAPTER THREE
CLARE

7/3/12

Dear Clare,

Sorry I haven't written sooner and this is just a note. I've been driving myself nearly crazy looking for a new place for us to stay. We live on the tenth floor of a high rise. It's so expensive out here though and I haven't found anything better. Everything is different. People are very friendly and everyone smiles and says "Hi," but I haven't made any friends yet. I asked someone to have lunch with me and she said, "Yes," and seemed really enthusiastic but didn't show up.

Stewart is doing well: working ten, twelve-hour days. He's bought a boat to take clients out. I go sometimes and have gotten a great tan but I get seasick. And it's a fast crowd.

I'm thinking about coming back to Coleton for a while. It's so hot here now. I'd just stay there for the summer then come back to LA in the fall and look for work. Stewart's so busy getting his clientele built up I hardly see him so that should be no problem. The only hitch would be staying with Mom and Dad.

How are Pap and all the horses? I miss riding more than I can say. It's too expensive here because there's no land. Take care of Lonesome, tell Dave I said hello, and maybe I'll see you soon.

Love,
Annie

MARCH 2014

There's a spot on the road, halfway up the mountain where the trees break and you can see the valley and the old Norwood farm. I was drivin to Pap's for supper and saw the light flickering from Annie's house. The farm went wild in the years she and Stewart was in California. It'd be hell getting it back. Take more than Annie to do it. Work yourself to death just keeping up the pastures. There'd be no time left over for running around, no time to ride a good horse just for the fun of it. I wondered if Annie knew what she was getting into.

The house was huge and real old too, but the walls was so solid it looked like it would last forever. It had been a mess when she and Stewart moved in, and they done a lot of work on it. He was an architect and it was supposed to be a way to make a name for himself. I liked knowin she was back inside that big old place. Solid and safe and permanent. She never did come for the summer. She wrote me another note sayin something about it not working out staying with her parents. No wonder. Most people didn't realize about her mom. They just thought she was some kind of eccentric who liked to stay to herself and maybe drank a little too much because of the accident. They forgave her a lot 'cause of that eye. Lost it riding her horse right after she got married. Actually, she was mean as a snake and gave Annie a hell of a time. And her dad didn't help any. He operated on my gram when she had cancer. A colder fish would be hard to find.

I remember one time Annie asked me to spend the night. She swore she'd asked permission. It was snowin like crazy and cold as hell. We was listening to tunes when Annie's mom called her out of the room and slapped her so hard I could hear it over the music. She said how dare she bring white trash into her house and to get me out of there or she'd call the police. She didn't even give me time to call Pap though Annie must of because he found me two hours later walking home through a whirling haze of white.

No, Annie didn't come back that summer. She stayed in LA through that winter and the next and when she couldn't stand it anymore, she moved back to the farm. Stewart had always been a hound, but I guess out in California it got so even Annie couldn't ignore it.

It was blazin hot inside Pap's. The older he got the more he cranked up the wood stove. From the sharp smell in the house, I could tell he had the kerosene heater goin too. With all the hay and grain stored in the front room like it was, he'd kill himself for sure one day with that thing. He was in the rockin chair with his glass of whiskey. He'd been waitin on me and by the look of him he thought he'd been waitin too long.

"Pap, you shouldn't drink when you got the stoves goin. You'll set the whole place on fire one of these days." He took a long swallow without looking at me, and said, "A man should be able to set and drink at the end of his years if he wants to. Wouldn't be a problem if he didn't live alone." He resumed rockin.

I found venison steaks in the icebox along with some bacon grease. I fried potatoes in the fat and opened a can of applesauce. Pap looked more and more cheerful as the food cooked. I helped myself to a beer. Poor Pap. I was the last of his kin he was close to. His brothers was all dead, my dad too, and the cousins didn't come around 'cause they thought he was above himself living up the mountain. They couldn't understand why he worked for a living. They was all on welfare. Pap maintained once you let the government into your life, you lost control and ended up settin in offices begging for food. He told me I ought to be glad he taught me a trade. I'd never have to take nothing from nobody. He couldn't understand how I could leave here and go live on someone else's place. Truth is, I'd of left the homestead with or without Raffino and his men showing up. Silver Storm Farm was just a lucky coincidence.

CHAPTER FOUR
ANNIE

By the time I woke the next day, the sun filled the room. I pulled on my boots and dashed out the door to tend my horse. A shiny red pickup stood in the driveway with a tall woman leaning against it. Even at this distance, I knew who it was. Clare stepped forward, waved, and when I came close, she put her arm around me. I anticipated then noted the springy feel of the black, tangled hair against my cheek. At least it smelled clean, not at all the way it looked, like the matted coat of a dog.

"So, you made it back," she said, pulling away.

I thought I had forgotten the dusky look of her skin, the way it could be both brown and rosy at the same time, but I had not. If anyone actually knew her background, I was unaware of it. French, some speculated or possibly Irish. Most favored the idea of American Indian in her past. She was raised by her grandparents after her parents were killed in a murder/suicide when she was just a baby. She never spoke of it and when pressed, said simply, "Pap says our family's always been here."

"Well, I'm back," I said.

"And Stewart?"

"Staying in LA like I told you."

"Oh well, that's more his style anyway."

I stuffed my hands in my pocket. "How's Dave."

"Gone. Sonofa bitch tried to hit me one night 'cause I'd gone out dancing with some friends."

So... the old pattern continued. "I'm sorry to hear it," I said. "I liked him."

"So did I," she said, and it was true. She liked them all for as long as she could. The trick was knowing when to move on, and none of them did.

"Hope you don't mind me bringin Lonesome back a day early. Like I said, we needed the stall." Clare shook her head. "The first of March and people are already bringing their horses—even the locals." She followed me into the barn and separated a flake of hay from a bale, put it to her face, inhaled, nodded her approval, and threw it into Lonesome's stall.

"How did Lonesome's legs seem to you?" I asked while scooping grain.

"They held up all right as long as I was careful but he's never going to be your bread and butter." Clare looked out to the fields. The land was still sepia toned from winter. "How's your fencing?"

"Better than I thought, but it needs repair and the weeds are taking over."

"Why not leave it the way it is? You've enough land to run a few horses on and feed them good."

"It would be hard to do business that way."

"It's hard to do business any way with horses. Do yourself a favor and leave it be." Odd coming from Clare with her fancy new job. She tapped her foot against the bottom board of the stall. When I didn't answer, she said, "You're too stubborn for your own good sometimes."

I ducked my head to hide my hurt.

Clare waited a few moments before motioning me to follow her. "Well, come on, let's go look at this truck. You won't find a better deal, I guarantee it. Mr. Raffino's spoiled rotten about his vehicles. Changes every year. The damn thing's like new, but he's got to have the latest model."

We drove out of my valley along the outskirts of town and soon we were on back roads. The scenery zipped past. I peeked at the speedometer then quickly sat back. We were doing nearly eighty. Clare patted the steering wheel. "What do you think of this baby? Rides like a car, don't it?"

It was the biggest pickup I'd ever seen, as red on the inside as it was on the out. I took hold of the armrest, concentrated on the farms sailing by.

"Jesus, Clare," I said.

"I guess you think nothing's changed but wait until you see my boss's house."

"Slow down," I said. "I can't see anything."

Clare looked startled, gave me a questioning glance, but did as I asked. Eventually, she pointed to a big, very modern house with cedar shakes and floor-to-ceiling windows opening onto a vast expanse of lawn. White boards fenced the long driveway and adjacent fields and ran along the road as far as the eye could see. There were no weeds in the thick brown pasture, and the fence looked as though it had just been painted. The horses wore winter blankets.

"Mafia money." Clare grinned. "My boss lives there."

Mafia money? Here? In the middle of nowhere? Where absolutely nothing happened and nothing changed for generations? I pictured dark, chubby men in pinstriped suits, the fabric stretched tight across their shoulders and back and black cars sliding along the valley road. A procession of them, penetrating quietly into the poverty. I liked the idea. I couldn't help it. I liked the idea of all that money and power insinuating into these forgotten mountains. It made coming back less risky. I had turned my back on Los Angeles for good reasons, I thought. I'd had no choice, I thought, and I'd returned to the place where I'd been happiest, trusting as well as I could that the old values were the right values. Yet, every night since I'd made my decision, I woke around four in the morning. The witching hour some people call it, or the hour of the wolf. I'd lie in a cold, sweating fear that I'd find I'd given up sparkle, bright talk, and adventure just to die of boredom in this backwater, too poor, too lonely, and too mind dead to look further.

We turned into the driveway. On the right were two training rings, a big one with jumps and a small one for breaking the youngsters. In front of us stood the barn, low and long and smartly white in the pale sun.

We stepped through wide doors into bright fluorescent light, colder than the outside. The aisle seemed endless. Twenty stalls on either side, and between the stalls eight grooming areas, two wash areas, a large tack room, a visitor's lounge, and an office. At the back of the barn the aisle opened onto a 200 by

150-foot indoor riding ring. Several neatly built darkskinned men pushed wheelbarrows heaped with bedding and manure along the aisle.

"Jamaicans," whispered Clare. She motioned me to follow her, and we went into a room that opened off the office. It was windowless, small and dark, and contained a bed covered by a stained quilt, one chair, a tiny refrigerator and stove. It took me a minute to realize this was Clare's apartment. She grabbed two cold beers out of the refrigerator.

"Welcome to my new home," she said, handing me one of them.

The can was frosty and the beer so cold I could feel flakes of ice on my tongue. I noticed a bag of empty beer cans as high as my waist lying in a corner next to the door.

"Let's see." Clare bent to look in the open door of the refrigerator. "We've got venison bologna and... yes, here's the mustard." She went to a small cupboard and rummaged through some things. "Yes, here are some crackers. I think they're still okay." She sniffed the open box.

We sat crosslegged on the bed to eat our snack. Clare placed the bologna on a paper plate between us. We took turns with the jackknife she kept in her back pocket. She cut thick slices of venison, smeared them with mustard and ate them straight, giving up on the crackers, which had traces of mealy bugs clinging to them. It was damp in the room and the bed smelled of mildew. I thought of the apartment in California with the early morning sun spread across the couch. I'd sat in that sun yesterday morning, my head in my hands, wondering how I was ever going to get on the plane and fly across the United States. I'd figured once I was at the farm with the hills, the familiar spaces, I'd be okay. Now, this poor, dark room felt like a weight behind my ribs. That same weight I'd felt on Saturday afternoons sitting in the shadowed living room of my parent's house listening to the tick of the grandfather clock while Mother slept it off upstairs and Dad was out somewhere being busy. I didn't understand, only recognized the dread. Clare ate with satisfaction, breathing lightly through her nose as she chewed. "Well, Annie," she said after studying me for a moment, "I couldn't live in LA either. Ain't nothing to do out there."

I burst out laughing, felt the weight break up and recede, so sincerely did she mean it.

"So," I said. "Mafia money. Are you sure about that?"

"No. But it could be."

"What are you doing here? I mean… this doesn't seem like you."

"Annie. The only places I seen horses like this is in magazines. I can't pass up this chance."

"What exactly are your job duties?"

"Give lessons mostly, polish up the lesson horses over fences. Break and train some of the local nags."

"Nags?"

"Compared to the ones Mr. Raffino brings in from out of town, they're nags."

"Do you get to ride them? Mr. Raffino's?"

"No, not yet."

"Stalls?"

"No stalls."

"Well, that's good."

"I don't mind doin stalls. Beats some of the lessons I have to give."

"Why did they pick here to build a place like this?"

Clare shrugged. "Cheap land I guess," she said and laughed. "And it's a good place to hide."

I raised an eyebrow. "And the pay?"

"It's okay. At least it's regular." She held the knife toward me, handle first. I shook my head, so she carefully licked the mustard off the blade, pulled her shirttail out of her pants, and wiped the steel clean. She returned the knife to her back pocket.

"Why don't you come and work for me? You could be my trainer," I said.

"Don't be silly… be your own trainer."

"No."

"You have no confidence."

"I can't do the tough ones."

"Who can?"

"You."

"I'm crazy, Annie. You know that."

I looked away.

"I wish you'd asked me a year ago. I'm settled here now."

"I know. I didn't really expect you to leave forty stalls for fifteen. I'm serious about a trainer, though. I put an ad in The Chronicle two weeks ago."

"What sort of business you looking for?"

"Boarding, training, lessons, sales... the works."

Clare looked at me quietly. "Why do you want to get into the horse business, Annie? You think you want to live like me?"

I didn't answer. Clare waved her hand in the air, brushing away the question. I helped myself to the last slice of venison to cover the awkwardness. It was mildly sweet, had come from someone who knew how to kill without souring the meat with the taste of fear.

"So, you had any replies? To the ad?"

"I have someone coming for an interview next week."

"From where?"

"Connecticut."

"Connecticut? All the way from Connecticut to the middle of nowhere?"

"I told her it was remote and she was all right with it. Said it would be a nice change."

"It'll be a change all right. I suppose you'll put her up in the garage. Lucky you have that. Or were you thinking of having her stay in the house with you?"

"No, no. The garage, of course."

"It might work out. I mean, I can see it workin out. Especially if she's inexperienced and trying to get started. Maybe a little desperate. What do you know about her? Is she just starting out or is she an old coot on the downward slide?"

"She sounded energetic on the phone. I liked her. And she sent a picture of herself going over a jump. She looked good."

Clare snorted. "Anyone can look good in a picture, Annie. I still think you should be your own trainer. If it was me, I wouldn't want a stranger living on my property."

"I'm not good enough to be my own trainer."

"Well, it's your business. I just wouldn't want some stranger underfoot unless they was tall, dark, and handsome. You know." Clare unfolded herself from the bed, went to the little refrigerator, and brought me back another beer. I started to refuse it, changed my mind, and was tilting my head back with the bottle to my lips when a man stepped through the door. He was good looking, heavily muscled and just starting to turn soft.

"Clare," he said, "I want you to ride that dark bay mare, the big one, this afternoon. If you can do anything with her, she's yours to train." His smile told me how generous he thought this offer. Clare's only response was to become still the way a wolf will when it sees something unfamiliar move into its territory. The man hesitated, then folded his arms, leaned against the door frame, and continued to smile.

I became aware of the sounds outside the little room—horses nickering and moving about in their stalls, the voices of the men calling to each other. In spite of the chilly dampness, I began to sweat. The man bent his head and brushed the front of his creased trousers. His hair was combed straight back from his forehead, the strands lining up in neat, oiled rows. He picked at an invisible piece of lint. When he raised his eyes, he didn't look at Clare, said matter of factly to the air, "See what you can do. She's worthless to me the way she is." He turned to me and made a small courtly bow. "I'm Mr. Raffino, and you are...?"

Clare stirred. "Sorry. This is Annie Walker, an old friend of mine."

Mr. Raffino made another small bow, more a nod. "Nice to meet you, Annie Walker." He turned back to Clare. "Like I said, see what you can do with her."

When he disappeared, Clare smiled, a sly smile not meant for anyone.

Lucky he didn't see that, I thought.

Stringtown had a fine, well-bred looking head and at seventeen hands stood unusually tall for a mare. She was four and had come from a racing barn. She held her head high when Clare led her out of the stall, the whites of her eyes showing. She jigged across the aisle on her toes, snapping her tail back and forth. When Clare brushed her flanks with a dandy brush, Stringtown aimed a sidelong kick at her, hunching her back away from the bristles. Clare switched to a softer brush. She had to step around the kicks. When she gently eased the saddle onto the mare's back, the horse bucked.

"This is all nonsense. She's been tacked up hundreds of times. Babied or bullied, she acts the same. Let's go outside. I hate that indoor arena."

A wind had picked up and blew Stringtown's mane and tail as Clare led her, prancing and shying, to the small training ring. When we got there the mare was already sweating along the neck. Clare pulled down a stirrup leather. The mare jumped sideways, lashed out with her back legs, eyed Clare intently and popped both front feet off the ground. Clare got in close to her shoulder and backed her up until finally the big horse stood still, her ears pricked and her expression alert and annoyed. She waited. I stepped back against a fence rail. Clare took hold of the mare's mane, tucked her toe into the stirrup and sprung lightly into the saddle.

Stringtown looked thoughtful for a moment then went up on her hind legs. Clare tapped the horse's rump with a crop. She burst into the air, front legs stretched in front of her head, back legs kicking out. Clare's feet came out of the stirrups, but she was sitting deep in the saddle. Stringtown landed, stood with her ears flicking backwards and forwards. Clare smacked her hard on her flank. Stringtown went straight up this time, hovered on the vertical. She's going over backward, I thought, and stepped forward, reaching for the reins. I was watching the hooves above my head as Clare jumped free. She landed on both feet, faced the mare, and using the reins, pulled her down. Stringtown watched Clare carefully. Fast as a cat, Clare was back in the saddle. Mr. Raffino had come out of the barn and walked toward us.

"It's no good," he said. "She always rears if you ask her to go forward."

Clare pressed her legs against the horse's sides. Stringtown reared and in one motion flung herself forward, landing hard on her front feet with her head down. She bucked the second she landed, twisting viciously. Before the mare had time to regroup, Clare smacked her again on the rump. Stringtown dropped her head so fast and so low she pulled Clare out of the saddle and onto her neck. As she tried to get her shoulders back into position, Stringtown went straight up. Clare tumbled off the back.

I jumped away from the fence and grabbed for the reins before Stringtown could bound off. The mare threw her head, yanking my arms practically from their sockets and trumpeted, stretched her neck, shook herself, and waited.

Mr. Raffino took a gold cigarette case from his pocket, retrieved a cigarette, tapped it against the case, held a gold lighter to it, and rested his elbows on the fence.

Clare was on her feet and took the reins from me. Stringtown jumped forward, knocking her down, then galloped around the periphery of the little ring, dragging my friend along with her. I grabbed the reins as she came by.

"For God's sake, Clare." There was blood on her jeans and I was shaking.

"She has the blood of kings in her veins," Mr. Raffino said calmly.

I looked at Clare. Her hair had come loose and hung in her face.

"She's out of Inca Gold and Sea Storm. No one has been able to ride her, though. She's thrown everyone who has tried." Raffino climbed over the boards and took the reins. "It's no go. She's a rogue. Dog food."

Clare stood. She put her hand on a post and eased some of the weight off her left leg. "One more try," she said. "I got an idea."

"It's no good. She's a rogue."

"Let me try something. I have to work it out with Annie first. But I got an idea and it takes two people."

I jerked my head toward her.

Raffino handed the reins to Clare. "She's no use to me the way she is now and too crazy to use as a brood mare. You can try once more, but I'm not feeding her indefinitely. I don't throw good money after bad." He turned to go then looked back. "You should see a doctor about that face and don't take aspirin—it will only make the swelling worse. I have some Tylenol if you need it."

I don't know what Clare did about her wounds that day. Blood oozed into her jeans on her left hip, and her hands were scraped raw. It looked as though her cheek would turn black and blue. It was already so swollen I wondered if a bone was broken. "I think you should see a doctor," I said. Clare shrugged me off. She washed Stringtown's cut with warm water, rubbed her down with a towel, and treated her legs with liniment. Her movements were stiff; she had to concentrate, where normally she moved with mindless ease. She was preoccupied and when she showed me the truck, said only, "Take it on trial. Tony said if you like it, you can go with him to the bank on Friday to work out the payments."

Tony? When had it become Tony?

I knew very little about cars and even less about trucks, but this one showed few signs of wear and the engine did not make any alarming noises. It was as bright red as his new one but I decided to buy it anyway.

And that was that. I would soon own a vehicle that could have been a fire engine and I was back here in the hills and apparently I was staying. Stewart or no Stewart.

CHAPTER FIVE

Two weeks passed before Clare came to me with her plan. Her idea was simplicity itself. The horse would not go forward, but she'd been born to run; it was in her blood. Once she'd got drunk on her own speed, Clare said, she would be cured. We had to find a way to motivate her over this hump, that was all. Stringtown was stubborn though, spoiled almost beyond hope. She would choose death before she would submit. We would have to use something more powerful than fear, more compelling than anger. Love.

Clare particularly liked the abandoned railroad that ran past my farm. The ties had long ago been torn up; only the cinders remained. Straight and level for more than a hundred miles, it invited horses to gallop forward to stretch their legs and fill their lungs with air.

"We'll wait until Stringtown is in heat," she said. "Then we'll put her in the field with Lonesome, give them a few days to fall in love, and with Lonesome leading, we'll head down the track."

"I don't know, Clare. Supposing Stringtown decides she hates him?" I knew of horses killed trying to make up to a disagreeable mare.

"We'll take it slow."

"Hasn't anyone tried this with her before?"

"Yeah, but they just walked the stallion back and forth in front of her stall. A half-assed way to do it. That wouldn't work with Stringtown."

We put them in adjoining paddocks to start. They snorted, nose to nose over the fence, blowing air into each other's nostrils. The tips of Stringtown's turned in and she squealed at the gelding, struck at the boards with a front foot. Lonesome stretched his neck over the fence, chortled deep in his throat, and sniffed the mare's arched neck. Stringtown wheeled around, presented her backside, squatted and spilled urine onto the ground.

Lonesome chortled again, moved along the boards until he could reach the mare's withers, and rubbed them with his lips. Stringtown dropped her head and allowed the caress. Without warning, she spun and slammed the boards with her back feet.

"It's working," said Clare.

I stared at her.

Two days later, we put them together in a field. Stringtown flared her nostrils, lifted her tail, and sidestepped toward the gelding. I held my breath. The mare bunched her muscles as though to kick but only gave a little buck instead. She bit him on the withers then rubbed the underside of her neck along his crest. She shook herself. Lonesome shook himself. They both dropped their heads to graze. By the next morning, they moved through the pasture together, form and shadow, inseparable.

Late March and the sky, a solid pearl gray, dropped close to our heads, draining the world of color. The trees were still bare as old brooms. Nothing stirred. Even the birds were silent and dropped rather than flew through the air. We watched the horses over the fence, Clare resting her foot on the bottom board. When she thought I wasn't looking, she still limped from her battle with the big horse. "They're as ready as they're ever gonna be," she said.

In the barn, we put them in cross ties. Stringtown nickered for Lonesome and kept her eyes on him even while she kicked at Clare. I took Lonesome to the mounting block first. Stringtown pranced behind. "Keep in front of me," Clare said, swinging her leg from the block over the saddle. "Not too far, not too close."

I set off on Lonesome, not looking back. Stringtown whinnied, so loud and shrill I jumped. Taking a deep breath, I turned onto the road. I heard the chatter of nervous feet on pavement. That was something, anyway. I glanced over my shoulder. Stringtown's eyes rolled, white rimmed and huge above the crimson nostrils. She looked demented but continued to jig forward. Clare absorbed the shock of those stiff legs with the small of her back, her hands quiet at the mare's withers. I continued to the right of way that led to the old railway bed. Lonesome remained steady, though now and then he looked over his shoulder. Clare had told me all I had to do was pick up a brisk trot once I hit the track. If Stringtown followed, I would move into a canter.

"One good gallop," she'd said. "And she'll catch the fever."

The footing was perfect. I allowed myself another quick glance over my shoulder. Stringtown pranced in back of us, tossing her head and blowing through her nostrils. I nudged Lonesome. He hesitated. I nudged him again and he moved into a working trot. I looked back. Stringtown was on her two hind legs. She hung there a second then lunged forward, exploding into her stride. Her hooves dug in, throwing up the dirt around them. In a few paces, she was next to Lonesome. Both horses slowed. "Go," Clare shouted, and I gave the gelding a kick. Obedient, he began to canter. Stringtown pinned her ears, kicked at him, but kept her pace. We moved side by side. Clare nodded and I signaled Lonesome to gallop. Stringtown stayed with him, moving shoulder to shoulder. I grinned at Clare, who grinned back, her white teeth bright in the growing dark. A wind had picked up, and it was all I could hear as it blew down the valley; that and the steady rhythm of the horses' hooves.

We had ridden about half a mile when Stringtown picked up the pace. For a few strides the two horses held steady, then the big mare pulled in front, flicked her tail as she passed Lonesome's head. She stretched her neck, dropped her body closer to the ground the way horses do when they mean to run. I gave Lonesome his head, and he strained to cover the distance between them. I could hear his breathing above the wind. I worried he might hurt himself, but not knowing what Stringtown would do when she realized she was alone, I didn't want to lose sight of Clare. We didn't have a prayer, Lonesome and I. Within seconds, Clare and Stringtown vanished into the dusk. All we could do was try to keep up with the sound of the pounding hooves. My legs and shoulders ached. The wind blew stronger, and suddenly it brought rain, driving it into my face.

In spite of himself, Lonesome slowed. He stumbled. I took back on the reins, but he pulled against me. Enough is enough, Clare, I thought. Turn the nag around. And so she had. Or perhaps Stringtown, noticing Lonesome's inability to keep pace, had turned back on her own. They appeared out of the rain, a dark silhouette flying toward us. Seeing Stringtown, Lonesome allowed me to bring him to a stop. Horse and rider blew past, Clare's face stony pale with her wet hair lashing behind her. She was riding to stay on, hands holding the mane and body hunched forward. Stringtown's nostrils drank the cold air.

I could see Clare struggle to turn the mare off the track and onto the right of way. They didn't make it and veered into the woods which bordered Cat Creek. A few feet into the woods there was a sharp drop to the creek below, and Clare would have little control once she was ducking trees. Cat Creek ran high and fast this time of year. I prayed the mare wasn't so stupid she'd tumble into the water. I kicked Lonesome, steered him down a steep bank to take a shortcut to the right of way. He scrambled over the rocks, going as fast as he could. Stringtown was in the trees now, and I lost sight of them. Lonesome and I made it to level ground and galloped on. I heard a crashing in the woods. Stringtown burst from the dark in front of us. The last I saw of her was her backside charging into the gloom.

When Lonesome and I got back to the barn, Stringtown was whirling in her stall, snatching bits of hay while Clare tried to rub her down with a towel. Steam rose off the horse's back. Clare's face was speckled with black cinders from the old track. The mare whinnied, a loud, piercing cry, as soon as we came through the door. Lonesome nickered softly. My fingers were so stiff from the cold I wasn't sure I could undo my tack. Stringtown was still sweating, but Lonesome and I had walked the final way home and at least he was cooled out. He stood still while I brushed the mud from his belly and legs.

Clare fetched a cooler from the tack room and draped it over the mare's back, who was quieting now that Lonesome was near her. The rain beat on the barn roof with a low, steady roar, and the last of the daylight faded. Clare rubbed the wool blanket over the horse's neck and back, absorbing the moisture from the rain and sweat. Both of us were as covered with mud as the horses, and our hair lay plastered to our heads. I thought of the chicken that I had left roasting in the oven and the warmth of the house. My legs shook, and I noticed Clare trembled from head to foot. But I knew Clare would not leave Stringtown until she was completely dry, so once Lonesome was clean and in his stall, I helped rub the mare down. The wool cooler gave off a warm animal smell but even rubbing hard to dry the mare, my skin stung with the cold.

"Isn't that enough now?" I said at last. Clare nodded. We were hanging the cooler over an empty stall when above the rain and wind I heard the sound of a car pulling into the driveway. We stepped outside and in the light over the barn door, a low white sports car came to a stop. The door on the driver's side opened and a white umbrella popped into view, followed by a tiny figure that stood under it, primly avoiding the rain. She wore a white leather coat and white wool slacks. Her blond hair was cut short and sleek and looked silver in the faint light.

"I thought you weren't coming," I said.

"But why?"

"You were supposed to start yesterday."

"Oh... well, it took longer to get ready than I thought it would. I didn't mean to worry you."

Lydia. My new trainer.

I should have told the girl to go, to turn around and go back from where she had come. I should have known that wanting something doesn't make it happen, that in the end people are who they are, that hate is hate and if you try to change it, people get hurt. Instead I pointed the way to the house. Taking great care not to get wet, the girl stepped back into the Corvette and drove slowly up the driveway. Clare and I followed on foot.

"Okay, let me guess. It's the Avon lady, right?"

"My new trainer."

"That is your new trainer?"

I nodded.

"That...?"

"Yes!"

"In a Corvette?"

"Seems that way."

"Annie, I've never heard of a trainer drivin a Corvette. Especially not someone twelve years old."

I shrugged. "The only other people who applied were a very overweight kid who brought her mother to the interview and a man from Germany who by his own admission would only stay a month."

"So you're actually going to hire her?"

"Looks like I already have."

"I guess the interview went okay. I mean, can she ride?"

"She can ride very well."

CHAPTER SIX

At some point in the farm's history, someone had built a free-standing garage. Another owner had turned it into an apartment for the hired hand. Stewart and I had never used it, even talked of tearing it down. It was too modern, the brick too even, too finely edged, Stewart had said. Now he lived in glass and steel. After seeing Los Angeles, I'd realized the pointlessness of carting our antiques to California. I just left them where they were, locked the doors, and turned my back. In the past weeks I'd hauled the lesser pieces into this garage apartment, searched out my old recipe for whitewash and covered the walls. The kitchen and living room were combined into a large room downstairs, with a circular stairway leading to a bedroom loft above the kitchen. When I was done, I stood in the middle of the downstairs and surveyed the results. I considered moving in here myself. It would certainly save money. The heating bill alone would be cut to a fraction. I could sell most of the furniture and some of the other valuables and pay off the truck. Or the heating bill. I had $187 left. I could divide the loft into two bedrooms, and Lydia and I could both live here. I walked to a window and gazed at the big house. I thought of the rooms filled with furniture we had found at out of the way antique stores, junk shops: the brass bed green with age, a patina we called it, the cherry wardrobe, the ornate Italian library table, the thick eleven-by-seventeen Aubusson rug we'd gotten at an auction for fifty dollars because it was too big for anyone else to consider. I remembered dragging it into the living room. The effort had warmed Stewart, and he took off his shirt. His shoulders shined with sweat. He noticed me watching him and laughed. "Annie, who knows where this thing has been."

Later, stretched out on the rug, he'd rested his head against my neck with one arm under my hair and sang against my ear: "*I guess I've been in love before, once or twice been on the floor, but I never loved no one the way that I love you…*" The sweet, sad sound of Simon and Garfunkel in true pitch. It was a strange fact about Stewart Walker that he always preferred the old songs. He sighed and pulled me tight against him.

So, no, I didn't move into the apartment, but stayed in the big house with its antiques, wonderful buys, and treacherous memories.

Clare ran her fingers over the girl's saddle. "Nice," she said.

I recognized this brand. Neither Pap nor Clare had ever paid as much for a horse. The long fingers lingered on the leather.

Frowning, the girl looked from me to Clare. "What happened to you guys, anyway?"

"We've been riding," I said. "In the rain."

Clare's hand was still on the saddle.

"A graduation present," said Lydia.

"Where'd you go to school?"

"Green Manor."

Clare tapped the saddle lightly. Green Manor Riding Academy cost $48,000 a year.

"We're dripping on the rug," I said. "You must be frozen. I've fixed some dinner for Clare and me, and it should be ready. Would you like to join us or are you too tired from your trip?"

Clare shot me a look.

"Oh, dinner would be lovely."

While Lydia freshened up, Clare dried herself and changed into a pair of my sweats, and I put the rest of dinner together: mashed potatoes, peas, gravy, rolls, and slaw. Clare came into the kitchen bare footed, ankles and wrists protruding from my clothes. She took a beer from the refrigerator, slamming the door shut with her hip. "So, that's your new trainer, huh. That's some saddle. And Green Manor. Wow. Course that really don't guarantee she can ride. And like I said, I've never known a horse person driving a Corvette. But who am I to say. God you look awful, Annie. Your face is all covered with cinders. It's a wonder we didn't scare her to death. Go change into dry clothes. You'll catch your death."

I slipped into a blistering bath, scrubbed away the soot, the mud, the chill, scrubbed until my hair was slick and sweet smelling. I piled it up on my head. I didn't take the time to put on makeup. I'd been looking forward to this evening for several days, had planned the menu carefully. I hadn't shared a meal with anyone since the snack on Clare's bed.

When I returned to the kitchen, Clare stood looking out the window, drinking her beer while Lydia inspected the label on the underside of my china. "This house is so big," she said, putting down the plate. "And where did you get all these antiques?"

"Here and there." I smiled, motioned them to the table. Lydia looked suspiciously at the food when I filled her plate. Clare held her fork in her fist and speared the meat as though she were holding down a living bird, cut off a piece with her knife, took a bite, and scooped up some mashed potatoes. She mixed the peas into the potatoes and sopped up the gravy with a roll. In between bites, she took long pulls on the beer. Lydia's eyes followed every move. "I can't remember the last time I've had a home cooked meal," Clare said, helping herself to more of everything.

When I served the strawberry rhubarb pie, Lydia looked at me in disbelief. "I didn't think you were allowed to eat this kind of food in the spring."

Clare and I stared at her.

"I mean, we have to be thinking about getting into our bikinis."

Clare looked at me and we both laughed. "What part of Connecticut did you say you was from?" she said.

"Not far from the city."

"Well, this ain't New York."

"No kidding." Lydia shifted in her chair. "But I see it as an opportunity. There's such a need here for professionals—people who know the horse industry."

The candlelight put shadows under Clare's eyes, making the angles in her face sharp as knives. She studied the girl carefully.

"You know how it is in the horse business," Lydia went on. "People pay slave wages, you live like a dog. You need to find a niche, be unique, find a place you can develop. Like here, where there is no competition."

The skin around Clare's eyes tightened and a flush spread on each cheek. She balanced her knife between her thumb and index finger.

I cleared my throat. "How long did it take you to get here?"

"About four hours. I made good time without the trailer behind me. My boyfriend will bring my horse tomorrow."

I didn't look at Clare, didn't want her to see my shock.

"Really?" she said. "What kind of horse?" I could hear the amusement in her voice, but we never did hear Lydia's reply. There was a sharp rap on the front door then a heavy tread through the living room. Mr. Raffino strode into the kitchen before I could say, come in. He was splattered with rain. I stared at him. So did Clare, her mouth slightly open. No one just happened by my valley. He looked all wrong standing in my kitchen with his Italian leather shoes making dark spots on the wooden floor. The points of his collar were too precise, the cuffs showing under the dark coat too white. He nodded toward me. "I am sorry about this intrusion, but your phone isn't working." He sounded both astonished and hurt.

"There's no reception out here. And the land line often goes out in a storm." I got up to check. Sure enough, the line was silent. "Yes," I said, "dead as a doornail."

"Yeah," said Clare, "all you have to do is piss next to the line and out it goes."

Lydia's eyebrows popped up.

"I've been trying to call the better part of the afternoon. I finally couldn't think of anything to do but drive out here."

Clare put down her fork. "Is something wrong?"

"I wouldn't be here if there wasn't," Raffino said crossly.

"Please," I waved toward a chair, "have a seat. Let me take your coat. Can I get you some coffee and pie?"

"No, no, thank you." He didn't take his eyes from Clare. "Prix Dot looks like she's going to foal tonight. I'd like you to be there." He hesitated, then said more quietly to me, "She's my best mare."

Clare did not get up. "Have you called the vet?"

"I don't think we need one yet. No sense calling one unless we run into real trouble."

"I would think if she's your best mare, you'd want a vet standing by," said Lydia.

Mr. Raffino glanced at her, took in the cashmere sweater, the silver hair and painted nails, then turned back to Clare. He stood big and obstinate in front of her. I agreed with Lydia, but Clare said, "Yeah, you're probably right. We still got time for you to have a cup a coffee and some pie, though, don't we? I mean, what's she doing?" Clare sliced herself another piece.

"She's restless, pacing in her stall."

"She still standing?"

"Well, yes."

"Been down at all?"

"She lay down once but got up again. She's restless, though."

"Anything showing? Feet, head, bag?"

"Well, no."

"We still have some time."

Mr. Raffino's face darkened. I considered offering the pie and coffee again but thought better of it.

"Here," said Clare, slicing a big piece, putting it on a plate, and shoving it toward Mr. Raffino. "Annie makes the best strawberry rhubarb pie you'll ever eat. Sit down and let me finish my supper."

"She's my best mare," he said again, as he pulled out a chair. He kept on his coat, wrapped the flaps around his lap as he sat. He pushed the pie away from him, watching Clare as she chewed, jostled his knee up and down, stared at the wall over Lydia's head, then turned back to Clare. "Weather like this, who can tell how long it will take us to get back."

Clare winked. "Trust me."

Mr. Raffino's head went back as though he'd been slapped. You could tell he didn't know what to do: shout at her, fire her, let it go, or smack her. "Let's go," he finally said and at the tone in his voice Clare looked at him carefully then finished her pie, took a swallow of beer and rose. "Let me get my boots on," she said.

Mr. Raffino got to his feet, concentrating on his trench coat as he buttoned it. While Clare pulled on her boots, he reached for the pie and took three generous mouthfuls, his little finger oddly dainty. He wore a pinky ring. "I believe Clare's right, that is the best strawberry rhubarb pie I've ever tasted," he said, placing it back on the table, smooth in victory.

He and Lydia weren't from around here, they didn't understand. They saw only a tall, unkempt girl, a hillbilly, bushwhacker, redneck, whatever you wanted to call them. She was better looking than most, that's all. They'd never seen her eyes go flat, turn inward like an animal's, or the sly wolf smile that was not a smile. They didn't know that when Ronnie Black's father drove his new Buick as far into the Holler as he could and walked the rest of the way to Pap's, he lost more than his new car. They were ignorant. They thought of Clare as alone, they thought of her as poor, which to them meant stupid, someone of no account. Biggest mistake of all, they thought of her as tame.

CHAPTER SEVEN

The next day, with the sun straight overhead, I walked out of the house to find the thinnest human being I had ever seen backing a horse down a trailer ramp. He wore his black hair shaved to the skin, making it no more than a dusky hue on his bony head. He himself was the color of coffee ice cream.

He tugged sharply on the horse's lead shank.

The gelding looked well built, solid with a dark, kind eye.

"Back," the man said briskly, though the horse was backing sedately down the ramp. From the creases in his lip, I judged him to be edging past his prime. He wore two blankets, over-the-knee shipping boots, a head bumper, and a tail wrap. But even under this he looked to have quality, plenty of substance without being coarse and the sleek coat, long muscles of a thoroughbred.

The door to the apartment banged and Lydia appeared, wearing the white leather jacket and skin-tight blue jeans. Her eyes were swollen and sleepy and the blonde bangs fell forward. It was the first time I had seen her that day.

"Hi, sweetheart," she said and patted the horse's neck and turned and kissed the man on the mouth. "You're here early," she said.

"It's noon, Lydia."

Lydia glanced at her watch. "Well, so it is." She smiled a cozy, lopsided smile.

The man handed her the lead shank, stuffed his hands in the pockets of his jeans, stepped back and surveyed the farm.

"This certainly is out in the middle of nowhere, isn't it?" He held out his hand. "I'm Rollo Smith, and I can't tell you how much I'm looking forward to being here."

"Ah… Lydia," I began.

"What do you think of him? Isn't he elegant?"

I looked uncertainly at Rollo.

"He's getting on in years. My dad bought him for me when he was thirteen. Otherwise he would have cost the moon. He was unbeatable for a while, though."

"He's lovely but, Lydia, I need to talk to you."

"He's gotten a little stiff this past year, but he didn't get turned out much where he was. These fields will be great for him." Lydia bent over, started undoing the leg wraps. "Rollo," she said, and he quickly moved to help her. While Rollo finished, Lydia ran her hand under the blanket along the horse's chest.

"Rollo drives way too fast. I wasn't going to let him bring the horse but he didn't want me driving him over the mountains by myself and he couldn't get away last night."

"What do you do, Rollo?" I asked.

"What say we finish this conversation after we've gotten the Doctor settled?" He looked around. "I assume that's the barn over there."

They set off down the driveway, Lydia leading the gelding, who walked quietly beside her.

So, my new trainer had arrived. A day late. With a horse covered in blankets and a boyfriend at least two shades darker than anyone else in this valley. I didn't call after them. I didn't yell stop. I stood and watched them walk away from me and all I could think was that Rollo had no behind at all.

They left the horse standing over the ankles in shavings, slowly working his way through twelve pounds of grain. My grain. Back at the house, Rollo and Lydia settled themselves on my couch while I made up my mind not to offer them refreshments. I gave Lydia a list of prospective training colts and students. After she had looked it over noncommittally, she handed it to Rollo.

He read it, then took a cigarette from his shirt pocket, lit it, held it to his mouth between his first three fingers and thumb, exhaled, squinted through the smoke and said, "How many of these names can we count on?"

I cleared my throat. "Ah, I hadn't been expecting this position to be filled by a couple. I mean Rollo... I can't pay anything extra. Most of the pay is on commission. Based on Lydia's lessons and training colts. It, well, you know, I mean, I hadn't expected a boyfriend."

Lydia looked stunned.

Even Rollo looked a bit startled for a moment before recovering himself. "We had assumed," he said, looking around for an ashtray and, finding none, tapping the ashes into his cupped hand, "that since you were providing a separate place to live, it wouldn't matter. My schedule is flexible, so I will be coming and going according to my own hours. We are planning to be married once Lydia is established."

I sat back, wondering what flexible hours had to do with it. Still, having a man here could be helpful. Lydia might adjust better to life in the country if she had her boyfriend for company. And there were always things that two women alone could not do. I looked him up and down swiftly from the corner of my eye. It was possible he was stronger than he looked. Little, wiry guys sometimes were. I glanced out the window. The wind and rain had gone with the morning, and it was clear, cold outside without a hint of spring.

CHAPTER EIGHT

CLARE

Tony, I mean, Mr. Raffino, was waitin on me when I brought Stringtown back from Annie's. No surprise. I'd been spending a lot a time away from Silver Storm Farm and he wasn't too pleased about it. He never said anything to me exactly, probably 'cause I never give him a chance. I just kept myself scarce or busy with customers. He wouldn't dare make a scene in front of customers. And I pretended I didn't see the notes he tacked to the bulletin board in the barn. I guess he saw my rig coming down the road. I'd taken my own, of course, since he didn't exactly approve of my takin S.T. off his place. He come over as I was walking Stringtown down the ramp.

"Well?"

"She's cured."

"Oh, really?"

"Yup." I kept my attention on the shipping bandages as I unwrapped Stringtown's legs.

"Cured?"

"Right. She don't rear any more or go over backwards."

"And?"

I stood up, faced him. "She goes forward just fine."

Tony took out a cigarette, tapped it against that gold cigarette case, lit it, inhaled slowly, and let smoke come out his nose. "Isn't that something? I have to admit, I didn't think it possible. How about giving me a demonstration."

"Sure. Anytime."

"How about now?"

"Now?"

"Sure. You don't have anything else that's pressing, do you?"

"No, Sir, I don't."

"I'll meet you at the breaking ring."

"How about meeting me at the cross-country course?"

He raised an eyebrow. "Cross-country fences? She's ready for that?"

"She's way beyond the breaking ring."

Course she wasn't. Not even close. I'd never even put her over a fence, just jumped over a few logs. Jumped hardly covered it. She cleared everything by three feet at least, pulling like a train. Truth was, I couldn't imagine spinning around in that small ring at the speed she went. The cross-country course wasn't all that challenging, anyway. A couple of tricky landings that could be trouble and it was best not to think about the in and out, but all in all pretty straightforward.

Tony has positioned himself right in the middle of the course, so he can see it all. I'm wondering why he's so damn interested in this when he's got all those other horses that are actually making him money as I make a big circle on Stringtown, warming up, which is a joke, there isn't any warming up on S.T. It's like being shot out of a cannon. She has her head up and is pulling my arms out of the sockets. She knows somethin is up, and she is one damn strong horse. The first fence is super simple, a little cross bar with wings and no distractions. She is galloping as we approach, and I can't for the life of me slow her down. She don't even seem to notice this little fence, gallops right over it without breaking stride, looking ahead at the next one, a plain brick wall no higher than three feet. She clears that by a foot, still without breaking stride.

We are gaining speed all the time and Stringtown's fighting the bit. She's all off balance as we come to the coop, which she hops over like a deer then it's the post and rail, which she takes two strides back, reaching, stretching, any other horse would never have made it but she's so big and scopey she lands easily on the other side, bursting away, and I can feel her muscles working underneath me, all hope of control gone as we come to the brush fence with the downhill landing, a great place for a horse goin too fast to stumble and fall. At this speed there'd be nothing left. The landing surprises the hell out of her. She doesn't stumble, just puts her head down and bucks. It's all I can do to stay on, and with me off balance, we head toward the in and out.

There is no way a horse all strung out can take this combination. I know that. And I know there ain't nothing I can do about it—short of bailing out, and at this speed I'd break something for sure, probably my neck. All I have are my instincts and everything Pap taught me, both of which are saying get yourself balanced and stay out of the way. It's too late now to do anything so just trust your horse and pray she can get the two of you out of this alive.

It's funny how it works. You got five, ten seconds maybe, but it seems like a lifetime as you're rushing toward whatever it is that's going to be your destiny. Destiny turns out to be Stringtown trying to take the two fences in one jump and landing on the second with the sounds of things breaking and she's hitting the ground sort of scrambling, and I start to jump free. Stringtown is getting her front legs under her, pushing up and kicking out and galloping again, all four legs working, all four legs okay, and I point her at the brick wall, an easy fence, as good a fence as any to end with, and she takes it, bold as ever, no hesitation, flying. And then it's over and Stringtown allows herself to be stopped and stands shaking her head, stomping her feet and snorting.

Tony comes over and hands me down. We both pretend this ain't unusual. He's not saying anythin, just looking at Stringtown's front legs, which are scratched from the fall. The cuts don't look serious, just superficial, but they are ugly. "Sorry," I say.

The mare is soaked with sweat so I start walking her. He falls in stride with me. We walk along in silence, heading toward the barn. I'm nervous 'cause of Stringtown's legs and the wild ride, which had to look totally out of control. When I'm nervous, things come into view that I don't normally see, get real clear, details I might not notice otherwise, stuff that doesn't seem to have anything to do with what I should be thinking about. So I'm lookin at the barn and the set up around it. How clean it looks, nothing out a place. I remember when they was building it, I'd come by just out of curiosity. I saw they used metal siding. I don't like metal barns, cold in the winter, hot as hell in the summer, but it sure looks nice now that it's done. I'm glad I have the chance to work here. I've taken liberties, I know. I'm regretting them a little now, after that show I just put on. Raffino might decide to just up and fire me. I'm thinkin this with the big horse walking along easily beside me, her neck bobbing with each stride, meaning she's moving well, using her back, and I know deep down inside I'd do it all over again if I had the chance.

"I certainly didn't expect to see anything like what I just saw."

I wait for what's next.

"I never thought the horse had it in her. I fully expected to have to take her to a sale."

"She's loaded with talent."

"It seemed a little risky there a couple of times."

"We missed our spot once or twice."

"Were you frightened?"

"No. Green horses are always a little rough around the edges."

"When she crashed through the in and out, did you see that coming?"

"Like I say, we missed our spot, got in a little close, but that will come with experience. The important thing is she likes to jump."

"You weren't scared when you realized you were going to crash?"

"No," I lie again.

"I think I would have been."

We walk in silence for a while, then he continues. "You really are a beautiful rider."

"No I'm not."

"Don't be modest."

I can tell he's watching me as we walk. "I'm not bein modest."

"You underestimate yourself."

I know I'm doing no such thing. I only know what Pap taught me. I've been riding since I was five, that's all, and I never had a horse that was already broke, had to do that myself, so I'm used to getting knocked around. I know how to get through it, that's all. I'm wondering if Raffino really thinks I'm all that good, which means he doesn't know much about riding, or if he's flattering me for some reason.

"You're doing a fine job here. I may have you work with some of the other training colts that have come in from New York."

I force myself to take a few steps before I answer. I tell him I'd like that very much, keeping my voice even, not too eager.

"And, of course, Stringtown. I want you to continue working with her. And don't feel rushed. We have all the time you need."

We? Tony's walking right in step with me and Stringtown's feet are hitting the ground in the four beat, squishy, yielding, athletic plop of a good horse walking on grass. He puts his hand on my shoulder, lets it drop away, a fleeting touch, but I know what it means. I've had more boys come on to me than I can count, and I won't pretend I haven't gotten certain vibes from him; I mean, I know the signs even if it's only the way guys hesitate a beat longer than necessary. Still, I'm caught off guard. And at once I can feel his solidness, the fit of his slacks, the span of his shoulders, the strong substantial wrists, curved lips, and the new, suddenly vulnerable bend of his neck. I feel all that strike, settle in, and become part of me.

CHAPTER NINE

ANNIE

The weather finally warmed for good and real spring arrived with all its magic. By May, the flowering trees were in bloom, and redbud and wild dogwood ran through the woods showing their pink and white blossoms through the splotchy sunlight. The light lost its winter glare as it filtered among the lacy new leaves unfurling along their branches. The grass turned the brief emerald green of spring.

There is a certain frenzied leisure at this time of year in the Allegheny Mountains as people realize winter is over for good and come out of their houses to feel the sun on their skin. People give parties and go for walks and open summer cottages and lie on the grass and take long rides in the country. They fuss with their gardens and put in their bulbs, wash their cars and get together with people they haven't thought about in months. Therefore it didn't surprise me when old friends from Coleton, people I hadn't seen since my return, called and asked me to a party. I quit early and washed my hair, scrubbed between my toes, tidied up my nails, put on pastel-colored clothing and shoes so delicate they weren't fit for walking across the yard. I climbed into the pickup—carefully so as not to get dirty—and drove through the balmy spring evening to the Drakes' lovely house on the lake.

There was music when I arrived. No one around here hired a band for parties except the country club, but tonight the Drakes had and it played light, shapeless tunes that drifted among the trees. A forest circled three sides of the house and someone had filled it with tiny white lights looking like frozen fireflies. Pale pink and cream colored Japanese lanterns hung from branches and the rafters of the porch.

The bar ran the width of one side of the house. Pots of hothouse red geraniums stood among the tawny, gold, and clear bottles of liquor. Weeks, the black man who had been catering parties in this area for so long he knew what most everyone drank, poured.

"Good evening, Mr. Himmler, Johnny Walker Red on the rocks, am I right? And for the lady, Chardonnay." His voice was as soft as the evening air. "And whiskey sour for Mr. Matheson… on the sweet side." He never measured; the knowledge acquired over the years lived in his fingers. He moved with such economic grace he appeared to stand still. Yet he could have your drink ready almost as he greeted you. Even so, there was a line. People not willing to wait helped themselves, grabbing bottles around the neck, pouring unceremoniously, tossing in the garnishes. Already cherry juice stained the white linen tablecloth with blood red spots and growing circles of amber spread under the bottles.

Weeks raised his eyes to mine and murmured, "Johnny Walker Red and soda with a twist." He was already pouring. He watched me to see how much scotch, and I let him fill the glass more than half full. I took a long swallow and was moving away from the table when John Drake called from the front door. "Why, it's Annie. And you look wonderful. Come here and let me kiss you. Darlene, come here. It's Annie."

"How thin you are," said Darlene. "Have you been sick?"

"Uh, no. I'm fine. Really, fine."

Darlene leaned over and kissed my cheek. "You ought to be kinder to yourself. All that striving on the farm and for what. We all work too hard. It's the curse of the millennium. The Townsends and Watkins are here. Have you seen them yet? And the Riverdales. You must have so much to catch up on with everyone. You naughty girl for not coming to see us sooner."

Sarah Townsend approached us, embraced me and said simply, "Annie, it is so good to have you back." Sarah was one of the kindest people I knew. Darlene and John left to greet another couple.

"You're looking thin Annie... thin but very fit," she said, giving my arm a gentle pat. "You're back on the farm." This was a statement, not a question. "I understand why," she went on and it was clear she had argued this with someone. "That valley is so beautiful... and so quiet."

I tried to remember if Stewart and I had ever had the Townsends out to the farm.

Bill Townsend emerged from the crowd, pumped my hand up and down vigorously. "Annie, it is so good to see you again. And how is Stewart? Gosh, I miss him." Bill looked surprised by this confession, leaned backwards slightly and blinked. His smile deepened. "When's he coming back here? Soon I hope." Bill winked at his wife, who shot him a look.

"Not soon, I don't think," I said.

"Well, I don't see him keeping himself away forever. Do you?"

The Drakes reappeared, bringing with them Bob and Lucy Watkins. The fading light subdued even Lucy's red hair. She had a broad, beautiful face and smoky green eyes. She touched her cheek to mine.

"What's that bastard up to these days? Boats is it?" Bob asked. "Boats are a wonderful thing," he went on, "and Stewart belongs on a boat. You can tell by the look of him. He's got that look. You know. Healthy." Bob patted his small but definite paunch. "Outdoors man, seaworthy. That's Stewart. Sailing, wonderful sport. Wouldn't think there'd be much money in it, though. Don't suppose that would bother Stewart. Next thing you know, he'll sail around the world. That's Stewart. There was always something about him. I've always admired him. He's got the sea in his eyes, so to speak."

"He's not sailing, Bob, he's selling, and not boats but something to do with computerized deep-sea equipment," said Lucy.

"Selling?" Bob looked somewhat disappointed.

I nodded.

"I know what you mean, though," John Drake said. "Now don't take me wrong, Annie, but I never did see Stewart staying on that farm... was surprised when the two of you moved out there, really. Back to nature is fine and all but Stewart's a party animal."

"Sea in his eyes," repeated Bob.

Lucy placed her hand on his arm.

Bob hesitated then continued with confidence. "Why, if it wasn't the sea, old Stewart would be a tennis pro or working as a spy for the C.I.A."

"Oh for heaven's sake," Lucy said.

"Well, you know… something exciting, lots of action, outdoors, plenty of… well, action."

"You've been watching too many movies."

"Of course, I know his parents were surprised he left. Surprised and disappointed. After sending him to architecture school. That farm was meant to help him get a start. I know he worked hard at it. You too. Wonderful designs. I just don't see him staying in the country, though. Or sitting at a desk. He's more a mover and a shaker, if you know what I mean." Bob rubbed his chin and shook his head. Momentarily out of epitaphs, he shifted gears. "And you're doing something with horses, I understand. Renting them. Something I've always wanted to do, ride a horse. Did once when I was a boy, but it ran right back into the barn. Nearly took my head off. Scared me to death. Don't mind telling you, I've been afraid ever since. Maybe I'll come and rent one of yours, Annie. That is, if you promise to give me the gentlest one you've got. One you'd put your grandmother on."

"She doesn't rent horses, Bob. She trains them." Bob glanced at Lucy, momentarily confused by the difference.

"I give lessons, too. I'll give you lessons on my gentlest horse if you like."

Three other couples drifted into our group. I knew them slightly. Each in their turn asked after Stewart. I had been drinking steadily from my tumbler of scotch and answered them, if not with ease, at least without making a fool of myself. Two women, mothers, inquired about riding lessons for their daughters. They had money, could more than afford it. I felt strings form, thin, tender as silk, weaving possibilities, a connection I was surprised to discover I wasn't certain I wanted. But I was flat broke and couldn't afford to be coy.

"How is business, Annie?" Bill asked. "Heard there is a fancy new horse barn out on Silver Valley Road? A multimillion-dollar operation, I understand. Isn't that your friend out there? Oh, what's her name? Tall girl, good-looking if a little rough."

"Clare," I said. "Clare Raffienne."

"Yes, that's right. Her grandfather was an old horse trader out in the Holler, wasn't he? That's certainly not his place. I always thought those people lived on the bare edge of nothing."

"Clare runs it for someone else."

"Something really funny about the place, I heard. You know… funny money."

Bill Townsend handed me a fresh drink. "I imagine it's hard to compete with that kind of money."

"I don't try."

"Doesn't it affect your business, though? I mean, there are just so many people interested in horses here. Not much of a client base, if you know what I mean. Not to discourage you, Annie." Bill patted me on the back. "Don't mean to do that at all. It's just that Silver Storm Farm is just so damn impressive. How did your friend get involved in that kind of operation? I've seen her driving the biggest, reddest pickup you've ever seen. We were in the feed store getting birdseed when she came in. I can't imagine her connected with that kind of money."

A fourth couple emerged into our cone of light. It was all but dark now, and away from the Japanese lanterns, people were no more than indistinct shapes. These two were strangers to me. He looked young, and she was all startled eyes and bony arms. The O'Sheas, Martha and Sean.

Martha looked at Bill. "Are you talking about Clare Raffienne? I take lessons from her. She's wonderful really. Can do anything on a horse. That Raffino knows he's got a good thing."

"Raffino? Is that the owner? Do you know him?"

Thin arms rolled her eyes. "I don't actually know him, but I see him there." She leaned forward slightly, and we all bent toward her. "He's connected to the mafia, I've heard, and I believe it. Strange men in suits coming and going." Bob leaned closer and listened eagerly.

"You should be there when he walks through the barn or around the grounds. Everyone hops to, you can be sure. The place is run like a military camp. Clare, now she's something else. I'm not sure he knows quite what to do with her." You could tell thin arms was pleased with this.

The caterers began bringing deep-dished crusty casseroles, pineapple-studded hams, huge crunchy skinned turkeys, gracefully curving shrimp in bowls the size of wash basins, and butter-glazed croissants from the kitchen. Small tables were arranged on the decks and patios, and I joined the Townsends and the new couple at one end of the porch. As people were finishing their meal, the band switched to dance tunes and a few couples swayed unevenly on the yard, then gave it up and moved to stand in groups around the house. Some of the men relaxed, loose-limbed, into lawn chairs while the women fetched sweaters or freshened their makeup in one of the many mirrored bathrooms.

The Drakes brought out champagne with dessert, which was followed by a mild stir of activity as people repositioned themselves. Groups formed, broke apart, reformed, and eventually shared all the gossip the town had to offer. The clusters began to thin and a few cars pulled out of the driveway. I could respectfully leave at any time now. Instead, I relaxed into a chair and put my feet up on a bench. I had a tall, fluted glass of champagne in each hand. I was glad I had come. I would leave when I finished my drinks and another evening would be gotten through.

A car pulled into the driveway, passed those parked along the semicircle, and stopped in front of the house. Several people approached the vehicle and stood in a cluster around it. The crowd was too thick to see the person as they stepped out of the car, but the group generated energy. Heads bobbed and individuals jockeyed for position. Eventually, they moved into the shadows and reappeared under a lantern. A larger group now, they focused on someone in their center. Odd, whoever it was should arrive this late in the game. Animated and cheerful sounds made their way through the moist night air. I thought I'd wait until the group dispersed before making my way across the yard to my truck. I sipped my champagne. I would wake shaking in the morning but tonight I would sleep well. I looked up to see a man step from the shadows to stand in front of me. It was Stewart. The evening that had been spinning into a fine mist was suddenly filled with sparks and the exquisite pain of hopes I thought had died.

CHAPTER TEN

The Drakes wanted us to stay the night. We did stay until everyone else had spoken to Stewart—shaking his hand, kissing him or clapping him on the back—and then left. As for me, I could barely look at him and certainly could not trust myself to speak. I could only nod and smile when people patted me or beamed their *we're so happy for you* looks in my direction. It was a spell so fragile, the wrong move from me could fracture it into a million pieces. I did not feel safe to drive. Stewart put his arm around me and said he would drive me home in the truck.

"Oh, stay," said John Drake. "You can go home tomorrow after you've had a good night's rest."

"John," said Darlene, "I think they might want to be alone."

"We'll give them privacy, all the privacy they could want."

"It's not the same," she said.

We pulled away from the house on the lake, left the unblinking lights behind and drove into the complete darkness of the surrounding woods. Stewart put his arm around my shoulders and drew me next to him.

"Stewart, I need to know what's going on."

"Nothing is going on. I just missed you, that's all. I wanted to surprise you. Aren't you glad to see me, Annie? Not even a little bit?" He touched me on the tip of my nose.

"You know I am. That's just it. I was getting used to it this way."

"That soon, huh?"

"It's been pure hell. I can't go through all that again."

"What hell? What are you talking about?"

I knew better than to go down that road but couldn't help myself. "I've missed you, Stewart." I looked at my hands in my lap. "You can't imagine."

"But, Annie, this was your idea. I've missed you too and wanted to see you again. I've come all the way from LA Can't we just enjoy each other's company for a while?"

"How long do you plan to stay?"

"A while."

At the farm, Stewart opened my car door, held out his hand, and asked for the house keys. I shook my head. "It's open."

"That's right," he said. "I'd forgotten that about here. In LA, there would be nothing left."

Inside, he looked around. "The old place looks even better than I remembered it." He indicated the couch. "You sit, Annie, while I make coffee." He tucked the blanket around my lap. When the coffee was ready, he poured Irish whiskey in his cup and a glass of red wine for me. I listened to the sounds in the kitchen, tormenting myself with the thought that the only person in the world who knew how much I liked to finish off the evening with red wine and coffee was puttering around in my kitchen. And in all likelihood would be gone within a week.

Stewart brought the drinks and put them on the coffee table.

"Are you feeling any better?"

"I must have dozed in the truck. I feel as though I've been to bed and now it's morning."

"It almost is." Stewart crossed to the stereo and pushed several buttons. Nothing happened.

"It's broken."

"What a shame. You've been out here all this time with no music."

"Not all the time, no."

Stewart picked up one of the boxes and turned it over. He examined the wires carefully, pulled the cord from behind the stand, and toyed with the prongs. He plugged it back in but still nothing happened. "Is the tool kit where it used to be?"

"You don't have to fix that now."

"But I want to."

He went to a closet in the hall and returned with a black metal box. He retrieved a tiny screwdriver and began tinkering with the wires in the stereo, stopping periodically to plug it in. The blackness outside the windows was becoming less dense.

"You never did tell me why you're here."

"Sure I did. I missed you."

"I want to know how long you will be staying."

"I don't know, Annie. Not long. I have to get back to work."

"Is it really that simple for you? Pop in, pop out whenever you like. No strings, no commitments."

Stewart glanced up from what he was doing, looked at me briefly, held the box upside down under the light, and peered at it closely. "The light in here is not that great," he said. After a few minutes, he placed the box upright on the stand, winked at me, and plugged it in. A love song from the fifties filled the room with the innocent, upbeat sounds of rock and roll in its infancy. Stewart straightened and stood next to the mantel, tapping it lightly in time to the music. He sang softly with the words. He had a beautiful voice. He turned toward me and held out his hand, smiling. I couldn't help myself. I smiled too. I rose from the couch, walked around the coffee table, and faced him. His smile deepened. He drew me to him, dipped and swayed against my body, catching me into the rhythm of the song. We danced between the furniture, stepping apart and together in a jitterbug. I moved awkwardly, my feet slowed by the rug, but Stewart kept me steady, guided me into the moves. His lips touched my neck. I stopped dancing and pulled back so I could look at him. Neither of us smiled. I could feel moisture above my lip, and I ran my tongue around my mouth. Stewart swallowed, still holding onto my hand. Then his smile was back, and he dipped me away from him once again, brought me in close, singing along with the words. His smell hadn't changed a bit. It was clean and sweet, as innocent as the song and, resting my forehead against his neck, I wondered helplessly how this could be.

When we stopped dancing, the outer rim of the sun, barely visible through the fog rising off the valley floor, was just showing over Hog's Back Mountain. I took a bath in scalding hot water and soaked away the long evening and alcohol. My skin felt clean and smooth as I slipped between the sheets. Stewart, wearing a pair of white boxer shorts, came into the room and sat on the edge of the bed.

"Want a back rub?"

I rolled onto my side.

He stretched out beside me and carefully massaged the area along the small of my back. Eventually he stood up, pulled the boxers to his ankles, and stepped out of them. He lifted the top sheet and slid warm and naked beside me.

"Ah, Stewart," I said, "why are you tan all over?"

"Shouldn't I be?" he said and moved in such a way that ended any discussion.

When I woke, the room was spinning. Stewart slept peacefully. His hair and thick lashes were streaked from the sun. I lifted the covers. Yes, he was definitely golden brown from head to toe. I could picture the situation. The women would be good looking, of course. And comfortable with the situation—with his boat, the ocean, and the sun sparkling off the water in hard chips of light.

I lay back with a sigh. I hated him.

Stewart stirred. "What time is it?"

"I have no idea."

"Why are you awake?"

"I just am, that's all."

"You sound angry. Why are you angry?"

"I'm not."

"Of course you are. You shouldn't be, but you are. Now come here." Stewart pulled me close. "Shall I sing to you?" He adjusted the pillow under my head. "There now... is that comfortable?"

When I returned from the barn later that morning, Stewart was dishing breakfast and Lydia leaned against the counter wearing a t-shirt and a pair of boxers. Her small breasts stood out under the shirt and her legs were muscled and perfectly shaped. She was barefoot. As soon as I walked through the door, she picked up a bowl from the counter and tilted it toward me.

"Coffee," she said with a sheepish grin. "I'm out and can't possibly get started without it. Neither can Rollo." Her eyes were smudged with sleep.

I didn't speak. Lydia looked from me to Stewart and back to me. She straightened from the counter. "Well, I better be going. It was nice meeting you, Stewart. See you later, Annie." She walked head down and, still smiling, pushed the screened door open with her free hand and glanced back at us before letting the door bang behind her.

I looked around at all the food sitting on the kitchen counter: eggs, bacon, toast, butter, jam, cheese, and a large pitcher of orange juice. Normally I had coffee for breakfast.

Stewart held out his arm for me. I stepped into him, leaned against his side, and laid my head on his shoulder. I scooped a spoonful of eggs into my mouth. They were tender, light, and mixed with cheese. I took another spoonful. "Where did you get all this food?"

"I went to that little store down the road while you were feeding the horses. Didn't you hear the truck?"

I shook my head. "Stewart, I have a show to go to."

"You've got time. Besides, let your new trainer go instead. I have to say I was a little surprised when she told me who she was. She looks about twelve."

"She's twenty something."

"Really? And how is she working out?"

"She's okay."

Stewart turned back to the food, began dishing it up. He was still smiling. "Well, let her go to the show. Isn't that why you got her?"

"We're both going. It's my business. I need to be there, too."

"And how is business, Annie?"

I thought for a horrible moment I might cry. He turned away from me and put a plate of eggs and bacon on the table and poured a glass of orange juice. "You have to eat, so sit down with me for a minute and enjoy it."

We ate in silence for a while before Stewart cleared his throat. "The farm looks a little overgrown," he said. "Should you hire someone to help with the fields?"

"No. It will just take me a little more time, that's all."

He pushed back his chair and winked at me. "You load up the horses and I'll drive you to your show... well, almost to the show. You drop me at the Drakes. The show is at Lakeside, right? And that way I can pick up my car. We'll bring the boat around and have a picnic. I've already spoken to Darlene. It's a gorgeous day. You'll love it."

"Stewart, I should be at the show. Riding."

"Come on Annie. It's not like I'm here every day."

"Stewart." Why was I feeling so fragile? It wasn't like me to go around feeling like crying. And here was Stewart looking so healthy and strong and sweet and rich. How did he do that? Stand there in a t-shirt and khaki shorts and look rich?

"Are you all right?"

"Yes, of course. But you know how it is with a business. I need to be involved. It's just getting started."

"It's just one show. Hand it over to your trainer. That's why you hired her. She'll take care of everything."

Rollo and Lydia were coming out of the apartment as we pulled down the driveway. Stewart cocked the rearview mirror and watched them climb into the Corvette. He hummed the love song from last night, checking out the options on the truck. "You know, this is the reddest truck I've ever seen. But I like it. Has everything, doesn't it? GPS, satellite radio, extended cab, engine sounds good, upholstery like new." He touched the tip of my nose. "You did good, girl." He tilted the rearview mirror again to keep the Corvette in view, an amused expression on his face. "Annie," he said, "have you noticed that your trainer's boyfriend is black?"

"Very funny."

"I like your style. Appalachia, white girl, black boyfriend. You've got balls, I'll give you that."

"That doesn't sound like you."

"I'm not talking about me."

I felt close to tears again. What had I expected? That he wouldn't notice? That no one would? "I didn't know about him until she moved in. Anyway, I could use a man to help out."

"I know but a black… excuse me… an African American? Here?"

I didn't trust myself to answer. Stewart patted my thigh. "At least the barn is still standing. For now, anyway."

CHAPTER ELEVEN

At Lakeside, the ring sits next to the shoreline. It's a popular show for that reason, with many people attending either just for the view or the prestige of being near the Yacht Club. When I arrived, Clare was there, dressed in the hunt seat traditional outfit: rat catcher shirt, black boots, helmet, black gloves. Even so, she looked all wrong. Her hair bunched out from under her helmet and a streak of dirt stained the front of her white shirt. She held the end of a lead shank, while at the other end Stringtown did airs above the ground. The amazing thing was that the big mare allowed herself to be contained at all. All four feet never touched the ground at the same time. Her dark eyes were rimmed with white.

"Get Lonesome off the trailer," Clare shouted when I pulled next to her, "so I can tack the bitch up."

With Lonesome tied next to the mare, Clare and I were able to throw a saddle on Stringtown, slip a bridle over her head, and tighten the girth before she could land a kick or break loose. I gave Clare a leg up. She fairly flew into the saddle, gathered the reins, and called, "I'll be back," as Stringtown galloped across the field and headed up the mountain toward the woods. She'd caught the fever all right.

Lydia and Rollo arrived, pulling the Corvette next to my trailer. Lydia gazed in wonderment after Clare. "Is she planning to show that horse?"

"It's the mare's first show. She'll probably just get her used to the atmosphere."

"Take her home and train her some more," said Rollo before putting a match to his cigarette.

I turned from them. White sails billowed against the painfully blue sky. A few boats were tied in the marina. The Drake's float boat squatted among them.

"Lydia," I said. "I'm not going to show today. Will you take Lonesome in the jumping classes?"

Lydia's lids flew open. "Not show?"

"That's right."

Lydia's eyes stayed wide open in mock horror.

"Something has come up. I'll be on that boat down there."

Rollo took a deep drag on his cigarette, which he held to his mouth in that three-fingered way I detested. "Do you think that's wise? It's your business, after all."

"I've never even ridden Lonesome."

"He's very easy… dead honest. Just point him at the fence. My tack is in the trailer. Just warm him up a little, that's all you'll need. I'll be down there," I said pointing, "if you need anything."

The float boat was complete with benches, chairs, tables, food, ice, champagne, and a waist-high railing. Stewart handed me up. Bob Watkins raised his head from where he lay in his swimsuit on one of the benches. "Hey, Annie, don't mind if I don't get up." He shielded his eyes before flopping down again. He was so large and luminously white I could hardly take my eyes off him.

"When does it start?" asked Lucy.

"What?"

"The horse show."

"It already has."

"Really?" Bob peered at the ring. "Looks like they're just warming up."

Stewart poured me a glass of champagne, which I drank while watching the show grounds. I could tell by the set of Lydia's shoulders that she wouldn't show Lonesome to his best. The hunt course here was long and flowing, made for my gelding who wasn't particularly handy. I could most likely get a second on him and a few times had even won the class, the long lines between fences exciting the greener horses or inexperienced riders to gallop too fast. All you needed was to sit quietly on Lonesome, and he would calmly do the job for you. Obviously irritated, Lydia was bound to override him, which would unsteady him, making him even less elegant. Everyone was busy: fetching water, tacking up, going to and from the warm-up ring. If there were conversations, they took place on the move. It was like an opening scene in a play, setting the mood: the hustle, the horses trotting around the warm-up ring or across the grounds, business like, some hopping over warm-up fences, mother's braiding their young girl's hair, older girls putting braids in their horses' manes or brushing their tails with long gliding strokes.

"Oh, look." Lucy pointed at the ring. "Something's going to happen. They're all lining up."

"That means the class is over," I said. "They are going to place the winners."

"Really? It's over?"

"What's over?" asked John.

"The class. It's been judged. There will be more, though."

"The whole thing's a mystery to me."

"It's sort of like watching sailing races, isn't it?" Lucy said.

Stewart sat on one of the benches and patted the seat next to him for me to sit down. Darlene passed around food and John poured more champagne. From where I sat, I could see Clare and Stringtown doing laps around the outskirts of the grounds. I heard Lonesome's name announced over the loudspeaker winning a fourth, but no mention of The Doctor.

Bob sat up, glanced down at his belly resting in his lap, pulled his t-shirt on, and swallowed some champagne. "So, Stewart, what's going on with you? Are you here for a visit or will you be staying?"

"Bob," Lucy warned.

Stewart put his arm around my shoulder. "Just visiting. Then it's back to work. You know how it is getting a business going… I'll be putting in long hours for a year or two. You'll watch out for Annie, won't you? Check on her once in a while?"

"Tell me again how you got involved in the deep-sea equipment business.

All the way in California. Talk about a one-eighty."

"Friend from college called. Thought I'd be good at it. Asked me to be his partner. Made me a deal I couldn't refuse. To tell the truth, I'm not really cut out to be an architect. I like knocking things apart and putting them back together my way, but sitting at a desk and drawing, not so much. And besides, I've always wanted to go to California."

Everyone looked at me. I turned away, stared back at the show grounds. I noticed Lydia's white-blonde hair as it caught the sun. She put her horse on the trailer, and she and Rollo walked down the hill approaching the docks, their hands over their eyes to protect them from the sun. "Here, Lydia," I called. She hesitated, and John scrambled forward, held out his hand. "Welcome aboard," he said, easing her carefully over the rails. Rollo followed on his own. Lydia patted herself back in place, smoothed her hair. Her face was set and blotched along the cheekbones. "I'm ready to leave. The judge says The Doctor's lame."

"Lame?"

"He's not, of course," said Rollo, "but there's no point in trying to convince this judge. We'd be wasting our time."

"What about Lonesome—you could stay and ride Lonesome."

"He'll never place more than fourth. The judge has picked his favorites."

"Lydia, each class is a new class. It could change."

Rollo flicked his cigarette into the water. "The best he'll place is fourth." He carefully enunciated every word. "If you have a moment, we'd like to wrap legs."

"Go ahead and wrap them."

Stewart cleared his throat. "Annie, why don't you introduce us?"

"This is my new trainer, Lydia. And this is Rollo."

John poured two more flutes of champagne.

Bob had gotten up and motioned Lydia to take his seat. "Annie told me she had a trainer, but I had no idea she was so young. What does your mamma say about you being away from home?"

"Mamma doesn't say anything since I'm over twenty-one."

"Really? And you actually train horses? It's hard to picture. You're so very little and they're so big."

"It's not a matter of strength," said Lydia.

Stewart sat in the chair across from her and stretched his legs out in front of him. Lydia and he looked straight at each other for a moment. "Where do you come from?" he asked.

"Connecticut, and you?"

"LA."

"LA?" I said. "You were born and raised here."

"And now I'm from LA."

"I've always wanted to go to LA," Lydia said.

"I bet you have," Stewart said.

"How long have you been in this backwater?" Bob asked.

"Close to two months, but it's not so bad. I like the slower pace."

"Aren't you up at the crack of dawn riding horses and doing whatever else you have to do to them?"

"I should say not."

"I thought that's what people in the horse business did," said Stewart. "You know, dawn to dusk, hardly a chance to take a bath, just stand their clothes in a corner at night, that sort of thing."

"Do I look like I hardly have a chance to bathe?"

"No, sweetheart, I should say not."

"Stewart." Darlene rested her hand on his shoulder. "Look at this boat coming here." A fine big boat, bigger and sleeker and far grander than anything else in the marina, was mooring into the slip next to us. Several dark, well-built young men hopped onto the dock to secure the lines. A man came up from below to watch them. He was tall, strongly built, and better looking than I remembered. We watched the men skillfully secure the big boat, their movements swift and sure. One of them, after a word from Mr. Raffino, jumped onto the dock and headed for the show grounds. He approached Clare, who slowed Stringtown to a jigging trot. The young man spoke to her while hustling alongside the mare, his head tilted upward at an awkward angle. He caught hold of her boot, gestured in our direction. Clare glanced at us, nodded briefly, and rode Stringtown to my trailer. She untied Lonesome from where Lydia had left him and put him inside and quickly let the mare bound up the ramp next to him. She secured the bar in back of the horses, lifted and secured the ramp, and walked down the hill toward the boat. Mr. Raffino, who had been watching since the young man went to fetch her, turned back to us, recognized me and managed a tight smile and slight bow.

John looked startled.

"He owns Silver Storm Farm. I was visiting Clare and she introduced us."

"They're buddies," Stewart said. My friendship with Clare had always interested him. "Why don't you ask him over?"

John waved, called him to join us. Mr. Raffino hesitated, seemed to want to refuse but John continued to wave and gesture so he acknowledged the invitation with another bow, and stepped from one boat to the other. He was amazingly light on his feet. Before addressing any of us, he turned to Clare, who stood on the dock, arms crossed, looking annoyed. Mr. Raffino leaned across the railing, held out his hand, and pulled her aboard. With the hat gone, her hair stuck out from her head in a crinkled mass. Her skin, damp and ruddy, gave off a sharp, animal scent. There were two wet half-moons under her arms. Bob stared at her as though she had stepped naked from the woods.

"Yes," Darlene said in a small voice, "please join us. Champagne?"

"No, thanks."

"You should try it," Tony said, accepting a glass.

"That's okay."

John stepped forward. "Anything else? Scotch, Pepsi, beer?"

"Beer's fine."

John bent over one of the coolers, dug up to his elbows through the ice and came up with a broad smile and a Coors.

"How did it go?" Mr. Raffino took a strand of hair that had gotten inside Clare's collar and smoothed it over her shoulder.

So that's the way it was.

"She didn't kill anyone," Clare said.

"Damn near," Rollo said.

"What on earth are we talking about?" Lucy asked.

"My horse." Tony held out his hand, smiling apologetically at his lack of manners, bowed yet again, and as he did so, collected himself, rearranged himself in some indefinable way so that when he straightened, old world charm stood out all over him. "By the way, you can call me Tony, Tony Raffino." He put his hand on Clare's elbow. "Clare here seems to think my horse has potential, but the mare's been unmanageable for everyone else."

"She's still unmanageable," said Rollo.

"She does have potential, though," said Lydia.

Clare tipped back her head and drank her beer in long, full-throated swallows. When she finished, she belched softly, deposited the empty back in the cooler, put one hand on the railing, and fast as a wolf jumped off the boat onto the dock. "Thanks," she called up to the Drakes, shielding her eyes from the sun before turning and striding back to the horses.

Tony looked at the dock where Clare had landed, blinked a few times, turned back to his audience. He smiled a shade uncertainly, shook hands with everyone while saying goodbye. He climbed off the float boat somewhat less gracefully than he had climbed on, spoke to his crew who gathered the lines, shoved the big vessel away from the dock, and left without a word.

Rollo and Lydia, on the other hand, stayed until the sun, coming at a slant across the lake, had lost its warmth. When Darlene began gathering up glasses and John put away the last of the food, Lydia rubbed her arms and, giving Rollo a nudge with her foot, said it was time they headed home.

Bob watched them walk down the dock and on up the hill. "She's a heart breaker, that one," he said.

"What do you mean?" asked Lucy.

"With that blonde hair and blue eyes. My, oh my. Seems awfully tight with her groom, though."

"That's not her groom," I said. "That's her boyfriend."

John whistled. "I wish you'd told us, Annie."

"Oh, you were all right," Stewart said. "Besides, I don't think they're all that tight."

"I would think Clare to be more your type," said Lucy.

"Clare?" Bob laughed. "She looks like she's got Uzis hidden in her hair."

CHAPTER TWELVE

CLARE

I saw the way Annie looked at me when Tony fixed my hair. She never approved of the way I was with boys. She wasn't mean, but it was her silence and the way she'd stiffen and look away every time I mentioned a new guy. There was only one man for her, though what she was going to do about that now I couldn't guess. I wished I had her loyalty. I don't know why I couldn't keep the good feeling going 'cause it was like nothing else when you was all new to each other, and kind of circling, and thinking about it, wondering if the guy felt the same way and finding out he does, and doing everything on God's green earth to get together, feeling like you'll bust if you don't and when you finally do, not being able to get close fast enough, all hands and mouth and flying clothes.

Tony was different. He sure seemed to be taking his time. After I'd rode Stringtown that day, he sort of vanished. I think he left the farm for a few days. I kept working the mare anyway, made up my mind to take her to a show. Except for gaming, where all you had to do was show up with a good horse, I'd never been much for showing. But Stringtown wasn't any game horse. She was too big; you needed something small and quick to game. The closest thing was the hunter classes, so I decided that's what we'd do.

Turns out I hated showing even in the hunter classes, but that didn't matter because Tony decided he loved it.

CHAPTER THIRTEEN

ANNIE

Stewart stayed a week. The day before he left, I lay next to him while he slept and figured out how many hours it would be before he drove to the airport. His plane departed at ten the next morning, plus the three-hour drive. I glanced at the clock. It was eight o'clock. I watched Stewart's easy breathing. Let's see. Twenty-six hours minus three. Twenty-three hours from now he would get in his rented car and go. I rolled onto my back, turned my feet upward, and stared at the ridges my toes made under the sheet. I breathed deeply until my belly stopped quivering. I could always go back to LA. I pictured the concrete and buildings and literally could feel myself coming up against those walls, the skyscrapers looming overhead, cutting off the air. Just crossing the street was an ordeal, parking something to be thought out and planned carefully. I visualized driving my red truck downtown, an easy target, so big, so red, so laughable. I could sell it, of course, would sell it should I move back. I could wake Stewart right now and tell him I wanted to return. I traced his fingers with my own and he frowned in his sleep, drew his hand away. Move back. To Stewart in bed next to me in the mornings. To late dinners in new restaurants. To boats and oiled brown bodies, to evenings that turned into mornings, to home in glass and steel.

The party was at the Watkin's place—a huge old house in town. The rooms were filled with people by the time we arrived. We'd brought Lydia with us and Stewart introduced her to a few groups, went to get a drink, and she settled into the melee without any hanging back, chatting and bobbing her bright corn silk head like a bird. Even though she was a stranger to these people, she moved among them with more ease than I did.

The last people to arrive were Clare and Tony. I spotted them on my way from the bar to the porch, under the chandelier, Tony's hand on the small of Clare's back. Lucy Watkins separated herself from the crowd and went to greet them. Clare nodded but didn't speak. Her eyes were wide, watchful, and she looked from one cluster of people to another. She had never been to a party like this. Her dress was low cut and shiny and way too tight. Everyone else was in sports clothes. I was surprised and furious at Lucy for inviting them. Tony bowed and smiled and shook hands, and though people watched him, watched him carefully out of the corners of their eyes, he got nowhere, seemed to be batting his Italian charm against a curious, smiling, barely polite shield. Unlike Lydia, a small, bright, cheerful novelty, who flitted here and there around the room, Clare and Tony loomed: large, foreign, vaguely threatening.

Stewart, on the other hand, drew people to him with the force of a magnet. Being next to him was like being at sea, rocking on waves, enclosed and protected, lulled by forces other than your own. We stayed out 'till nearly dawn that night, and poised next to me in the truck, cheerful and wide awake, Lydia suggested going somewhere for breakfast. Stewart didn't have to turn his head, didn't even have to shift his eyes briefly in my direction to know my reaction. He laid his hand on my knee and said, "How about a rain check, Lydia, girl?"

We didn't sleep at all that night. "Time enough for that on the plane," Stewart said, looking like he could go forever. In the early morning, he packed his belongings, folding his clothes neatly into the suitcase. My eyes kept closing in spite of myself. I blinked them open, but they closed again, and the next thing I was dreaming of the ocean, transporting my shiny red pickup across it on a barge, then Stewart woke me with a touch on the shoulder. I saw his suitcase on the rug in front of the bed.

I said nothing so as not to beg him to stay.

He kissed me lightly on the lips. "I'll be back," he promised.

"When?"

"I'm not sure, but soon."

He carried his bag down the stairs while I followed with his briefcase. Outside, the sun was just showing itself over the hills, already dispelling the nighttime chill. The day would be bright and cloudless. I stood by the car while Stewart tossed his bags into the trunk and settled himself into the driver's seat. He rolled down the window and I rested my hand on the sill. He patted it gently and started the motor. I stepped away, watched as he backed up and turned around and waved as he drove out of the driveway. I looked down the road long after the car had gone from sight, unable to pick up my life in the house or in the barn or among the fields.

CHAPTER FOURTEEN

JACK

"Wake up!"

It was Dad. I slit an eye just enough to see him leanin against the bedroom doorframe. I didn't move, just lay still as I could, kept my eyes closed. He jabbed me in the side with his cane. Someday I was gonna kill the son-of-a-bitch.

"Get up outta that bed. It's seven thirty." He jabbed me again, harder.

Seven-thirty. Not still drunk but coming down off it, which would make him mean as cat shit but too sick to do much about it. He jabbed me twice this time. "Get outta that bed, now, you hear me."

I rolled over. "I'm up. I'm up."

"Good." He turned and gimped down the hall, dragging that wooden leg and muttering about me being a lazy good for nothin. I waited until he was in the kitchen yelling at Mom about gettin the Goddamn coffee ready before I slipped into their bedroom and got the rifle.

Harry was waiting on me at the end of the driveway. We was startin up Hog's Back when I happened to look back, and there it sat, low, white and fast looking. A Goddamn Corvette. There'd never been anything like it in the valley. Even setting still, you knew it would beat anything around here. At first I thought it must a belonged to that Walker woman. She was starting some kind a horse business, but Harry said, no, he heard she'd hired a trainer. Someone from out of town. Figured. You'd have to be from out of town to own a car like that. Sleek and fast and new. Later, when I got to know Lydia, that car and her seemed to be one and the same.

Harry and I spent the rest of the morning shooting. We had no luck at all. We seen three squirrels and two rabbits but the sun was hard and bright and must of shown off the barrel of the guns when we raised them because the squirrels cocked their heads, flicked their tails, and skittered out of sight. Same with the rabbits. They froze the way they do, but as we squeezed the trigger, they bounded off. Harry took it okay, but I was spitting nails. We hadn't brought dinner, thinking we'd be back home in a couple hours, and I was getting hungry. I told Harry I was goin back and he said, "Hell, what for?"

"I ain't had no breakfast."

"Me neither."

"We could go home and get something to eat and come back in the evening."

"I ain't hungry."

"Well, I am. I don't have any fat to live off like you. The hunting sucks anyway. Might as well go home."

"Yeah, you is skinny."

I was about to say something, but Harry cradled his rifle under his arm and turned down the mountain. It was steep going and shale rolled under our feet. We half slid down, grabbing onto saplings to keep our footing. Harry stopped, hanging onto a tree. He dug his heels into the ground to keep his balance, propping his gun next to his knee. He was breathing a little heavy. He stood with his hand resting on the barrel of his rifle, looking down on the valley. "Look at those horses down there. How much do you think they're worth?"

"I dunno. Hundreds. Maybe thousands."

"Where do you suppose she gets that kind a money?"

"Her old man's rich. His daddy's a doctor in Coleton and his momma is too. And so is her daddy. You know, high society folks."

"How do you know?"

"Mom heard it at work."

"Your momma still works?" Harry made it sound sinful.

"So what if she does."

"Nothin."

"So why did you say it like that?"

"I didn't."

"You did."

"I didn't mean nothin."

"Yes, you did. You're just too chicken to say it."

"My Dad would never let my mom go to work, that's all."

I didn't say nothin. I knew his folks would lose their welfare checks if either one a them went to work. It was like that with everyone in the Holler. My dad was always yelling at Ma about the same thing. Harry steadied himself, moving his heels back and forth in the ground. He let go of the tree, took his rifle from his knee, cocked it, then raised it to his shoulder. He aimed at one of the horses. "Bang," he said. "There's your dinner."

"You couldn't even hit a horse from here."

"You can't do no better. Shit. You missed everything you shot at today." He closed his one eye again, sighting on a chestnut horse grazing in the field. "Bam. There goes 1,000 dollars." He moved the rifle slightly to the left, aimed it at a big dark horse who must have heard us 'cause it raised its head, pricked its ears in our direction. "Bang. There goes 2,000 dollars." He moved the gun again. "There's 3,000 dollars." He set the butt of the gun on the ground.

"I can shoot a hell of a lot better than you," I said.

"Shit."

"I shot Jeannie's cat from five hundred yards the other day."

"You shot your own sister's cat?"

"Yeah, from 500 yards."

"Shit, you couldn't hit no cow from 500 yards."

"Bet ya."

"Bet your rifle."

"Not my rifle."

"Right. You never shot no cat, specially not from five hundred yards."

"Okay, it's a bet."

"Right."

"I'll even show it to you. What's left of it. It's in the woods in back a my house."

"You're sick, you know that. Your sister know you shot her cat?"

"No. Not unless she went into the woods. And she never goes into the woods. She never does nothin but sit around that house watchin TV. She's been calling that cat for days, though." I laughed.

"You really are sick."

My stomach was churning so I put my gun under my arm and began sliding down the mountain. Once we was on level ground, we followed the right-a-way around the Norwood farm. You could see that white Corvette plain as day. It stood out in the sun, all sparkly and fine. The Walker woman was living out here by herself, I'd heard. Her old man wasn't with her.

"Hey Harry, is that trainer a man or a woman?"

"Woman most likely. Only fags ride horses. Course, it could be a fag."

Fags didn't know anything about cars. Cars like that need someone who knew what they were doing looking after them. Next thing you know it wouldn't be worth a damn with some fag taking care a it. Or a woman. I'd never worked for a woman. No sir. But looking at that Corvette and thinking how it needed proper care, I started to think how maybe they might need a hired hand. I figured it might be worth a try. If it was only two women or even one woman and a fag, they'd need someone to take care of things, including that car. Change the oil. Tune it up. They might even need someone to drive them around.

Harry lived deeper in the Holler than I did and he kept going once we hit my place. Mom's blue Ford was next to the house. I scraped the mud off my boots on the cinder block in front of the door. I could smell hamburgers frying. I opened the door and stepped up into the kitchen and propped the rifle against the wall. Mom was standing at the stove flippin burgers. My eyes took a while to adjust to the dark after bein outdoors. I could barely make out Jeannie lying on her stomach in the living room, watchin TV.

I got a Mountain Dew out of the refrigerator and sat down at the kitchen table. Mom put the burgers and some fries in front a me. "Does your daddy know you took that rifle?"

"Yeah. How about some ketchup?"

She got the ketchup out of the refrigerator and put it on the table. "You sure your dad knows?"

"I said yes for Christ sake."

"He'll beat your ass if you took it without permission."

"How's he gonna find out?"

Mom put another plate on the table and started scrubbing the frying pan. "Jeannie," she called, "come and get your dinner."

Jeannie didn't move. She was like that when she was in front of the TV.

"I'm leavin for work in fifteen minutes. You haven't eaten by then, you don't eat."

My sister still didn't budge so Mom wiped her hands on her dress and went in and turned off the set.

"Mom!"

"Come and eat. I got to leave in fifteen minutes."

"I just want to see the end of the show."

"You don't eat now, you don't eat."

Jeannie got to her feet, acting like she could barely move. She came in and sat at the table, leanin her head in one hand.

"You're still in your pajamas. Ma, it's noon and she's still in her pajamas. How can you let her get away with that?"

"It's Sunday," said Jeannie. "Leave me alone."

I took a bite of hamburger. Maybe I'd walk back to the Norwood farm. See about getting a job. I looked at Jeannie picking at her French fries, her head still in her hand. She was about the laziest thing I ever seen. I reached over and pulled her hand away so she'd have to sit up, at least.

"Leave me alone."

"You was getting ketchup in your hair."

"I was not."

I flicked a fry at her. The ketchup landed right where I wanted it to, in the strands that hung under her chin. She shrieked like I knew she would.

"Mom. You see that? Make him stop." She started sucking at the ends of her hair, trying to get the red out. Mom clattered the fryin pan into the sink.

"Jack, ain't you getting too old to be actin that way?" She went into the bathroom, maybe to cry but prob'ly just to get tidy for work.

Jeannie stuck her tongue out at me. "You made Mamma cry."

I sat there looking at her with the ends of her hair still pink. She was too old to just lay around the house all day. She should be helping Mom; she could be doing the dishes, at least. That's what got Mom upset, havin to work and cook and clean too, not my scrappin. Jeannie couldn't even take a little teasing she was such a baby. She needed to grow up and stop whining and do her share. She needed a good kick in the ass.

"What you starin at, Jack? You think it's funny you ruined my hair?"

"No, it ain't that. I was just wonderin if you found that cat of yours yet."

Jeannie snatched up some fries and pitched them at me. "You know I ain't."
I could see the tears in her eyes before she high-tailed it into the bathroom.

CHAPTER FIFTEEN

ANNIE

By late May, people began coming to the farm. All the students were beginners. After demonstrating how to put a bit in the lesson horse's mouth for the fifth time in one day, Lydia eyed me stonily and told me she hadn't expected all her students to be so green.

"I'm raising my prices," she said. Her face was flushed and the skin on her nose looked burned. It had been very hot.

"How much?"

"Twenty dollars."

"Lydia, that's almost double. No one around here charges that much."

"I'll only raise my present customers fifteen, but the new ones will be forty-five a lesson."

"You'll lose business," I said, but I suspected that was the idea.

Around this time, Jack came to the farm. He heard I was starting a horse business. He figured I could use someone to do the heavy work; I told him I could use someone to clean stalls. He didn't hesitate. He could start today.

"I can't pay more than minimum wage," I said.

"Cash?"

"Yes, I suppose I could do that."

"That will be just fine."

I'd heard about him but couldn't remember from whom. I had the impression he was a decent kid. You could turn your back on him and he didn't steal you blind. I was pretty sure that's what I had heard. "We'll start just a few hours a day," I said. "See how it goes."

Rollo left again and that same evening, Lydia banged on the front door right around suppertime.

I stood on the other side of the screen, a plate of pizza in my hand.

"Thanks for Jack," she said.

"Oh, yes. Well. I figured we could use the help with the heavy stuff."

The girl didn't move from the door.

"Would you like some pizza?"

"Sure, that would be great."

I handed her my plate. "I'll get the box."

Lydia had settled herself in one of the rockers when I came back. I sat next to her, blew on the piece of pizza, and took a bite. The day was still hot but the porch was in deep shade at this time of evening and there was a breeze. It was comfortable sitting protected from the sun.

Jack drove out of the barn on the blue and white tractor with the manure cart attached to its hitch and pulled it to the pile on the other side of the road. He hopped down, tipped the cart so that the back end rested on the ground, and dug into its contents with the pitchfork. He held it like an oar and his shoulders rose and fell as he swung. Even from a distance the power of those strokes could be seen. He had it all out of the cart in six moves. After climbing back on the tractor and parking it alongside of the barn, instead of getting on his bicycle and riding home, he walked up the lane to the house, buttoning his shirt. He strode across the yard and stood at the bottom of the steps. "I'm finished," he said. His broad cheekbones were flushed, and his mouth was so dry his words sounded furry. His eyes dropped suddenly and briefly to Lydia's bare legs then focused in the distance.

"Would you like some pizza? It's from Dominos." I didn't expect him to say yes—I had the idea folks from the Holler were too shy to eat with strangers—

but he gave me a brief nod. When I handed him a slice, he started to sit on the bottom porch step.

"Don't be silly. Sit up here with us."

He wouldn't sit in a chair, settled, instead, on the floor in front of Lydia. He folded the slice and finished it in three bites. I handed him another.

He ate this one more slowly while losing the battle to keep his eyes off Lydia's legs. I leaned my head against the back of my chair and stared down the valley.

"Lydia," I said, eventually, "I got a call about a new training horse."

"It had better not be another Appaloosa."

"No, it's a Thoroughbred. Three years old. They want it as a hunter prospect."

"Really? A Thoroughbred?"

"Yes, off the track. Too slow and easy going to race."

"A Thoroughbred. Just think."

"Lucy Townsend was asking me when Tara would be going to shows."

"You're not serious. She's hopeless."

We sat back against the rockers, not saying anything. I had plenty to do. I should have been cleaning tack or paying bills or checking the fence in the north field. It had looked to me that a board might be down. But a breeze was moving through the porch and I stayed on. Eventually, Lydia said, "Tara's a nice little girl and all but she's not that interested in riding. I think she just likes the clothes. Lord, I wish I had some students that could ride."

"How many do you have?"

We both looked at Jack as though he had just materialized out of the air, he had been that quiet.

"Oh twenty, twenty-five, I guess. I don't know."

"Guess that's pretty good, ain't it?"

"It wouldn't be so bad if they all weren't beginners."

"It must be hard getting people started."

"It's not hard, just boring." Lydia stretched her legs out in front of her.

Jack hesitated. "People ain't so used to horses around here. It's kind of new to them."

"No kidding."

"How long do you figure it will take before your students ain't beginners anymore?"

"Oh, who knows? With most of them it would take forever." Lydia kicked off her shoes, put her head back, and rocked with her arms out from her sides in order to catch the breeze. The shadows had gotten longer and moths fluttered against the porch light. She swatted at them as they flew by.

"You need one a them bug lights, the yellow kind. I could get you one in the mornin. I'll ride my bike into the village first thing."

"That's not necessary, Jack. I can pick one up," I said.

"Guess Rollo took that Corvette with him when he left."

Lydia looked at him. "Of course he did."

"He's a pretty good driver, I guess."

"He does all right."

"How fast that thing go? Hundred? Hundred and fifty?"

"At least."

"Even in these mountains?"

"Sure."

"Car like that must need a lot of maintenance. I could look after it for you. Check the oil, stuff like that, tune it up."

Lydia leaned her head back against the rocker. "No way."

Crimson spread along Jack's cheeks. "I guess you really trust that black guy, lettin him drive a car like that."

Lydia frowned. Suddenly she leaned forward. "Jack," she said. "If you are going to sit here with us in the evenings, you are going to have to bathe after you muck out the stalls." She held her nose in case he missed the point.

I went hot and cold at the same time and Jack looked so stunned I thought he might tumble backwards down the steps. I could see the threads of self-confidence shatter. I knew once he had collected himself he would disappear, never set foot on the porch again. He might even quit. I searched for something soothing to say when Lydia added matteroffactly, "You want to use my shower? I don't mind. You can come by when you're done with work. Whenever Rollo's not here, that is. He's funny about people in his home, very private. Me. I'm not like that at all."

I was sure he would turn her down. He was too shy even to walk through my door for a drink of cold water, put his upturned head under the pump instead. I was sure he would never do something as intimate as taking a shower in someone else's house. But I had misjudged him. The next day, he walked stiff legged up the driveway, stopped across from the porch where Lydia and I sat. She had brought us another pizza. He stood at a distance, shifting his weight from one foot to the other. Lydia waved him toward the apartment. "Go ahead, door's open," she called. Her eyes followed him briefly then returned to the pizza box. She helped herself to another piece. "Funny how this stuff is good any time of year. Even when it's this hot. Where does Jack come from, anyway?"

"The Holler. Not the really bad part. Sort of on the edge."

"The Holler?"

"It's the next valley over. Indigents live there. Well, not indigents exactly. Welfare people."

"All the welfare people around here live in the same place?"

"No. It's hard to explain. The Holler people are a law unto themselves really. But he's all right. He doesn't live right in the middle of them. I'm pretty sure he has worked for some of the farmers around here."

"He's kinda cute, don't you think?"

"He's only sixteen."

"He's still cute though."

CHAPTER SIXTEEN

After that, **Jack brought** a change of clothes each day. Once he was done with the barn, he walked straight to the apartment and stayed a good half-hour. When he emerged his hair was wet, slicked back, and he smelled strongly of cologne. He settled himself against a pillar where he could look up at Lydia. As the evenings grew longer, he became steadier. The silences between them shortened. Through dusk and long after dark I listened to their voices—hers light and steady, his a jumble of ranges, but growing more persistent all the time—until my eyelids drooped and I went to bed. In the bedroom, their talk filtered through the window screen, indistinct, wordless, part of the other night sounds.

Rollo returned late one afternoon and drove the Corvette straight to the apartment door and disappeared inside. With the instincts of a cat, Jack sensed the change immediately. As soon as he finished in the barn, he jumped on his bicycle and was gone.

Lydia and Rollo, dressed alike in pale blue cotton shirts and white slacks, spent the evening in town.

I made myself a peanut butter sandwich and a scotch and took them to the porch. I was very hungry, having only had a leftover piece of pizza all day. I could feel the scotch hit my stomach, spark and spread an instant glow. The tree frogs were out in full force and the birds called to each other as dusk settled in. It had been very hot all day but was finally cooling off. I couldn't remember it ever being so hot here this time of year. It was nice sitting quietly on the porch. I tipped myself back and forth in the rocker, not thinking of much of anything, and finished my sandwich. I considered making another, but didn't feel like bothering, so I went to the barn and saddled Lonesome and rode him that hour before dark through the fields. I had only meant to prolong this pleasant state of mind and seduce sleep, but as soon as we turned off the driveway, I could not help noticing the solid sound Lonesome's hooves made striking the ground. My gaze shifted downward. The ground had become dry, cement hard in places and, even worse, turned to fine dust in others. It was only June. I looked back through the days since my return in March. We'd had a few dark days with rains so light they amounted to little more than a mist. The rest had been clear, the clouds high and white and barely moving. It had not rained a good hard rain since the night Lydia arrived.

I rode Lonesome through the field. He picked his way carefully, giving me time for a close look. I saw that the good grass had been eaten down to the dirt. On the farm we had one lesson horse, two training colts, six borders, The Doctor and Lonesome. That left four empty stalls I had to fill if I was going to do more than meet expenses. The land was barely supporting the eleven we had and soon the weeds—heartier than grass—would take over.

The next afternoon around three, I put on a big straw hat and walked to the barn where we kept the blue and white tractor. It was another bright day with the sun forming dark, crisp shadows under the trees and around the buildings. The horses shifted in their stalls, awake after dozing through the middle of the day. One or two nickered for dinner. A bale of hay dropped from the hole in the ceiling onto my head, knocking off my hat and crushing it. Jack dropped out of the hayloft behind it.

"Annie. Gosh, I didn't see you. Are you okay?"

I brushed at my shoulder and arm where the hay stalks had raked my skin as the bale bounced off my head. My neck hurt worse than the scratches. I rolled it from side to side. It seemed all right, just sore. "Yeah, I think so," I said.

"Sorry."

"Just yell the next time you throw down hay, okay?" I leaned my hand on a stall door to steady myself. "Listen, I want you to hook up the brush hog to the tractor for me. I need to mow these fields. The weeds are taking over."

"I could mow them for you."

"Maybe next time. First I want to see how bad they are."

"I'm a real good mechanic. Honest. You can ask Eddie Clites. I work on his vehicles all the time. And I've done mowing for lots of folks."

"That's okay. I want to get a feel for it myself."

"Lydia's gonna let me work on her Corvette."

"Really?"

"Yeah, she knows I'm good with cars. I keep my mom's jalopy running for her and it's got over 200,000 on it." Jack didn't take his eyes from mine. I was certain Lydia hadn't said he could work on her car, and even if she had, Rollo would never allow it.

"You've seen me drive the tractor lots of times. Pulling the manure cart. You know I'm a good driver."

"The Brush Hog has many more moving parts than the manure cart and it's more temperamental than a ballerina. And this farm can't run without it."

"Can't run without a manure cart either."

I laughed. The boy had been arriving earlier and earlier, working steadily until he parked the tractor next to the barn in the evening. And he was thorough. The stalls were spotless; the bedding banked against the walls the way I had shown him. I'd never seen him hanging around idly.

"All right, but this is strictly on a trial basis. You get rowdy pulling that brush hog and you're done in a heartbeat."

We started on the field next to the barn that bordered the road. Jack drove and I walked beside him. I had to tell him to slow down twice, but then he settled into a nice pace. Swallows swooped and dipped close, looking for insects frightened into flight. Without the hat, the sun beat on my arms and the back of my neck.

It took us three hours to finish the first field. Jack drove steadily, slowing whenever I raised my hand, nodding when I pointed to a rock. The days were at their longest. We could get in another three hours.

We went to the field on the other side of the driveway. Jack drove slowly and when a weed popped up, he backed the brush hog over it. It was slow work, and we took turns on the tractor. It was nearly dark when we finished. He drove into the barn, his face gray with dust. Underneath the dirt, his nose and cheeks were burned dusky red. "Looks like a front yard, don't it?" he said, and so it did.

My arms were shaking from turning the stiff steering wheel. I drew a steaming tub of water and standing in front of the mirror I saw, like Jack, I wore a mask of dust. The fine gray dirt was inside my bra; coated the welts along my arm. I put on a bathrobe and sat on the edge of the tub. My feet showed the marks made by the laces on my boots. I put my elbows on my thighs and rested my head in my hands. Then I went downstairs and called Stewart's number. It rang six times before the answering machine came on.

I gazed out the window across the fields that looked like lawns to the back fields with their thistle, ragweed, choke weed, and at the sky turning red and the mountain in back of Crab's Eddy filled with nothing but trees and hung up without leaving a message. Upstairs, I added more hot water to the tub and settled into it. I stretched my arms along its rim. I slid under the water and ran my hands over my dusty face. After I had scrubbed, I washed my hair, rinsing it with a large plastic glass and rested my head against the tub's curved back. *What would I have said if Stewart answered?*

At 7:30 the next morning, there was no sign of Lydia. I fed the horses and walked across the lawn to the apartment and knocked. There was no answer. I knocked again, louder this time. I heard some noise behind the door, a muffled voice. Lydia opened the door a crack and peeked around it. Her hair was tousled and her eyes were smudged with sleep.

"It's almost eight," I said. "You're going to be late."

"For what?"

"The show. At Somerset."

"Oh, I'm sorry. Didn't I tell you?" Lydia rubbed her eyes, let the door swing wide. She was wearing a man's t-shirt and nothing else. "I'm not going."

"What?"

"You've been there. It's a terrible show, really small, and the ring and grounds are horrible."

"Lydia, you can't decide which show you will or will not go to. That's my decision."

"That's not in the contract."

I stared at her. "Listen…," I began.

"I'll go to the show next weekend, promise. It's too late to try to get there now, anyway."

"Who's that?" Rollo's voice called down from the loft.

"It's just Annie," Lydia said over her shoulder. "She wanted to know why we weren't going to Somerset."

"Cause it sucks," came Rollo's answer from above.

CHAPTER SEVENTEEN

CLARE

I made up my mind I wasn't going to wait on Tony to make the move. I liked those strong wrists, the groomed hands, the well-fed muscles that ran along his shoulders, filling out his shirts. I liked the way he smelled, so different from the stale tobacco, kerosene smell I was used to. Comparing him to everyone before was like comparing a world class show horse to the rough coated, scrawny two-year-old colts that have lived on weeds all their life.

I stood at his front door. "It's hotter than hell out here," I said. "I'm soaked through. I thought I'd use your shower to clean up."

We looked at each other for several moments before Tony stepped back and opened the door wide.

The bathroom was like nothing I'd ever seen. Mirrors everywhere. I half expected to see one on the ceiling, but no. The shower was huge, with places to sit and places for the soap. The tub was the size of a small boat, with holes along the side. I found out later what that was for. The water surprised me with its strength and the way it pulsed. I kept my head under the shower, feeling the hot, heavy beat running along my neck, my back, the dip before my butt, down and around my thighs. I sat on the marble bench and used the sponge to scrub between my toes. Once I was sparkling clean, I took a man's bathrobe off its hook; toweled my feet dry and pulled on my boots. I left my dirty clothes on the floor.

"Would you like to see the bedroom next," Tony said when I walked into the living room.

He had a king-sized bed and the room was done entirely in leopard velvet: the bedspread, the heavy drapes, a blanket on the back of a leather chair. There was even a leopard rug. I sat on the bed and pulled off my boots. Tony sat next to me and pushed the robe off my shoulders, rested his hand on my arm for a moment. He unbuttoned his shirt, folded it, and laid it on the back of the chair, keeping his eyes away from me, focused on his task. It was that taking his time and the careful way he treated himself and his clothes, the not hurrying, being in control, that I liked about him. His body was as good as I'd hoped, and I wanted to feel the solid curves. He never looked at me, sat on the edge of the bed to take off his shoes. I began to feel a little foolish, so I slipped under the covers. I ran the tips of my fingers along the valley made by the muscles along his spine. I kissed the place where his neck met his back, breathed deeply of the warm scented skin. He didn't turn around.

A male voice called from the bottom of the stairs. "Hey, Tony, you there?"

I couldn't believe it. He got up from the bed, put his shirt back on, zipped his pants, and slid into some loafers. There didn't seem to be a question about just waiting for that fella to go away. I didn't say anything while Tony was putting on his clothes or when he told me he would be right back. He shut the door quietly behind him. I sat on the bed under the sheet with my knees tucked up against my chest and waited. I could hear low voices below. I sat watching the door and waiting. Must have been business. Important business to take him away like that. Shady business, no doubt, monkey business, or more likely mafia business. I wondered if Tony really was in the mafia. Seemed far-fetched. When I asked him about the farm, he just mentioned investors and changed the subject. I wondered if he'd ever killed a man. Maybe he just hired people to kill them. Hard to imagine, tender as he was. Yet not so hard, when I really thought about it. I mean, where did all this money come from, and who were all these men? A clock ticked. The last light faded from the window and as it did, a whippoorwill sang in the distance. Tender or not, I was sitting up here in this huge bed by myself. I waited a minute longer. Business my ass.

And what business did I have sitting here in some Italian's bed, when I'd never sat around for nobody. I jumped up and put on the robe, jerked on my boots. I was reaching for the handle when the door opened quietly and Tony came back in the room. He put his hand on my shoulder, kind of guided me to the bed, and sat me down without saying a word. He kneeled, took my heel in one hand and the toe of my boot in the other, and easy as you please just as gently as a momma with her kid, worked that old boot back and forth 'till it eased into his hand, free. No one, not ever, not in my whole twenty-six years, had ever helped me with my shoes like that.

CHAPTER EIGHTEEN

ANNIE

"The judge said he's stiff, doesn't move well, if you can believe that. He cleaned up on the A circuit just two years ago. The A circuit, not some rinky dink little local show. Where do they find these judges?" Lydia watched me closely. I continued undoing Lonesome's leg wraps.

"The Doctor's getting too old," she said. "If we want to make a good impression for the barn, we need something younger, something fancy, something with a lot of potential."

"Rollo, please don't smoke in the barn," I said.

He hesitated then flicked the cigarette out the door onto the dry grass where it caught making a small smoky fire. He and I jumped at the same time to stamp it out.

"You should throw a bucket of water on it to make sure," I said.

He watched me without moving. "Right," he finally answered. He filled the bucket to overflowing and threw it on the charred ground with enough force to splatter my legs.

"Anyway, wouldn't you like having a first-class horse here?" Lydia said, as if nothing had happened. She leaned against a saddle rack, her bangs falling over one eye. "I know this woman," she continued. "She has sold some of the best horses in the country. I've made an appointment for Thursday. I'll take

The Doctor to see about a trade in."

"You'd trade in The Doctor?"

"If I find the right deal, he's a goner. I mean, I'm talking real quality animals." Lydia listed several names. I'd heard of them all and seen a few featured in the national horse magazines.

The girl read my mind. "They start around fifty thousand for the really green ones."

"Geez, Lydia. Are you sure?"

"She's not sure of anything yet. It's just a thought." Rollo looked up from the dark water marks on my jeans. He smiled.

I put Lonesome in his stall, refreshed his water bucket. "Well, it's her money," I said. "I just think it would be hard to trade in your horse." I knew the Doctor could be fine with a little regular work to loosen him up. But if Lydia wanted a new horse, I wasn't going to talk her out of it. And I didn't think Rollo would be able to either.

As spring turned into summer, the rain still refused to come and our battle against the weeds deepened. I was bent down running my hand over the stiff grass when I noticed from between my legs four tires with sparkling rims pull into the driveway. A brand-new black Lexus parked in front of the barn. Darlene Drake stepped out along with the thin-armed woman from her party. They both cupped their hands over their eyes and looked around. They spotted me and waved, saying something to each other. Martha opened the back door, and a wispy little girl climbed out. The two women and the little girl wore sundresses. I tried to tidy my hair, pushing strands into the ponytail with one hand and tucking in my shirt with another as I walked toward them.

Martha wanted to know about lessons for her daughter. She put her arm around the girl and pushed her slightly toward me so I could get a good look at her. She was about ten and so skinny and big eyed she reminded me of a bug. Lydia was not in the barn, so I walked them through and introduced them to Sadie, who stood in a shady corner of her stall with her back to us.

I brushed at the dust on my face and legs while trying to retrieve something from the edges of my memory. What was it? Yes, now I remembered.

"Weren't you taking lessons from Clare?"

"I was, but she's not doing that part anymore."

It was a sign of my preoccupation with failing pastures that I couldn't muster the curiosity to pursue this information. I hustled Sadie out of her stall, gave the little girl a brush, and set her to grooming, our standard introductory lesson. Darlene stood uneasily in the center of the aisle well away from any dirt or debris.

Martha patted Sadie's nose, looked at her hand, and wiped it on her skirt. "What do you think, Nancy? Would you like to take lessons here? Sadie seems nice, doesn't she?"

"Mmmmmm," said Nancy. Her voice was barely above a whisper, giving the sense she couldn't muster anymore because of being so thin.

In the end, I invited them into the house for a cold drink. I avoided the kitchen, which was piled with dirty dishes and pizza boxes, and settled them in the living room while I filled glasses with ice and Pepsi. When I came out with the drinks, the three of them were lined up on the couch, the little girl in the middle. I sat across from them and struggled for something to say.

Martha shifted in her seat and said, "Your house is very pretty."

"Thank you."

Silence.

Darlene looked around her. Sighed. "Have you heard from Stewart?"

"Yes, he's doing well, business is booming. He's working seven days a week."

"Will he be coming east anytime soon?"

"Yes, soon," I lied.

"I imagine you're very busy too," said Martha. "Horses are so labor intensive. I don't know how you do it."

"They certainly are. It's not just their routine care. There are the fields. They have to be maintained."

"Really?"

"Yes. Horses are selective grazers. They won't eat the weeds. It's protective really. So many of the weeds are poisonous, even the most innocent looking. For example, that front field, where it dips low, there is a marshy spot, even in dry weather. Must be a spring under there. Well, those flowers that grow there in late summer, the ones that look like Queen Anne's Lace only a little thicker, that's water hemlock. A deadly poison. So deadly that horses have been known to die with it in their mouth. Normally they wouldn't eat it, only if they were starving and there was nothing else. But what happens, you see, is they eat the grass around it right down to the roots, and this gives the weeds a chance to take over. You have to keep your fields mowed so the weeds don't shade out the grass. That way the weeds don't choke out the good stuff. And, of course, the more you keep after it the more the grass has a chance to push out the bad stuff."

"I see." Martha took a sip of her Pepsi. "So. You actually mow the pastures?"

"Mommy, I want to go home."

"We're leaving in just a second."

"I don't mow them. Jack does. He works for me. He's very good. And you don't mow them exactly. Not with a lawn tractor. We use the big one and a brush hog. The brush hog really pulverizes the weeds, makes it harder for them to come back. Once they're mowed, you take a harrow, that's one of those things that looks like a bed spring with spikes, and drag it over the field… sort of a harrowing experience you might say." I chuckled but the silence continued. "Well, anyway, that aerates the soil. Ideally, after that you seed with whatever grass you want."

"How interesting."

"You certainly seem to know a good deal about it." Darlene looked at her watch. "We should be going, Martha. I've got an appointment in town."

They rose in unison and started toward the kitchen with their nearly full glasses.

"I'll take those, just leave them here." I steered them out the front door, out into the front yard, down the driveway toward their car. "You see there." I pointed. "That's where the water hemlock comes up every year. Tons of it. I've mowed that field but couldn't get into the really marshy parts for fear of getting stuck. It's amazing. Even in this dry spell, it still lies wet. And if I got stuck, I'd be a goner. I guess I could pull the tractor out with the truck and come-a-long. I don't even know where that thing has gotten to. It's just a huge, heavy-duty chain. I can barely lift it. What a hassle it would be to get stuck. So

I just let that part grow up. It will surely be thick with water hemlock come August. Over there is the tractor I use and the brush hog behind it."

"Yes. My. What dedication." Martha started the car. Darlene rolled the window down and leaned out. "Thank you for the tour and the Pepsi."

"Mom." A plaintive voice from the back.

"Yes, Nancy, we're leaving. I'll have her here next week for her lesson, and thanks for everything." I watched the Lexus pull away, sleek, elegant, born off on the flood of my words. Not even the exquisitely lethal water hemlock interested them.

CHAPTER NINETEEN

That summer, **Clare Raffienne** was taken up by the town's people. There was talk in the feed store. It was natural they were drawn to the bright glow of wealth and nowhere did it shine more brightly than at Silver Storm Farm.

Few people from Coleton rode. My mom, before the accident, and a handful of her friends. Now men who had never given a thought to horses found themselves harassed about riding lessons, Jodhpurs, Jodhpur boots, hard hats, riding jackets, rat catchers—all kinds of things they had never heard of. And they were nagged about leasing or even buying ponies. At first the persistent chatter and requests for things that made no sense, and words sounding like a foreign language came from their daughters whom they thought they could ignore into eventually giving it up. However, not only did these girls, usually so flighty and easily led, prove to be astonishingly tenacious on the subject, they were soon joined by their mothers. The wives were subtler than their children, but in their own fashion were just as relentless. Come to the barn, won't you? Melissa is doing wonderfully. You really ought to see her put Barney through his paces.

Barney?

And so these middle-class men found themselves, in spite of their reluctance, on evenings, even weekends, standing bewildered and in varying degrees of annoyance among the well-ordered and hectic world of the professional barn. They observed with amazement what went into the maintenance of the pampered and elite of the equine world. They noticed the attention to detail, the hard physical work, the tediousness and endless repetition. And because the love of horses was not born to them, their attention wandered. It was natural they found out a thing or two closer to their hearts. A young woman for one. A young woman good looking enough to keep their glances returning as she mounted a horse, pulled on a boot, turned a stream of hose water on a horse's leg or tucked her hair yet again under her helmet.

Throughout June, Tony took Clare to the shows. They stayed in a mobile home with a wide canopy. Tony served soft drinks, beer, and thick deli sandwiches to anyone—and there were many—who stopped by. I no longer brought Lonesome to Clare's trailer. The new Clare disturbed me. I did not know how to talk to her. I wanted back the days when no one knew how to approach Clare Raffienne but me. If others found her accessible I didn't know, only that the silences between us, always impressive, had become wide chasms hard to cross.

Still, Clare would not let the bonds be broken. Or perhaps it was only Stringtown that bridged the gap. She cried for Lonesome, pulled back and snapped the tie that held her and galloped to my trailer. Clare did not take her back to the mobile home and canopy, secured her instead next to my gray gelding.

Stringtown had been making a fool of Clare since the beginning of the season. The horse arrived with her ears pricked and her head high. She ran from fence to fence, out of control, flicking her tail and jumping way too high. The smaller fences she simply charged through. All Clare's strength could not hold her. At one show where the course was set up in an open field, she bolted after her third fence, galloped over the hill and disappeared. The audience, the riders, the judge all waited with their faces pointed toward the crest. When Clare finally rode Stringtown over the hill into sight, her lips were parted in a smile. That was the trouble. It was hard to say who enjoyed these antics more.

After Stringtown knocked down four jumps in one class, kicking back and splintering one so badly it could not be repaired, Tony called Clare over and had a talk with her. Clare rode to my trailer and asked me to help her in the practice ring.

"Raise the jumps a foot," she said.

Stringtown charged over them.

"More," said Clare.

I raised the vertical and widened the oxer.

Stringtown ran at them off balance, going way too fast. Still, she cleared them with room to spare. When Clare turned her around, the horse's ears pricked toward the jumps with interest. People had gathered around the practice ring to watch. They leaned on the top rail. "That's way too high," said one man. Lydia walked over and stood next to Tony, her elbow on the rail touching his.

"Higher," said Clare.

Stringtown cleared the jumps by a foot.

"Just lucky," said Rollo around a cigarette.

"She jumps higher at home," said Tony.

Clare sat still in the saddle. "Another foot," she said, but I hesitated. This was out of our league. The mare wasn't balanced enough to manage jumps this high. I tried to catch Clare's eye. Tony motioned me to help him. We put the fences up to their highest notch.

Clare circled Stringtown. The big mare's ears pricked forward, taking in the situation. She raised her head, seemed to consider a moment. Instead of charging at the jumps, Stringtown slowed, rocked back on her haunches, collected to make the effort. Her muscles bunched, strained with force. A soft gasp rose from the audience as she cleared the vertical, rocked back again and cleared the oxer.

Tony measured while Clare dismounted. The vertical stood at a little over five feet five inches, the oxer at five feet with a four-foot spread.

It was Lydia, leaning against the fence, who mentioned timber racing. Clare's eyes widened briefly. Timber races were in a different world than ours.

"I know some people who timber race," said Tony.

"People pay all kinds of money for a good timber racer," said Lydia.

CHAPTER TWENTY

It **was not long** after Lydia put the idea of timber racing into Tony's head that Clare walked naked through the Silver Storm barn. I'm not sure of the sequence of events. I don't even know if Clare liked the idea of traveling east and racing point-to-point. She stopped going to the local shows, and while I watched the grass on my farm turn brown and crisp, she galloped the big mare up and down the mountains to get her fit.

She had called me that afternoon, asked me to drop by sometime soon. This was so unusual that a number of images and possibilities hummed in my thoughts while I hurried to finish my chores. Even with my haste, it was dusk when I drove to her valley. The lights were off in the barn. I could barely make out a figure backing down the stairs from the loft. As she turned, I saw that it was Clare. At first I thought she wore a buff colored outfit; tight buff breeches, tight same colored T-shirt. With a blast of adrenaline, I realized she wore nothing at all. My skin tingled the way it does when you almost hit someone with your car. My thoughts took over, absorbed her loose-limbed walk, her jaunty carriage. What was she up to? My eyes flicked around. Where was Tony? Should I turn around and beat it out of there? She waved, called casually she was on her way to take a shower, just give her a couple of minutes. I kept my focus away from her, embarrassed and annoyed. I glanced in her direction as she passed through the last pale light of evening coming in a window, her naked form reflecting the light as though she were made of marble.

I saw no one else in the barn. The clients must have all gone home, thank God, but a young man I recognized as one of Tony's workers backed down the same stairs. He wore tight jeans on his narrow hips, no shirt or shoes.

Clare walked past me and into the wash stall.

"God it's hot, don't you think, Annie?" she said. The sound of water sluicing onto the concrete cut off any answer I might have given. The young man walked toward us, hesitated, confused. He wanted to stop, would have leaned over the wash stall door and spoken to Clare had I not been there. I held him off with the hardness of my stare.

He shifted his weight from one foot to another, looked away, flicked his eyes at me sidelong. He was a nice-looking boy, young with a full mouth and smooth olive skin. I held my ground and by the time Clare stepped from the shower, wet and smooth as a seal, he had turned his sheepish face and gone. I started to speak but she beckoned me to follow her to her apartment.

Opening her fingers, Clare showed me the earrings: two large teardrops joined at their points, so they swayed and caught the light. She drew back her hair and put them on, demonstrating their sparkle against her throat as she moved her head. She reached under the bare mattress and brought out an envelope and handed it to me; gave a little backward hop onto a stool, crossed her legs, and smiled. The envelope contained Stringtown's papers.

"My birthday present," said Clare. "He gave them to me with the earrings." She reached up, pulled them from her ears, and dropped them into their velvet-lined box. She tossed it above the sink, onto the only shelf in the place.

Her wet hair hung across her shoulders, clung to the front of her, accentuating her nakedness. I tossed her the dirty quilt that had lain in a heap on the floor. She mocked me with a smile but wrapped it loosely around her.

"Where's Tony?"

"The hell with Tony."

"Seriously? Is that any way to repay him?" Raffino was at the end of a long line. Just before I'd left for California, one heartbroken boy Clare recently dumped drank so much he passed out in the V.F.W. parking lot and froze to death. I was sure that wouldn't be Tony's way of handling things, though.

Clare's lips tightened and she looked away. "We've been friends for a long time, so I'll pretend you didn't say that," she said.

I sat down on the other stool. "I'm sorry. You're right. You scare me sometimes, that's all. What if Tony was to catch you?"

"He's out of town. He went ahead to the point-to-point to see some people he knows. So you can stop worrying." Clare adjusted her blanket. "That Stringtown is some horse, you know. She got fit so fast. She's an aerobic machine."

"Where's the race?"

"Timonium."

"What do you think your chances are?"

"Who knows? I don't know the other horses. I don't know the people. Not that the people matter." Clare paused. "I'm not worried about the jumps—or the time. It's just we haven't seen anything like it before. It'll be strange, is all. I haven't figured out the rules yet. And if the truth be known, I hate showing."

"I thought you liked showing."

"Whatever gave you that idea? I like riding, is all. Riding and Stringtown. God, I'm crazy about that horse. But I hate the clothes. They're hot and impossible to keep clean. And those stupid rules. No. Going to shows is Tony's idea. He likes to show off."

"Is that why you're mad at him?"

"I'm not mad. I'm just restless." Clare flung her hair back over her shoulders, spraying water on me. Her black brows drew together. She looked past me at nothing in particular.

"You think he might be seeing someone while he's down there?"

"Shit, I don't know."

"Would it matter?"

"No."

"I thought Tony might be different."

"Oh, he's different, all right."

"What if he finds out about that boy?"

"How would he do that?"

"Guys talk. Especially young ones. They brag. Hell, this will go through the barn like wildfire."

Clare looked at me for a long while.

"I just worry about you, that's all," I said uncertainly.

"Well, then. Keep those papers for me. I got no place really private."

I put them in my pocket, gave it a pat. "They're safe with me," I said.

CHAPTER TWENTY-ONE

CLARE

Annie didn't understand why I started running around on Tony. Neither did I, to tell the truth. He never got possessive or acted jealous. All I know is I felt really jumpy the few days before the race and that kid was so sweet and good looking. It just happened. We were upstairs throwing down bales of hay together. He had his shirt off and was all glisteny with sweat, and when he come up behind me to help with a real heavy bale and let his hand slip and touch my breast, I just turned around, moved in, and kissed his pretty mouth. Afterwards, I was so itchy with hay and sweat I couldn't wait to get washed off, so I just climbed down the stairs naked. I could've taken less chances, I know, but it just seemed natural with it being so hot. Anyway, no one else was in the barn except Annie, and she'd never say. Course, it wasn't as simple as I'm making it sound. I just know I'm no good at the girl-guy thing for the long haul. Anyway, that pretty boy helped settle me down. I didn't worry about the race even though that's what I was working toward every day, getting S.T. in condition. And packing for the trip. Making sure I had the right bit, plus a spare, bandages, leg wraps, S.T.'s vitamins, a clean and pressed shirt for me, a girth cover, plenty a fly spray. And water, lots of water in case S.T. didn't like the change. And, of course, her grain and hay.

And there were my evening clothes. Apparently, there was some big shindig after the race. And a dinner before. Tony took me shopping, bought me a black dress, plain as mud. I mean it was just two pieces a cloth sewed together, low enough in front to show some cleavage and that was it. No beads, no bangles, nothing shiny, and that little bit a nothin cost over five hundred dollars. I had to laugh.

He bought me another dress for the big shindig and this one was bright red and had sequins. I seen it in the window at Kaufmann's, the best store in town, and told Tony that was the one I wanted. At first he said no and had me try on a bunch of others, but that floaty material just looked silly on me. When I walked out of the dressing room wearing the sequins, Tony was looking through a magazine. He glanced up and stared at me.

"You're right," he said. "No point in being subtle."

Louie and I headed out the day before to give S.T. time to settle in. He was the gardener, which meant he pointed out where the younger men could plant things. He was old as dirt. He'd stand there with the hose just staring at the flowers while he waved the spray over them. He was never around when it was time to unload the plants or grass seed or fertilizer. That day before the race, he limped down the hill as I was climbing into the driver's seat. Tony had assigned him the job as my babysitter for the trip.

"Better let me drive," he said.

"No way I'm going to be a passenger all the way to Timonium."

Louie shrugged and climbed in the other side while S.T. danced around in the trailer. I put the truck in gear and poked the gas. Louie's head snapped back, and he grabbed his hat. He gave me a look. You could hear the mare scramble to get her footing.

"That ought to keep her still for a while," I said.

"You'll be lucky to ever get her in a trailer again."

Great. A gardener who was an expert on horses. This was going to be a long trip.

But Louie slouched against the seat and pulled his hat down and said no more. Soon he was snorin gently. He didn't wake until I slammed on the brakes so I could get on 695 making the circle around Baltimore.

CHAPTER TWENTY-TWO

The party was held in a two-story yellow house with many adjoining parts and a long front porch with yellow and white striped awnings and white wicker furniture. Inside was yellow and white too and full of evening light with filmy curtains moving in the breeze and fresh flowers everywhere, and even with the windows open it was still cool because of the porch and all the big trees.

We ate in a room made of screens and glass, and there were candles running down the middle of the entire table and more silver and glasses than I'd ever seen lined up at each plate. The waiter kept pouring different colored wine. What I really wanted was a beer or some champagne, which is just a faster kind of beer, but they didn't serve that until the end of the meal with the cake, if you can believe it. Tony hardly looked at me all night, though I'd overheard the hostess say, "Your girlfriend is stunning—in an unconventional way."

Everyone was talking about the race, saying the black was bound to do well, or the chestnut was a sure thing. Apparently, most people hired jockeys instead of riding their own horses. I didn't mention that I was riding Stringtown. Tony didn't either. Instead, he talked about what good lines she had.

"Flat racers don't necessarily make good timber horses." This from an older gentleman sitting at the head of the table. Tony raised his glass and said, "Let's just wait and see about that."

CHAPTER TWENTY-THREE

At dawn, the air was so wet it seemed to resist me as I walked toward the truck. "Sleepin," I told Louie when he asked where Tony was.

Stringtown stood at attention in her stall, her ears flickin back and forth. She seemed to be waiting for me. I looked in her water bucket. It was full. Not good. I reached through the bars and flicked the water with my fingers.

"Drink, you fool."

She flicked an ear and turned away from me, her face to the wall.

I went outside and sat on the mounting block. The race wasn't till the afternoon. I could sit for hours, waiting. Tony was supposed to meet me at the grounds at eleven. If I took S.T. there early, she'd wear herself out tearing around or fighting me. Louie came over, motioned with his hand that I should make room. Eventually, he said, "Let's load up the hay and the water and be on our way." I realized I'd been feeling something I'd never felt before. An ache deep in my stomach.

"What'll I do with Stringtown?"

"They have stalls. Portable stalls."

"Why didn't you say so earlier?"

"I thought you knew."

"I don't know nothin about this stuff."

When I led Stringtown out of the stall she was at attention again, all firmed up and muscle hard, her head in the air. She kicked out when I put the wraps on her, but she was distracted, her mind on the gray next to her eating his breakfast. Flies was everywhere in that heavy, determined way they have when the air is damp. I coated Stringtown with repellent, and they buzzed around her, zinging into the invisible barrier, veering off, and trying again. My shirt was wet with sweat and stray ends of hair curled and clung to my face, making it hard to see.

The ache moved up into my chest when we arrived at the grounds. Not a lot was going on since it was only nine o'clock. The stalls was made out of canvas, lashed on to metal polls, right out there in the open. S.T. loved it. She stuck her head over the top and hollered a couple a times then lipped hay while she watched what was going on. After munching for a minute or two, she stuck her nose into the water bucket and took a long drink, her ears moving as she swallowed. I put her grain bucket down for her and she took a mouthful, chewing slowly over the bucket with her eyes half closed. It was too late to be feeding her before a race, but I couldn't see making her go the distance on an empty stomach. When she finished and had another drink, I took all the hay and water out of her stall and left her to go walk the course.

There were a few others, very businesslike, taking big strides before and after the jumps, sometimes discussing it with someone else. I didn't know what all that striding was for. I was just curious what the fences looked like. They were solid, lots of logs, coming off twists and walls that wouldn't budge if you hit them, strange angles, several oxers, only the first two coming from a flat approach, the rest down or up a hill, a no stride triple in and out and something that looked like a picnic table. Most of the course was in the woods. It would be easy to get lost or off course, and the route favored a nimble horse, not one like S.T. who ran flat out. If I didn't have Tony's expectations sitting on me it would have been fun, just dashing helter skelter, jumping what we could, not needing to win.

By the time I got back to the stall, Tony was there watchin S.T. "She looks settled."

"Yeah."

"Did you tranquilize her?"

"Nope."

"How does the course look?"

"Just fine."

"Not very talkative, are we?"

"It's pre-race jitters." Louie had come up behind us.

"Is that right? Clare? Are you nervous?"

My instincts told me I'd better not show a sign of weakness. Even a little jumpiness before getting started would have put me in a place with Tony I didn't want to be. "I'm just hungry. I haven't had anything but coffee."

"Well, that's pretty foolish." He pulled out a cigar and lit it. I'd never seen him smoke one before. I hated the way they smelled.

"I'm gonna get a hot dog."

Tony walked with me, puffing on the cigar. I ate standing in front of the concession stand. Tony pointed to several men getting out of long, black cars. They walked toward us in a group, wearing dark suits, a solid mass with coat tails flappin, making its way past the slim riders in their skin-tight breeches and the coaches and grooms wearing snug jeans, polo shirts, slender no-nonsense clothes, and all with the slightly bowed loose-limbed legs of riders, looking light, almost airborne next to the bulky, over-dressed men advancing in our direction, elbow to elbow. They made me think of them Muslim women who go around wrapped up in cloth, only their eyes showing. Seeing those women always made me angry. I wanted to rip the fabric right off of them, tell them they had nothing to be ashamed of, there was nothing evil about their hair, and they didn't need to hide anything about themselves just because some man thought he owned them. Course Tony's buddies weren't tryin to hide anything, but they at least could make an attempt not to look so stupid.

I ate my hot dog. The men's cologne mixed with the cigar smoke, and I thought my stomach might send the food right back up. I sipped the Pepsi, which was lukewarm. I could feel the sweat on my upper lip and running from my armpits down my sides.

Finally, it was time to get ready.

Stringtown let me put the saddle and polo wraps on her without having to chase her around the stall. I changed in the trailer while Louie kept an eye on the mare. Britches, boots, gloves, hardhat, vest, number. At least I didn't have to wear that stupid coat.

I put my foot in a stirrup, swung on board while Stringtown stepped forward and there was the sudden comfort of movement, a gathering up, the familiar swinging, eager walk. Stringtown was all eyes and ears, wondering what was happening here. She started to walk a little stiff legged, prancy, neck arched. into an awkward trot because she was too busy looking around to move forward.

Then, of course, the worst thing happens. She's sucking back, starting to jig in place like the old days. I try the other direction and it's worse. She whinnies to the gray who is cantering in easy, collected strides. I trot the mare to a practice jump. She minces to it and jumps like a deer, flat bellied, back stiff, shaking her head as she lands. The whole thing feels awkward. I can't get in sync, there is no rhythm to her movement, and she pays no attention to my legs or hands. As I'm struggling, I notice the jockeys—small, perfect little humans with tiny hands and feet. Where do they get their boots, I wonder. At the same time I'm feeling sick because S.T. is getting stiffer and stiffer under me. I put my heel into her hard, and she kicks out behind. I do it again and she bucks. The loudspeaker announces it's time to head to the starting gate. S.T. falls in behind the gray, chortling steadily. She uncurls just a little. The bell sounds and is followed by thunder as thirteen horses lunge forward. Stringtown saunters after them, surprised and curious. But even ambling along, her large stride brings us next to a blood bay a few paces ahead who stretches out to stay in front, and something in Stringtown clicks. The mare leaps forward, hind legs well under her, head up, hooves digging into the turf, sending clumps of dirt and grass flying. She shakes her head, pulling on the reins, passes the horse and flicks over the first jump, a straightforward log fence. Her ears are pricked and she sails over a coop, clearing it by several feet too many. We pass three horses—the rider's bright colors a blur—come to the water jump, which two horses ahead refuse. S.T. leaps, lands, splashes out of it not even hesitating. It's not so much that she has figured out this is a race as she has been waiting all her life for this, and it's everything before that's been confusing. She wants one thing and one thing only: to get in front of every horse there.

She pounds past three more horses, is over an oxer into the woods and I worry about goin off course, but there's no need, she knows instinctively to stay with the others. I hear her breathing, harsh but not labored. She passes two more riders going up a bank to a stone wall. We fly over a creek, not even a hoof in the water, and pass two more horses. It's a blur of fences—a coup with flapping flags on top, a stone wall with a downhill landing so steep that I feel like we're flying into space. Not Stringtown. She doesn't even hesitate, lands and gallops on, head and neck moving like a piston between her shoulders and taking what looks, as we sail over it, like a spring house from back home. We come up behind the gray and I'm thinking, don't stop, don't stop, forget him, keep going, this isn't the time for love, this is a race. She doesn't even flick an ear. Her breathing gets louder but there's no feeling of her getting tired. We're out of the woods much quicker than possible. Stringtown has her neck stretched out, her body lowering toward the ground, galloping, galloping, catching up to the only horse in front. He's black and as big as she is. But heavy too. I see the big haunch muscles, the sturdy, almost coarse legs. More to lift over a fence.

My shoulders and back burn and I'm almost out of breath. We pass the black. Stringtown's strides are starting to feel labored, not so smooth, not so effortless. My ears are roaring, or is it her breathing? I sit back in the saddle as we approach the triple, try to collect her. She pays no attention to me, doesn't change her position at all, and we are there. From a deep distance she takes off and I think helplessly here we go again, only this time the fence is *huge*, a mile high triple. She is taking the combination all at once. She reaches, stretches her head, neck and legs as she realizes she can't make it. A leg catches in the last fence. She pitches forward and is down on her knees, sliding, scrambling, her nose in the grass, neck twisted, I'm sure it's broken and am ready to jump free when unbelievably, she's got her feet under her, is pushing herself back up. Once again. Galloping. A miracle. But the black has passed us and though I can feel the muscles coming together and stretching out with enough power to get us to the moon or at least to the end of this race, she can't catch him and we finish second.

I jump down, snatch the saddle off and am sick at the sight of the heaving sides. She stands still, watching the crowd and looking bewildered. All her muscles are trembling. Her head drops and for a second her legs start to buckle. Louie comes from out of nowhere with water and we both sponge and sponge between her front legs, behind her ears, and suddenly a vet is beside me taking her temperature, listening to her heart. He fills a syringe and puts somethin into a vein. He offers her a sip of water with electrolytes in it. He doesn't say nothing, just keeps checkin her temperature and heart rate. He gives her another injection. By this time, Tony has arrived with his flock.

It was so close, he says. If she hadn't caught that leg she could have won, he says. Second isn't too shabby for her first time out though, he says.

I look at the vet.

"I've seen worse. Her temperature is starting to come down and she's not breathing so hard." He offers her another sip of water. "Watch for signs of tying up. Stiffness in the back hind legs, extreme pain. Keep giving her sips of water with the electrolytes. I'll give her a shot of Bute for the soreness, and you can walk her for half an hour. Let her have a drink every few minutes."

The outcome of the race comes over the loudspeaker and it's official. Stringtown is second. I tell Tony to pick up the ribbon; I have to walk the horse. Stringtown walks with her head down and there isn't any fight left in her.

Louie and me are at the stable before daylight. I let him drive home. There's too much in my head. As we get further along and are climbin into the mountains, they don't look the same to me and I realize I've never seen them from this direction.

It was dark when we got back to Silver Storm Farm. Stringtown walked quietly into her stall, an ordinary horse. I didn't go up to the big house, opened the door to my apartment instead. It was hot as blazes and stunk to boot. Even so, I flopped down on the mattress, kicked off my boots, and lay there for a minute. I went to the refrigerator and took a look. Good luck. A six-pack left. I took two beers back to the bed, lay with my head and shoulders propped against the wall. I finished them off. I made two more trips to the fridge that night, and afterwards I finally fell asleep.

CHAPTER TWENTY-FOUR

ANNIE

The invitation stood out from the usual bills piled in my mailbox. It arrived in a large, oyster colored envelope, edged in gold. Dinner at nine, it read, with a handwritten note at the bottom. "Come early, we never seem to have time to talk. As ever, Tony."

My first dinner invitation to Silver Storm Farm. I finally settled on a sleeveless black dress, stepped over the other choices lying on the floor, and headed out. I had not talked to Clare since the night she gave me Stringtown's papers.

I parked my truck in front of the cedar shake house a few minutes after nine. The weather was hot and heavy, threatening a storm. Nothing stirred. Overhead, in the trees, there was a high-pitched hum as though from locusts, an August sound though it was only June.

Floodlights lit the driveway, making it bright almost as day, but there was not a light on inside the house. Tony answered the door himself, bowed, gracious, and solemn. He was dressed in a pale linen double-breasted suit and white shirt. His cuff links winked in the candlelight. He ushered me into the dining room with a hand just below my shoulder blades. Candles flickered on the sideboard, from sconces on the walls, along the table set for three. He pulled out a chair, indicated with his hand I should sit. "I thought it should be just the three of us tonight. So you and I can get to know each other." Clare slouched at the table. A woman in a black-and-white uniform brought out a bottle of white wine. Tony poured it into glasses the size of bowls.

"Annie," he said, "You're Clare's best friend and yet we hardly do more than say hello."

I eyed Clare uneasily. She wore a gold lamé dress that looked like something out of the thirties and cowboy boots. The dress was torn under the arm, and I thought I remembered it from a dance we had gone to in high school. She pulled her chair closer to the table and put her feet, with a loud clunk, on the chair across from her.

"You know how it is in the horse business," I said. "There is never enough time."

"So I hear from Clare. Maybe that is why she came back early from the point-to-point in Timonium. Said she had to get Stringtown back. Left me a note on the dresser of the motel. The mare wasn't happy, she said, was out of her element and needed to get home to rest, didn't like being transported and could only rest back here. So she said. Did you know Clare came back early, Annie—the morning right after the race? Did she get in touch with you?"

"Some horses don't travel well," I said cautiously.

"I thought she might have called you when she got back. Have you bring that gray gelding over—or taken Stringtown over there. The two are so attached."

"Your race went well?" I asked.

"Brilliantly. Who would have thought the bitch had it in her?"

I froze, glanced from Tony to Clare. Tony refilled his glass. "Came in second. Unheard of for an unknown. You should have seen her taking the jumps. And what jumps. Nothing scares her. And to think she was all but dog food before Clare took her on."

"Will you race her again?" I asked politely.

"Oh will we." Tony looked at Clare. "We can't afford to waste talent like that. I may not have Clare ride her, though. She's so tall. Most people have professional jockeys, anyway. Clare could act as groom."

"She was a mess afterwards," said Clare. "Shaking and sick."

"She'll get used to it."

"She won't last. She'll use herself up."

"How do you think those other horses do it? You said yourself how quickly she got fit." He turned to me, touched his head with a finger. "Clare doesn't think the mare has the—what did you call it, Clare?—mental make up for this kind of competition. Twenty thousand dollars she won for second place. I say she has the mental makeup. In fact, she's made for this sort of thing. That Lydia knew what she was talking about. The mare is a timber racer all right. Galloped out of nowhere, would have won if she hadn't stumbled. We were so close, just a stumble away. I wonder how you could have prevented that, Clare. What do you think? Of course, she might not have stumbled at all with a different rider on board. No offense, Clare. It's just your size, like I said. You're so much bigger than the other riders. Without that extra weight, she might have made it over that last jump. What do you think, Annie? A lighter rider can make all the difference, can't it?"

I said nothing.

Tony snapped his napkin and put it in his lap. He motioned to the young woman in uniform who had been standing discreetly in a shadowed corner. She brought shrimp cocktails from the kitchen.

"Marta has something for dinner that doesn't wait well, so we'll go ahead and start, Annie, if you don't mind. I was hoping you could have gotten here a little earlier so we would have more time before dinner to chat." He poured more wine into the glass I had barely touched and refilled Clare's.

"Drink up, Annie," he said, "this is a celebration. You should have been there. Those blue bloods didn't know where that mare came from. She galloped out of nowhere. I celebrated down there with some buddies, but Clare had to come right back here with Stringtown, so this is our first chance to celebrate together." Tony kept his voice pleasant.

I focused my attention on the food. The shrimp were served in a bowl that rested in another filled with crushed ice. They were huge, firm, and cold, and the sauce just spicy enough.

"Taste it, Hon," said Tony mildly. "Clare loves shrimp, Annie. It's about all she'll eat that Marta fixes."

Clare took her feet from the chair, sat up to the table and picked up a rosy tail with her fingers. She looked tired, had dark circles under her eyes and I noticed with a stir under her nails as well.

"How's your appetite tonight, Clare? She's been off her feed lately, so to speak. Hasn't had much appetite for anything. Isn't that right, Clare?

Clare remained silent and would not take the bait.

"We're really glad you could make it tonight, Annie," Tony went on. "You probably won't be seeing much of Clare for a while. She will be on the road with Stringtown. The horse seems to have recovered now that she's been back a few days. Don't you think, Clare? I know you were worried about her. That's why I called you. Did you get my messages? I called you several times."

"I got them."

"Oh? I would have thought you would have returned my calls."

"I didn't know how to reach you."

"All you had to do is look at the number on the cell phone."

"I lost it."

"She's so careless, Annie. Oh well, never mind. Clare has other attributes, doesn't she? You know what I mean. You grew up with her. Are all the local girls like her? But you're local too, aren't you?" Tony emptied the bottle of wine into his glass, motioned for another. "You're not the same though, are you, Annie," he said, watching Clare.

Leaning back in his chair, his wrists resting on the table, he addressed his empty bowl of shrimp. "By the way, Clare, I've let that young fellow who works in the barn go—what's his name? Miguel Vasquez. He left this afternoon."

Clare picked up her glass. For the first time, she looked directly at Tony.

"Don't matter," she said. "There will be another one along just like him."

Tony sat still for a moment, meeting her gaze. He half rose, one hand at his waist to keep his napkin in place, and in a gesture so smooth, so calm, so filled with old world grace that for a second I thought he was going to bow, he back handed Clare across the mouth. He put all his weight behind the blow. Her head snapped back.

She was on her feet before the blood started running. Her eyes lit up and as dark crimson suddenly gushed, she wiped it with the back of her arm.

She smiled, a hideous smile, her mouth smeared red. She spit, spattering the tablecloth with a spray of pink foam. She raised her knee, placed a booted foot against the table, and shoved. Crystal, china, sputtering candles, and hot wax flew across the room. Tony leapt out of the way, brushing furiously between his legs, where a candle had landed.

"Get out of here," Clare hissed to me.

I had jumped up, knocking over my chair, no thought to anything *except* running. It is not with pride that I say I went down the long hall so fast that the candle flames wavered. Outside, the hot thick air hit me like a door. In my haste I nearly flooded the truck, got hold of myself enough to cease stomping the gas pedal, and thought I heard the engine catch. It was only thunder rumbling in the distance. I held my breath, counted to ten, tried again. Nothing. Something small and dark flew past the windshield. A bat, I thought, but it was too small. Another darted past, then another, insects of some sort. I tentatively turned the key. The engine stuttered, caught, and I was down the hill and on the road.

A mile or two away from Tony's house, the world reassembled itself. The houses lining the road were plain and reassuring. My skin began to dry. I took several deep breaths. Were they insane? I pictured Clare with the blood smeared across her mouth, along her arm. I slowed. She's a big, strong girl who can handle just about anything, I reminded myself. I drove on. I wondered if Tony had a gun. Of course, he had a gun. Clare is fast as a cat, I told myself, is probably halfway to the Holler right now. I pressed harder on the gas pedal.

As I turned into my driveway, the headlights shined through the willows. The farmhouse looked quiet, solid and secure sitting behind them on the hill. After I parked and turned off the engine, I sat in the truck for a while. It was dark with no moon. Eventually I went inside. I turned on the lights in the hall and the living room. I also turned on the lights in the upstairs hall. I turned on the light next to the bed. I'd just sleep with the lights on for a while.

I woke with an image of an afternoon in back of Cat Creek sharp in my mind. I remembered the feel of a hand lifting me onto a horse, the warmth of the hide underneath me and the texture of a girl's shirt onto which I clung. I rose, climbed into my clothes; went straight down the stairs, out the door, and into my truck without giving myself time to think.

As I pulled into Tony's valley, the wind picked up suddenly, slammed out of nowhere. It tossed debris, leaves, and twigs against the windows. I could feel it beat in gusts against the truck. As I drove, I heard it shriek through the trees. Branches tossed and dipped. A few smaller ones broke away and flew in front of the headlights. It was utterly dark beyond the cones of light. Three or four swollen rain drops splattered onto the windshield, not enough to beat down the dust.

When I reached Silver Storm Farm, the lights were on in the barn and under the dusk to dawns, I saw the empty place where Clare's truck and trailer had been parked. The main doors to the barn hung open and inside the horses were awake, moving restlessly in their stalls. I called Clare's name. The center hallway caught the wind, drew it through the barn with the force of a train. Dust and bedding blew into my eyes. I was blinded for a moment. When I could see again, I noticed that Stringtown's door stood open. It banged against the wall with a crash that made me jump. Her stall was empty. I had the presence to look for her halter, which normally hung by her door. It too was gone. Wherever Clare had gone, she had taken the horse with her.

I started pulling out of the driveway when the lightning hit, followed by a crash of thunder so loud the truck quivered. It didn't zigzag through the sky, it burst next to Tony's house like a bomb.

CHAPTER TWENTY-FIVE

I **woke with a** start to the sound of Lonesome hollering and the sun blasting in my face. I heard my horse's deep whinny again; before the sound had a chance to fade, it was followed by a high, strident reply. I rose immediately, dressed, and went to the barn. Lonesome stood by the pasture gate, pawing and pacing in short, frantic lines. When I entered the barn, a dark, sleek head greeted me over the stall door. Stringtown.

She paced, hollering for the gelding until he was next to her, chortled through the slats, ignored her grain and circled, stopping with each turn to peer at him. Lonesome put his nose to the boards that separated them, woofed once, and settled quietly into his breakfast. The other horses pranced into the barn, ears pricked, necks arched, jigging at the end of their lead shanks as though they were world class. The big mare certainly could stir things up.

I had just returned to the kitchen when Clare walked in, letting the screen door bang behind her. Her lips were swollen rose and purple sausages, the top one split in the middle. She pulled out a chair and sat down.

"Christ, Clare. Are you all right?"

She just looked at me.

"Tea?" I indicated the mug.

Clare shook her head. "A beer?" Her words were fuzzy.

I twisted the cap off, handed her the bottle.

Clare shook her head. "Glass?"

"Oh, right. Of course."

She carefully opened her mouth, held the glass so it barely touched her lips, and let the liquid flow into her throat.

"How bad is it? Are your teeth okay?"

"Front's loose."

"Oh, Clare."

She shrugged, drank more beer.

"What are your plans? You can leave Stringtown here as long as you like. You can stay too. God knows there's room. I'd love it if you'd stay. I don't know why I haven't said something sooner. It would be perfect. God, Clare, I'm so sorry I left you."

Clare shook her head. "I'm goin to Gram's."

"Stay here. Please. I want you to. You can leave Stringtown here forever. Free. Should you see a dentist? A doctor? I'll take you."

Clare looked out the window.

"I did come back later. But you were already gone," I said miserably.

"Annie, I swear." A bright drop of blood appeared in the middle of her upper lip. She touched it with a fingertip.

I went to a drawer and pulled out a dish towel and handed it to her. "Clare?"

"Hmmm?"

"I'd like it if you stayed here. Where you'd be safe."

She shook her head and licked the blood away with her tongue. "Come with me," she said through barely moving lips. "To Gram's old cabin. To look it over."

"Of course. Anything, anything you…"

Clare held up her hand. "Stop,"

The road, if you could call it that, to Pap's cabin was gouged, its deep ruts filled with rocks, and the climb was straight up. We drove on one side, straddling the worst part for as long as we could before the woods closed to the very edge of the path. We bounced over the rocks. Branches scraped and screeched along the top of the cab, and several times I hit my head on the metal rooftop. After five miles, we came to a cleared meadow surrounded by woods with barbed wire strung from tree to tree. A few horses grazed in their shade. Pap's cabin stood at the edge of the woods, protected by the mountain from the north wind, but open to the morning sun. It was a small, two-story clapboard building. It had been painted white once, but time and the elements had scrubbed the boards until they were all but bare.

An empty twig rocker faced us from the porch. Our boots, as we went up the steps, made a hollow ringing sound.

Inside, the wallpaper had faded to a dusty, mottled gray. The kitchen contained a woodstove, small refrigerator, sofa, another rocker, a table, two beaten up mismatched chairs, and a couch. A faded rug covered half of the wide planked floor. The room next to it was stacked from floor to ceiling with bales of hay and bags of grain. Pap sat in the rocker reading a newspaper. I had not seen him in years. He was a little thinner, but you could still sense the wiry muscles under his shirt and pants. His shoulders sloped downward more than they had. His skin, its resilience stolen by the elements, draped under his neck, but his eyes, though watery, were the same pale blue, hawk eyes I remembered, and his jaw like Clare's looked as though honed with an ax.

"Annie," he said after glancing at Clare, "it's been a while." He looked me up and down. "Though you've hardly growed since that first day Clare brung you here." He rose stiffly, put down his paper, took two mugs from their hooks, plopped tea bags into them, and poured water from the kettle simmering on the woodstove. He added three heaping teaspoons of sugar to each and handed them to us. Clare and I sat at the table while Pap settled into the rocker. He watched me as my eyes slid to the hay and horse feed in the other room.

"An old man's needs is few," he said and looked at Clare. "Once his family has gone." He turned back to me. "I'd like Clare to stay here but she thinks she's too old to live with her Pap. I could open up one of the bedrooms upstairs, both even; it could be her own apartment. She could ride for me again. I'm an old man. I can't be training horses forever."

"I just want my own place. You should understand that."

"That old place ain't fit for more than rats or coons. Your lip is bleeding again."

Clare licked her mouth. "Annie don't want to hear us fighting."

Pap crossed his legs, adjusted his shoulders against the rocker, and sighed. "I don't do much anymore, Annie, just sell a few horses here and there."

I had grown up knowing his name. Jim Raffienne was a small-time legend in Coleton. He knew all the old ways with a horse, the ailments and rank behaviors and how to cure them, the special secret tricks that put a bloom to a coat, cured lameness, or fooled those he thought deserved to be fooled. If he chose, he could match pony and rider so well the relationship lasted over decades but those who showed up in high heels and said they wanted a horse with spirit got exactly what they asked for.

"At least you left that place," he said to Clare.

She shrugged.

We sat in silence, Pap gently rocking. Outside, I heard a sound, a high metallic hum—the same sound I had heard last night at Tony's. I was puzzling this over when Pap stopped rocking, stretched his feet in front of him and asked me what my plans were. His voice was mild, but I felt as I always did when he looked straight at me with those pale blue eyes.

"I hear you're at the Norwood farm."

"Yes."

"Starting a horse business."

"I am. I've got fifteen stalls and a great old barn. Great land."

"Yes, yes, I know the place. Go by it all the time. Big old wooden barn sits up on a hill. Has 'burn me' written all over it."

I slopped tea on my lap, scalding my leg.

"People around here are set in their ways, Annie. They don't give up their hates easy."

"What have you heard?"

"You know how it is, old men hanging out at the feed store, they gossip."

"About?"

"Like I said, people don't give up their hates easy."

"My trainer has more lessons than she can handle."

Pap nodded.

"The parents bring chairs and sit next to the ring and watch their kids ride. No one has said anything to me."

Pap said nothing.

"I mean, they don't snatch their children away when they see Rollo. Rollo comes and goes... he's barely ever there. And even when he is, you hardly ever see him. People probably think he just helps out from time to time."

Clare was looking at her boots. Pap nodded again.

"She turns business away," I said.

"Just be careful, that's all. It's been dry lately. Fire's always a worry when it's dry like this."

I picked at my pant leg, wiggled it, and stirred the air around the place where the tea had landed. It stung like crazy. There was nothing I could do about Lydia. She was here. I couldn't start all over again.

"No one is going to burn down the damn barn." Clare licked away more droplets of blood.

Pap looked at me, impassive.

I continued trying to cool my leg. "So," I said, not looking up, "how long do you think this drought will last?"

"Droughts come, droughts go. They generally last seven years."

"Seven years!"

"Have you talked with Cecil lately?"

"Cecil?"

"Yes, you know, Cecil, Cecil Lowry... your neighbor."

I shook my head.

"Run into him last Saturday at the feed store. He was buying a new irrigation system. Going to tap into Cat Creek. His old one will be for sale. Probably give a neighbor a break."

The Lowry farm was huge by our valley's standards, over 1,500 acres of corn and alfalfa and long, low buildings that housed the hogs. Four generations lived on the land. Recently, one of the brothers started a full-scale milking operation and now they had all the modern equipment. The Lowrys never went to a movie, ate a meal out, took their children to a park, or went on vacation. Every penny went back into the farm. Men and women both wore shirts and blue jeans day in, day out, the only changes being their state of repair, the stiffness or limpness with which they hung. They often smelled of cow manure or, even worse, pig. No, I had not talked with Cecil lately. I did little more than wave as we passed on the road.

Outside we stepped off the porch into the bright daylight and the high-pitched whine that had begun last night closed around our heads. It ran along my spine and set my nerves on edge.

"What is that sound?"

"Don't you know," said Pap, genuinely surprised. "It's the cicadas. It's the year of the cicadas, Annie."

Gram's cabin was farther up the mountain, almost at the top. We could easily have passed the small building without seeing it. The clearing around it had grown over and the shadows from the trees fell on its roof, spread concealing stripes along the walls. It was one story, tiny, with two small rooms. The door was unlocked but we had to push it open due to the trash and broken furniture piled against it.

Inside, through the dim light, we saw an old mattress on the floor and boxes filled with clothing. The pipe to the cook stove had disconnected and leaned toward us like the eye of a camera. The damp rooms smelled of mildew and mice. Clare banged at a window, shoved it up and open. The panes were so covered with grime they had kept the place dark. As Clare raised them, light entered the cabin. It spread along the floor, exposing little bundles of shredded fabric, soft piles of mattress ticking, leaves and twigs and small black pellets everywhere. It filtered through dust motes, illuminated cobwebs. With the light on them you could see they were torn and gray, encrusted with dead flies and filth tangled in their delicate strands. Gram had turned her back on the place as soon as she could. From the little Clare and Pap would say about her, I gathered she was a vain woman. "Full of pride," Pap said fondly. With the force of her will, she had grabbed as much land as she could, talked Pap into building a decent house, insisted on paint and wallpaper. She wouldn't have her son or granddaughter raised the way she was raised.

Now, instead of helping Clare, I watched her let out the stale air. I didn't move. I stood in the middle of the room so still you'd have thought my feet were nailed to the floor. If Clare noticed, she gave no sign. She banged against the casements, leaned against the frames to loosen the windows, giving a soft grunt when she shoved them open. There were two windows in each room, four altogether. Clare stepped over boxes as she went from window to window, cobwebs dragging in her hair. What was I doing here? This wasn't a fairy tale. Last night a strange man with strange money had nearly knocked Clare's teeth out and now she was going to live in this place with real rat shit on the floor and real bats lying in corners, broken winged and decaying, some no more than a fine web of bones. Was I insane? I could see the polish and glitter of LA; remember the cool temperature of the buildings, the clink of ice in glasses, Stewart's easy, come hither smile, the way he sat, open legged and inviting. Did Clare really not realize how dreadful this place was? Did I not realize? I could see the muscles along the back of her neck and shoulders tighten with effort. I went to one of the windows and pushed. It didn't budge. Clare walked over and pushed with me. The window creaked and, with a loud crack, shattered into pieces. I jumped back shocked, but Clare burst out laughing and after a second, so did I. "Well, I guess we're done," she said and walked past me to the truck. We climbed in and bounced back down the road.

CHAPTER TWENTY-SIX

Clare dropped me at home, and as she pulled out of the driveway, the screen door to the apartment banged open and shut. Lydia, moving faster than I'd ever seen her, came across the driveway and stood in front of me. Her eyes followed the rusty truck. She rocked up on the balls of her feet then down. I thought she might do a little jig.

"Have you heard?" she said.

"What?"

"Clare didn't say anything?"

"*What?*"

"Tony's house burned to the ground last night."

She couldn't wait to tell me. Lightning had struck it, slammed into the house like a meteor, bursting it into flames. The cedar shakes exploded off the roof and the windows blasted out, spraying glass all over that huge yard right on down to the road. People said it was like an arsenal, doors flying, furniture, glass, just one explosion after another. Fire companies from three counties came, but it was too late. By morning it was just a pile of ashes. Lydia rocked up on her toes again.

"What about Tony?" I asked.

"Oh, he's all right. He and the servants came running out of the house as soon as the lightning hit. They must have been downstairs. Certainly, they weren't asleep or they would have been fried for sure. He was a mess though. Who wouldn't be? People said it was unbelievable. Actually, someone called the police. Nothing would burn that quickly on its own." She looked at me steadily. "They're considering arson. Lightning generally doesn't do a whole house like that. They're going to look for evidence. People always leave evidence. No matter how careful they are, there's always evidence. Clare wasn't there, was nowhere to be seen, which was really odd. You would have thought she'd have been home that time of night."

"She was with me."

"With you? Really? Well. Anyway, it's been on all the scanners." Lydia's morning lesson had told her all about it. The kid could hardly pay attention, almost fell off when she was trotting, her mouth was going so fast, jabbering about the fire. And the mom just went on and on about how she'd always suspected it was a shady operation. I mean, where did these people come from anyway, with all that money? Maybe it was a payback sort of thing. You know, a mafia thing. The whole town was talking about it.

Lydia rocked back and forth again. "And Clare was with you? That was pretty lucky, considering the investigation and all. What were you doing?"

I stared at her. "That's not something you need to worry about," I said finally.

"What'll she do now? Does she still have a job?"

"How would I know? I have to go, anyway."

"Do you think Tony will keep the farm going after this?"

"How do I know? You know more about it than I do. This is all news to me."

"So, Clare spent the night here with you last night, huh?"

"That's what I said, isn't it? I have to go, Lydia."

"Don't you think it's something though?"

Yeah, I thought it was something all right. I went in the house and shut the door behind me. I headed instinctively for the phone but remembered before my hand touched the cradle that Pap had gotten rid of his years ago. Good Lord. Tony's house blown to bits. How could lightning do such damage? I felt like I had a cold rock in my stomach. I went to the gun cabinet and took out a bottle of wine to dissolve it. It was already open and tasted stale and sour. I drank a glass anyway. I pulled the thin curtains across the windows and the heavy ones over those. I turned on a light and took a novel I had neglected for months and sat down with it on the couch. That and the wine. I tried to lose myself in the story, but it was no use. *What was Stewart doing now*, I wondered. It was three hours earlier in California. Sunday morning. He was probably just getting up, maybe fixing himself a cup of coffee, reading the paper in bed. Something civilized like that. Something sane. He'd probably had dinner in a restaurant last night. A nice restaurant with polite people making polite conversation.

That night my dreams were full of flames. Flames and cries drowned out by police sirens; Clare in shackles, laughing, sitting with Pap in his living room drinking tea while the house burned around them and somehow, though the walls were all in flames, the police pounded on their door. They pounded while Pap rocked and Clare waited, inscrutable as a cat, and the pounding grew louder and louder until it woke me and I realized it was my own door that was being beaten. My heart leaped, nearly matched the beating fist but curiosity shoved me out of bed, propelled me down the stairs before I could catch my breath and think. Jack stood on the other side of the door, fierce and trembling. In the porch light, I could see the sweat running along his jaw line.

He didn't wait for me to invite him in. He practically shoved me out of the way, propped the edge of his bottom on the nearest chair, and leaned toward me, his wrists and hands hanging off his knees. I placed myself on the edge of the couch, mirroring his pose. The minute I did so, he burst out, "You heard about Raffino's fire, right? Well, the guy's driving around looking for Clare. Thought I better warn you. She's prob'ly at Pap's. Raffino don't know where that is, does he?"

"Why is he looking for Clare?"

"Cause Clare done it, that's why."

"Don't be ridiculous."

"Police said ain't no way it was lightning."

"Do they have proof? Will there be an investigation?"

"Prob'ly. Naw. I dunno."

"How do you know he's out driving around and, even if he is, how do you know he's looking for Clare?"

"I run into a guy from the Red Run said Tony was there askin questions."

I sat back. First Tony slams Clare in the mouth, and now he's out in the middle of the night going to local dives and asking questions about her. Some foreigner from God knows where. Well, no one would talk to him. Not to a stranger. Clare might be from the Holler but she was from here. I was sure no one would point the way to Pap's. But this farm. Tony already knew how to get here. And it didn't take brains to figure out this would be a good place to look. Clare wasn't here, but Stringtown was walking around my pasture this very moment. I had an image of someone driving quietly to the barn, putting her in the back of a trailer, and driving off while I slept in bed.

Jack shifted closer to the edge of his chair. "Should we drive to her Pap's and warn her?"

"Stringtown is here."

Jack understood immediately. "I'll stay here in the barn."

"I'll stay with you."

"No need. I won't fall asleep. I stayed up all night lots of times. If anyone shows up, I'll shoot off my gun."

"Gun?"

"My rifle. It's on the porch."

"You brought a gun with you?"

"Course."

"Look, I don't want you shooting that gun."

"I'll just shoot it in the air."

"Not here. No shooting at all. I'll spend the night in the barn with you. But no guns. Do you understand?"

We found some flashlights in a closet and, armed with these, we went to the barn and settled in amongst the hay bales. They scratched but other than that made a comfortable bed. Jack lay with his arms behind his head, staring at the ceiling. Our feet faced each other.

"Is he her groom?"

"Who? What are you talking about?"

"That nigger. I never seen him do no work. Why's he stayin with her if he ain't gonna work on the farm?"

Did he really not understand what was going on? Should I tell him they'd talked of marriage? If I did, it would spread through the Holler like wildfire. I stared at the rafters. How old they were. At least 150 years. Probably older. How quickly they would burn. If Jack didn't know the relationship between Lydia and Rollo, perhaps the others in the Holler weren't sure either.

"Listen Jack," I said, "Rollo doesn't work here. He has another job. He's a salesman of some sort. He's on the road a lot."

"How come he comes to the farm?"

"Well, he and Lydia have a relationship. I think maybe her parents adopted him. Or maybe he was their foster child."

"Ain't right. Everybody says so. Even if they's just friends. He shouldn't stay in the same house with her. You shouldn't let them. People are talking, saying you should do something about it. Or else they will."

My whole body became alert. "What exactly are they saying?"

"People used to hang niggers for less around here."

I waited, not breathing.

"Course, if they're like brother and sister. Been raised together and all. That's bad enough. But if people thought there was something between 'em, it would be real bad. Lydia and me are friends, you know that. I been telling her it ain't good having Rollo here. I imagine he won't be hanging around much longer. But you could hurry things along, tell him he ain't welcome."

"I'm not going to do that, and I don't want you getting in the middle of it. It's none of your business and nobody else's either."

Jack scrunched his shoulders into the hay. "Well, I was just telling you." He rolled onto his side and muttered something I couldn't quite make out. Soon his breathing became slow and regular. He slept quietly, like a child. I listened to the soothing rhythm, the night sounds, and finally the birds as they woke in the hazy light. Tires crunched along the gravel driveway. I poked Jack. We scrambled off the hay, emerged from the barn with stalks, dried leaves, and shattered clover sticking to our clothing and hair.

Tony's red truck and trailer greeted us like the glow from a furnace. He opened the door, walked around and leaned his backside against the near door. He crossed his arms. He looked dreadful, had a day's growth of beard, bloodshot eyes, and badly rumpled clothes. "Is Clare here, by any chance?" he asked matter-of-factly.

"No."

"And Stringtown?"

I said "Yes," and Jack said "No," at precisely the same time. We looked at each other. I frowned at him. There the big mare stood plain as day in the middle of the field. "Yes," I said, "of course she's here."

"She disappeared during the fire. You have heard about the fire, I presume."

"Yes."

"I'm quite sure Clare took the mare and I'm looking for both of them. But now that I've found Stringtown, I'll just take her with me."

"You will not," I said.

Tony moved his backside away from the truck and stood straight. "She's my horse, Annie," he said softly.

"No, she's not. She's Clare's. And no one touches her without Clare's say so."

"Why don't you just tell me where Clare is, and we'll get this straightened out." He brushed at his pants, looked up at me, smiling. "I hate to see you in the middle of this, Annie. I just need to talk to Clare, that's all. There is nothing to be alarmed about. And I certainly hate seeing you in such an awkward position. So if you'll tell me where I can find her."

"I don't know where she is," I said. I wanted to add, and don't give me that I'm an Italian gentleman crap, I saw you nearly knock Clare's head off.

"Annie," he said still softly, "I don't believe you."

"Don't matter if you believe her or not. Clare ain't here and you ain't touching Stringtown, so you might as well clear off."

Surprise, then disbelief moved across Tony's face, the first spontaneous emotions I'd ever seen him show. He looked at Jack for the first time that morning. I stood immobilized. Tony outweighed Jack by at least fifty pounds. The boy stared back, not moving. We stood locked in a triangle that seemed to hold us together with an electrical charge. I didn't dare look straight at either of them. Time hummed, whirred in my ears while Tony scrutinized the boy. I waited, expecting him to flatten this kid from the Holler, but instead he stepped back, lowered his eyes, and ran his hand along the fender of his truck. "I'll find Clare eventually," he said. "And, Annie, watch your back," he added, glancing at Jack.

We watched as the red rig pulled down the valley road. I touched Jack's arm. "Thank you. I'm not sure what would have happened if you weren't here."

"I'd better be goin. I'll just get my gun and head home."

"I'll drive you. You must be exhausted."

"I got my bike. I'll do fine."

"We can put the bike in the back of the truck."

Jack had turned away and was walking to the house. I followed behind him. When we were inside, I reached for the gun, meaning to put it in the truck. Jack yanked it away from me.

"What is it?"

"I don't need no lift."

"But…"

"Jesus Christ. I don't need to have Paw see me drivin home with some woman after daylight. Christ all mighty. Specially you."

"Me?"

"He hates nigger lovers worse than he hates niggers. I'll come back later, but I got to get home now."

"People need to mind their own business," I shouted after him, but he was already out the door, on his bike and pedaling hard.

I told Clare the next day that Tony was looking for her. She put her tongue to the back of her top teeth and exhaled a disgusted sound, so careless in her dismissal I could only marvel.

Tony returned two days later. He was as clean and crisp as ever. He followed me through the barn as I did my chores, stood talking a fastidious three feet away while I bathed Lonesome. He told me it was Clare's complete carelessness that had first attracted him. Her looks helped, of course, but he'd known countless pretty girls. It was the way she couldn't even be bothered to comb her hair that drew his attention. "You know how much time women spend on their hair. And money. My God, the money they spend making it those awful colors. And stiff as wire. Half the time Clare doesn't even run a brush through hers. You could get lost in it. And she isn't vain about her clothes, either. She'd wear the same thing day in and day out. She's more like a man than a man in some ways," he said sounding surprised. "Men wear cologne and jewelry."

I could imagine him glancing at his pinky ring.

"Men are the ones that stray," he went on. "At least most of the time. Women can be such sneaks. Not Clare. Right out in the open. She even walks like a boy. Have you ever seen her wear heels? She absolutely won't wear pantyhose. Flat out refused at the party in Timonium." He'd bought her fancy dresses that she'd left on the floor of the motel. Given her lingerie and she never wore it. "In fact, I'll let you in on a little secret. Most of the time she doesn't wear underwear at all." Raffino seemed to ponder for a moment. "Of course, she's all woman in bed."

I peeked through the boards of the bathhouse at him. He stood patiently, speaking to the air. "She's like a wild thing, something that just walked out of the woods. It's like grabbing hold of a savage. I'll tell you one thing. I never expected to find anything like her when I came here. I thought every woman would be fat with only a few teeth." One of the things he missed most was making love in Clare's apartment. It was airless, rank; the bare mattress underneath them stained. I could picture it all.

I even found him sitting in the dim light of my kitchen at dawn one day. "You've got to stop this," I shouted. "You can't just walk in here anytime you like. You scared me. At least knock or something to let me know it's you. I sleep with a gun. I could have shot you." He had the grace to look abashed for a moment. "Oh, Annie, you'd never shoot anyone." He waved his hand. "Clare, on the other hand…"

I sank into the chair next to him. I told him about the boy who, heartbroken and blind drunk after Clare dropped him, froze to death in a parking lot. "And she maimed another," I added.

"Froze to death? Well, I've certainly no intention of doing that." He frowned. "What do you mean she maimed a guy? With a gun?"

"No, she bit him."

Tony looked thoughtful. "That's something a woman would do," he said, sounding almost disappointed. After a tense pause, he looked at me and said, "Now listen. I'm rebuilding the house. Clare can come back. I want her to come back. To work for me again. It's crazy. I know it's crazy. I mean, she walked out on me. No woman ever walks out on me. Of course, I don't believe for a moment those rumors about her burning down my house. That's just nonsense." He hesitated. "Tell her I'll even give her her share of Stringtown."

I told Clare she could train for Tony again, and she laughed. "Are you nuts? Tony don't want me to work for him again. You are so gullible, Annie."

"What's he want?"

"I don't know but it ain't got nothing to do with what he's saying."

"He wants to give you your share in Stringtown."

Clare stared at me. "My share? Did you say my share?"

When I told Tony Clare wasn't interested in his proposition, an edge crept back into his voice. He stood in my yard and looked up the mountain. His imagination seemed to hum. "No phone, no electricity," he murmured. "Do they even have a road up to that place?"

"Not really."

"Not really? Well, they must get up there somehow." Tony turned away from the mountain to look at me. Smiling, he shook his head.

He stopped coming round after that and once again Jack climbed back on my blue and white tractor, and we spent most of our days going back and forth through the dusty grass.

CHAPTER TWENTY-SEVEN

You could not say that Stringtown settled easily into life on the farm. Clare stayed away, busy up the mountain fixing her place. She had no fences, no pasture, no hay or feed. She asked me to keep Stringtown while she took care of these things. In the meantime, Stringtown dug holes in my stall floor, went through more grain and hay than three horses, ripped up my pasture with her lunging and spinning, fought and bloodied the other mares, and refused to be separated from Lonesome. If we took him out of the pasture, she simply jumped the fence and galloped after him. If we took him from the stall next to hers, she kicked the boards until they came down and her back legs were swollen and bloody.

One Saturday when Lydia gave Sadie a break and used Lonesome as a lesson horse, Stringtown tried to climb out of the stall. We had to bring him back into the barn.

"Is Clare just going to leave that horse here?"

"We'll just have to use one of the boarders," I said, untacking my horse.

"If she's not going to do something with her, she should sell her. A horse like this is wasted on Clare. And all the horses are too tired to give another lesson."

"Reschedule Tina. We'll give her a free lesson?"

Lydia's eyebrows shot up.

"Go ahead, give her another time."

"When do you want to come back?" Lydia shifted her weight to one leg, her hip out.

Tina tucked herself against her mother. "I want a lesson now."

"Sadie is too tired now. Do you want to come back for another lesson?"

Tina nodded against her mother while gazing at Lydia. Mrs. Robinson, her hand under her daughter's chin, tilted the child's head upward. "What do you think? Would you like to come back tomorrow?"

"Tomorrow won't work," said Lydia.

I looked at her.

"Rollo and I are going to spend two days this time looking for a new horse again. In Connecticut. I told you about it."

"Nooo, I don't think so." I thought over the last few days. It was possible she had told me and it had slipped my mind. I didn't think so, but it was possible.

"Sure I did. Remember? I'm taking the Doctor as a trade in. Anyway, we'll only be gone a couple of days."

"Ah, Mrs. Robinson, would you like to return in a week? Same time?"

"I want to come back tomorrow," Tina wailed.

"How about this coming Wednesday? It's only a few days. You'll be back then, won't you, Lydia?"

"Yeah, sure. I guess."

"Yes or no? Which is it?"

"Yeah, sure, I'll be here."

When the Robinsons left, I said, "I did *not* know you were leaving."

"I'm pretty sure I told you."

"Do the other students know you'll be going?"

"Most of them."

"Well, make sure they all do."

"Okay. But I did tell you. I don't know why that kid is taking lessons, anyhow. She's not interested in horses at all."

"I think it's you she's interested in."

Lydia left the next morning. I was about to begin feeding when Jack arrived. His face was open, totally lacking in guile and full of alarm as he stepped out of the sun into the shade of the barn.

"Was that Lydia's trailer going down the road?"

"She'll just be gone a few days to look for a new horse."

"Rollo went with her, I suppose. When's she gonna get rid of him?"

"Jack. We've been over this."

"Ain't right," he muttered.

When we were done in the barn, the boy followed me to the kitchen. On the way, he talked of Lydia. He spoke to the air, walking slightly in back of me, confident his words would reach their target and I would absorb them, send them back to him altered in a way that would help him understand her. I poured him a glass of tea as he sat at the kitchen table and stared out the window at Lydia's apartment. Once again, I began to doubt what I was doing, saw myself becoming dry and crisp as parchment, flat enough to reflect other's yearnings while my own turned to powder. I was shadow without substance, slept alone only to wake in the morning to watch the land around me turn to dust.

Lydia returned two days later. Jack must have been lying in wait for he pedaled his bike furiously behind the trailer as it bumped down the road. Even though Rollo was out of the truck as soon as it stopped, it was Jack who lowered the ramp, came around, and walked The Doctor down it.

"Lydia." He looked in the truck window. "Do you want me to put him in his stall?"

She nodded, slid from her seat, too disgusted it seemed to speak. She had not intended bringing The Doctor home.

"Anything decent starts at fifty thousand," she said after staring at me. "That includes The Doctor as trade." Rollo came round to our side and leaned against the truck, watched Jack remove the horse's shipping boots. Lydia paid no attention. "We're selling this rig," she said, giving it a smack.

Rollo raised his eyebrows, but otherwise did not move. "No way," he said.

"How else are we going to get the money?"

"Not by selling this rig. And it isn't worth fifty thousand."

"Whose rig is it?" asked Jack.

Lydia looked at him blankly then turned her attention back to Rollo. "We could use it as a down payment."

"Let's talk about it later," said Rollo quietly. He lit a cigarette and carefully picked a piece of tobacco from his lips. "It's been a long day. I think I'll take a shower." He looked at Lydia through the smoke, his eyes half closed. "You might want to do the same," he said before walking off to the apartment while Jack drove to the pump and hosed out the trailer.

"He's head over heels in love with you, you know," I said, inclining my head in the boy's direction. Lydia only made a clucking sound at what she already knew. Her eyes followed Rollo. She turned to face me briefly, a darting glance, showing the hint of a conspirator's smile.

"He'll come around. You just watch."

The days now were endless, the sun not going down until after nine. Sometimes thunder rolled in the faded hills, even brought with it a hot wind. It was always a false promise. Afterward, the gnats dashed at our eyes with still more fury. And all day, every day, the air was filled with the cicada's metallic cry.

Clare brought Pap to my farm. They wanted to take me to the Lowry's to talk to Cecil about that irrigation system before he sold it to someone else. They stood in my kitchen like two trees. Pap smelled the soup cooking on the stove. Sick of peanut butter sandwiches, I'd thrown chicken bones and vegetables in a pot to simmer, even though it made the room nearly unbearably humid.

"Ah, a woman's touch," he said.

Clare didn't want to take the time, but Pap couldn't resist. I filled three bowls with the soup and three big glasses with iced tea. I put these and a loaf of Italian bread on the table. Pap dipped his bread into the soup, closed his eyes as he sipped.

"It's a sin for a man to have to cook for himself when he gets old," he said.

Clare tossed her hair, bent over her soup.

"How old are you, Annie?"

"Tsk," Clare clucked. "She's my age, you know that."

"Time both of you realized you're women, not little girls playing with horses."

Clare's spoon clattered against her bowl. "Pap, you're the one who wants me to train for you."

"Granddaughter, it's better than having you get your teeth knocked out."

Clare let it drop.

Pap helped himself to more soup. "No man's going to live with you in that cabin a yours. You're the last of us, Clare. I'd hate to die thinking our family was dying out."

Clare jerked to her feet, went to the sink, splashed water into her bowl. Pap turned to me. "You married, Annie?" he asked, all innocence.

"Yes... ah, no. Well, sort of."

"Well, either you're married or you ain't."

I didn't know what to say.

"I see you still got your wedding rings on. Must mean you're more married than you ain't. The way I see it, making this farm your only bed fellow ain't natural. You girls ought to be settling down, raising families."

I glanced at Clare, expecting trouble. Instead, she stood absorbed, lost to her surroundings. I can only guess what she imagined standing so still and distracted at the sink. She may have been wondering about her tiny cabin so far up the mountain with no electricity, no phone, nothing to connect her to the outside world; she may have been wondering about how finely she had stripped life, about choices she had made, choices that were meant to keep her free. If we could have waited, she might have told us what was going through her mind, but it was at that moment Tony called hello and walked through the kitchen door.

His face was rosy. A smile hung at the corners of his mouth and his bare brown arms swung at his sides. He raised an eyebrow. When I spoke his name, he had to force his eyes from Clare.

"Tony, this is Mr. Raffienne, Clare's grandfather."

Tony held out his hand toward Pap.

Pap pointedly put his hands in his pockets. He leaned back on two legs of his chair. "So you're the man who knocked my granddaughter's teeth loose," he said.

Tony stiffened.

Pap waited, tipped back in his chair, watching him.

Tony turned back to Clare. "I've been looking all over for you. I want to talk to you about Stringtown. I know she's here and I could have taken her at any time. But I wanted to talk to you first. I'm willing to give you payment for the work you put into her. You helped, after all, made her worth something." He looked pleased with himself, as though he expected surprise, even gratitude. He glanced briefly at Pap then back to Clare. "Can't we talk? I've been trying to for weeks."

Clare stared at him. Her dark look was in place, pure and clear.

Tony accepted and tolerated the stare a moment, then a moment longer. He waited and I heard the clock on the stove ticking. He straightened. "You've stolen my horse," he said with careful nonchalance.

No one spoke. The silence pushed him farther. "I've come to take her back."

"I've got papers," said Clare.

Tony was ready. "You stole them along with the horse. You've got no bill of sale."

From the way her nostrils flared, I knew Clare realized she was caught. More than that, she saw Tony had counted on her foolishness, had used it as insurance.

I felt only recognition as I watched Clare reach for the butcher knife I had used to cut the bread. She moved so easily, flicked her wrist with such unhurried skill that it looked almost casual. The knife swished past Tony's ear, landed in the wall behind him with a solid thunk.

The man's face drained of color, then red burst on his cheeks and ears. He opened his mouth, closed it; took a step, not toward Clare, but Pap who remained seated. He leaned over him. "Your granddaughter is crazy. You know that? She should be locked up." I thought he might grab Pap by the shirt collar. "I'm not some local hick you can push around. I can put her behind bars."

Pap settled his chair back on four legs, rose slowly to his feet. Tony stepped back. He blinked to cover his surprise at Pap's height.

"Don't make threats you ain't prepared to keep. A well insured pile of ashes ain't the worst thing that can happen to a man."

I believe it was Pap's age that held Tony's hands still. Yet his fingers opened and closed and his eyes, hard and black as beads, darted around the room.

"You're both crazy," he said eventually. When no one spoke, he turned and shoved open the screen door with the palm of his hand.

I ran after him.

"Annie, take some advice. Get these people out of your life." He took several deep breaths, settled himself enough to continue. "She meant to kill me."

I had to laugh.

This was not the first time I had seen Clare Raffienne throw a knife. Years ago, on an afternoon as hot as this one, we had stalked the second story of my barn, positioned ourselves on the hay, back amongst the shadows and the dust. We listened to the pigeons cooing in the rafters. They had taken residence in the spring, settled in and multiplied. They ate my grain and covered the barn with their filth. Time and time again that day, I saw Clare's knife flash through the air and land with a muffled thunk as it pinned a fat breasted bird to the floor. The pigeons continued to flap to the floor seeking the corn we had tossed, even though death picked off their companions one by one. By dusk, not a pigeon moved.

I told Tony if Clare had meant to kill him, he'd have a knife in his heart.

This did nothing to mollify him.

"I came to offer her a reasonable deal. I saw her truck from the road and actually hoped this would be a chance to talk to her. And she throws a knife at me. And he, he threatens me. The old man threatens me!"

"Well, you did split his granddaughter's lip."

Tony looked disgusted at this trifle. He slung himself into his car, a Cadillac every bit as red as his truck. "Don't think for a minute, Annie, that I'm afraid of the Raffiennes," he said, leaning his elbow on the window frame.

"Are you really planning to take Stringtown?"

"She's worth something now. Clare was working for me when she trained her. I'm within my legal rights." He shifted gears. I stood back from the car.

"Take my advice, Annie, get away from these people. They're small town, but they can still cause trouble. Not for me. Not in the long run, anyway. But you. You're just a woman alone." His tires spit gravel as he left.

Clare and Pap came out of the house. Nothing in their manner spoke of what had happened in my kitchen. Pap held the door to Clare's truck open for me and I climbed into an oven. He draped an arm along the window, swatted at the flies that had gathered. He looked at my fields as we passed them, shook his head at the curling brown grass. "You shouldn't have cut it so close," he said. "The weeds could have offered some shade. Now the grass will just burn up in the sun."

"I didn't know."

"Should've asked."

CHAPTER TWENTY-EIGHT

The Lowry farm, in contrast to mine, was still green. We saw their tractor from the road and the spiky apparatus behind it. The image quivered in the heat, but I could make out the three Lowry men: grandfather, father, son. They worked at the far end of the field, too distant to hear us shout. We made our way carefully across the tender new growth. Halfway to them the Lowry's saw us, straightened from their task, leaned against the tractor, and waited for our approach. Mr. Lowry took a handkerchief from his overall pocket, wiped it across his forehead. Mike, Ken's seventeen-year-old son, climbed onto the tractor seat, slouched down until his head rested on the back, and closed his eyes. Even his eyelids were sunburned.

"Jim," said Cecil Lowry and held out his hand. "What brings you down the mountain into this heat?"

"Not farming, you can be sure."

"Be glad of that."

They were close in age, had the same dried out, sinewy look.

"This your new irrigation system?" asked Pap, tapping a metal tube with his foot.

"Damn thing's hung up on these rocks. Pay a fortune for this stuff now a days and it doesn't work as well as the old."

"Speaking of the old stuff, you still got yours?"

"It's in the barn," said Ken.

"I'd be interested in it," I said, "if it's not too much."

Ken looked at his father.

Cecil wiped his face. "From the looks of it, you'd better do something soon or it'll be too late. You'll lose the roots."

Before I could answer, a bell rang, sharp and clear, from the big house across the road.

"Dinner time," said Mr. Lowry, running his hand through his hair before putting back his hat. "You can borrow it for a while. Just bring it back when you're done. I can always use the parts."

CHAPTER TWENTY-NINE

Four o'clock in the morning and I was still awake. I gave up and went to the barn and brought in the horses and put Lonesome in cross ties, went to the tack room for my brushes. I started with the curry comb then stopped, ran my hands over my horse's chest and flanks. I could feel his ribs so clearly I could have counted them if I wanted to. He'd lost one hundred, maybe two hundred pounds. "Only one flake," I had told Lydia and Jack. "When you bring the horses into the barn." I was very strict about it. "This hay has to last all summer and through the winter," I'd said, "or at least until the rain comes."

Now I wrapped my arms around my horse's neck. "Oh, big guy, I am so sorry." Lonesome shook his head, fidgeted with his feet. I rubbed my knuckles between his eyes; ran my hands along his ears then went through the barn checking the others. The big, rangy ones had obviously lost weight. It wasn't so obvious in the smaller animals, but I noticed with dismay that their coats no longer glistened the way they had in the spring. I would have to buy hay, good hay, and lots of it.

I called around as soon as it was a decent hour. Many of my contacts weren't selling hay; they were hunkering down for a hard year. I finally found an alfalfa timothy mix that cost fifteen dollars a bale, more than I had ever paid. Next I called an auction house. Would they be interested in a large antique Italian library table, an Aubusson rug, a chifforobe, a tavern table, several pedestal tables, a dry sink, porcelain wash set and other porcelain pieces?

"I can't say until I see them," the voice on the line said, crossly. "How do you know they aren't reproductions?"

"Some are family pieces and the others—well, the others are genuine. I'm sure of it."

"Have you anything else? Wouldn't be worth sending a truck out for what you just mentioned. The stuff doesn't all have to be antiques. Any collectibles? Dolls? Toys?"

"No dolls or toys, but I have some lamps, bookshelves, and end tables." I mentally went through the rooms. "I have a dining room table, matching chairs, and a Victorian desk." I also had a full set of Havilland china that had been my grandmother's, a sterling flatware set in the Old Rose design, a full set of Venetian crystal glasses that I never used anymore. All my grandmother's. There was no response, so I continued. "Some paintings, chest of drawers, a highboy." I couldn't think of anything else.

"We charge fifteen percent."

"Okay."

"I'll send someone out this Tuesday."

Three men arrived armed with a roll of red sticky circles. They began the minute they walked through the front door. "Does this go? This? What about that over there? And the paintings, what about them?" They slapped a red circle on something each time I said yes. And, caught up in their detached, irritable haste, I found myself saying yes more than I had planned.

When the men finished loading the truck, the crew leader handed me an inventory list. It was long. We sat at the kitchen table while I looked it over.

"You got some nice things," the man said. "You want to put an amount you won't go below? That rug won't get much but the rest is nice. That china and crystal, the flatware, you might want to save that for another auction. One in a big city where people would appreciate it."

I thought a minute. "No, that's okay. You go ahead and sell it," I said.

"Well, dealers come sometimes. If they do, you should get a good price."

I nodded.

"The sale is Saturday. You can have a check by Monday," the crew leader said gently.

"Thank you." I signed the inventory and handed it to him.

When the men were gone, I looked around. The only furniture left was the table and two chairs in the kitchen, a couch, matching love seat, gun cabinet, and lamp in the living room, the sprung couch in the parlor, the brass bed, night table, and lamp upstairs. That was fine. I didn't need that other stuff anyway. This time next week I should have a barn full of hay, good hay, the kind of hay that would put a bloom in a horse's coat. As I walked through the house, I willed myself not to notice the echo of my boots.

CHAPTER THIRTY
JACK

Friday night the old man came home early from the V.F.W. That only happened twice before and both times was bad. I had the boom box goin and didn't hear anything 'till that old cane hit the kitchen wall.

"Jack! What the hell you doing?" I could hear him stumping down the hall. I scrambled to get the boom box under the bed. I was just straightening up when he appeared in the door.

"Gimme that goddamn thing."

"What?"

"You know goddamn well what. I seen you put it under the bed. Now get down on your knees and get it and give it to me. I'm gonna break the fuckin thing in a million pieces."

"No."

He staggered toward me, leaned that wooden leg against the bed for support, and raised his cane.

"Oh, yes you will."

Mom came in the room. "Os, stop that. Stop it. Leave the boy alone."

"Goddamn lazy, good for nothing. You gimme that fuckin boom box or I'll kill you."

"Just give him the box. Please, Jack."

"No, I ain't."

"Os, come on, I'll fix you somethin to eat." Mom reached for the old man's arm. He jerked away from her, swayed all his weight onto his good leg, almost lost his balance.

"Os, come on now. Forget the box. Jack won't use it again. Ain't you hungry? I got hamburg."

"Jesus Christ. Is that all you ever fix?"

"I can make chili if you want. Come on Os, come sit in the kitchen and I'll make chili."

I'd straightened and was looking at him, so I managed to duck the blow.

"I'm gonna get some supper and when I'm done eating, that fucking boom box better be on the table."

I looked in the truck. Yeah, the drunk old bastard had left the keys in it. I climbed in, released the brake, and let it roll downhill. I started the motor and headed toward the abandoned general store at the edge of the village. That's where kids hung out at night. They'd park their cars and trucks back from the street where it was too dark to see 'em. There was two pickups when I pulled in. Harry, Blair, and Chad sat on the tailgate of one of them. I squealed rubber, skidding and fishtailing up to them. I leaned out the window. "You got any?"

"Does a bear shit in the woods?"

"How much?"

"Three six packs."

"Shit, that ain't enough."

"You was supposed to bring some."

"I couldn't." I jumped out of my truck and hopped up with the others. Chad reached behind him, opened a can, and handed it to me. It was warm but beggars can't be choosers.

"How come you couldn't get any with that fancy new job of yours? Workin for Ms. high-and-mighty society lady from Coleton?" asked Blair.

"She ain't like that. Anyway, I couldn't find no one to buy it for me. An my old man come home early."

"What about that blondie you're so hot for? Couldn't you ask…?"

"She's already got a boyfriend." Harry cut in. "That skinny ass nigger what lives with her." He threw an empty into the back of the truck bed and opened another.

"He don't live with her."

"Jack would like to think he don't, but I'd like to know what you call it."

"You had any of that?" asked Chad. He was younger than the rest of us, only fourteen. There was somethin wrong with his head. He wasn't crazy, but he couldn't learn. Leastwise not in school. He hung around with me as much as he could, which wasn't much now that I had a job. The other boys didn't like him much, but they tolerated him when I was around.

"That's for me to know and you to find out."

"You like sharing with a nigger?" said Harry.

"I ain't sharing with nobody. So keep your fucking mouth shut."

"What do you call it? You think they're just friends?"

I reached behind him and got another beer. "I don't share."

"Does that mean you ain't doin her?" asked Chad.

"Let's change the fuckin subject, okay?"

Blair got himself another beer. "My pap says the KKK used to be big around here."

"Yeah," said Harry, "I heard that too."

"What's the KKK?"

"Don't you know nothin, Chad? It's them guys that dress up in sheets and hang niggers."

"But there aren't any niggers around here."

"That's 'cause we run 'em out, dumb ass."

"Well... maybe we should do that now."

"Chad, take this beer and drink it. That ought to keep him quiet for awhile." We all laughed.

Blair belched. "Seriously, though, it ain't right. Something should be done about it. We don't need to hang 'em, just give 'em a message. Didn't those guys in sheets use to burn crosses in people's yards?"

Harry had that sleepy look he got when he was feeling mean. "Yeah, and burn down barns."

"Dry as it is, it would be easy to burn that old barn."

"They got horses in there," I said.

Harry finished off his beer in a couple of long swallows. "Let's drive over there and take a look."

"And then what?"

"Nothin Jack. Just take a look."

"Ain't nothing to see. It's just a barn. We're gonna be out of beer soon, anyway. I know someone in town who can help us out." I didn't really want to go into Coleton, but I knew this would distract them.

"I'll come with you." Chad jumped down from the tailgate, ready to go. Once inside the truck, he saw the boom box right away. "You holding out on us, Jack?" He put it into his lap and started fiddling with the dials.

"Careful with that."

"How come you left it in the truck? You holdin out on us?"

"Quit saying that. I left it in the truck because I wanted to and if you don't like it you can go home anytime."

The Porters lived on Decator Street right in Coleton. I parked next to a steep hill where the houses stood so close you could have reached out one window and grabbed the person in the next one.

We climbed up the stairs to Porter's back door. It was darker than pitch. I knocked several times and after a long wait an old woman in a housecoat opened the door a crack. I thought she might shut it on me when she seen she didn't know who I was. I asked for Bill real quick and told her I was a friend of his. She opened the door enough for me and Chad to slip through and shuffled off, her heels glowing fat and white as the underbelly of a fish, stepping on the backs of her slippers.

"It sure is dark in here."

"Shut up, Chad."

"But why they keep it so dark?"

"I guess they like it that way." I pulled out a chair and sat at the kitchen table. There were dirty dishes everywhere.

After a while, Bill came through a curtain hanging in a doorway. "Yeah?"

"I was wondering if you got any beer for sale."

"Naw, it's all gone."

"I got plenty of money."

"Who's that with you?"

"Chad Mallow. He's okay."

"You know I don't like you bringing strangers here."

"He's okay. He runs with us."

Bill took a drag on a cigarette and proceeded to cough like he'd never stop. Finally he spit in the sink and that ended it.

"Well, if you ain't got any beer, I guess we'll be goin."

"I got some Daniels."

"Yeah?"

"It'll cost you."

"I got plenty."

He reached under the sink and brought out a quart. "This is all I got."

"How much?"

"Fifty."

"Holy shit."

"Take it or leave it."

Chad had the top off the bottle by the time I started the truck. He took a swig and choked.

"Don't waste the damn stuff."

When we got back to the parking lot, Blair and Harry was still sitting on the tailgate. I hung onto the neck of the bottle and swung it back and forth in front of them.

"Hot damn," said Blair.

Harry grabbed for it. That bottle kept us busy for about an hour. By that time Harry and Blair was just itchin to go to the Norwood farm. I didn't see how I was going to hold them off. Chad started pukin and I'll be damned if Blair didn't too. He spit on the ground. "Let's go up on the Pensye and raise some hell."

"You just got done pukin and you want to raise hell?"

"I'm fine now." He straightened up; drew a deep breath and exhaled. "And the night is young."

"I want to go home," said Chad before he leaned over the side of the truck again and emptied his stomach. He threw up until he got the dry heaves.

"For Christ sake," said Harry. "You guys are a hell of a lot of fun."

"Hell, it's early yet. I'm up for anything. Let's go." Blair held the bottle to his eye and peered into it, tilted back his head, and shook the last drops into his mouth. He leaned over and emptied his stomach on the asphalt again.

All that good liquor I paid for gone to waste. "I'm going home. Come on Chad, I'll take you back to your place."

Harry had taken the bottle from Blair and was shaking it upside down. "You have turned into such a pussy, Jack."

"We're out of liquor and everyone's pukin their guts out."

"How about you, Blair? You all right now? Let's go raise some hell."

"I want to go home," Chad said again.

"Come on, I'll take you. Let's get out of here before you all start making me sick. God, it stinks around here." I seriously thought I might throw up myself.

"You go on home. You and Chad. I swear, Jack. You are messed up."

When I turned on the barn lights at seven o'clock in the morning, Jack was waiting for me, his face white and pinched. "The horses are gone," he said.

I stared at him.

"The boards are down, and the horses gone."

I looked across the driveway to the field. The gate was closed with the chain around it. Everything was in order. Except the field was empty. I turned back to Jack.

"When I came, they wasn't at the gate. I thought you'd brought them in. When I didn't see them in the barn, I started looking and seen the boards down by the road." Jack's words came out in a tumble and as he talked, he hustled past me. "Come on, I'll show you."

The boards were stacked neatly against the closest fence post. It seemed someone had taken the trouble to arrange them in a way that left no doubt as to the intent. I stared, motionless. I couldn't think of a thing to do. I thought I should cry but not even tears would come. Jack watched me closely. Where does one look for a herd of missing horses?

"They probably headed down the road toward the village," said Jack.

I knew I should do something, but I didn't seem able to move.

"Probably someone from the valley did it. You know, because of Lydia and Rollo." Jack was still, watching me closely. "I'll go get the truck," he finally said.

We spun out of the driveway in the direction of the village, Jack driving. Halfway there we sighted them, fidgeting next to a metal bridge with no sides. They were pumped up from their adventure and wanted to keep going but the open network of iron gridding had them buffaloed. They stared at it with their front legs spread, heads down, snorting. I counted eight... all that had been in the field. "Careful," I said.

We eased out of the truck. Stringtown's head went up. She looked at us over her shoulder. She understood immediately what we were up to. She bunched her muscles, gathered her legs underneath her, did a brief furious dance and jumped. She cleared the bridge by a foot. Whinnying, head and tail high, she galloped up the hill toward the village a mile away. Lonesome looked at me, hesitated, then turned and trotted over the iron bridge after her, his feet clattering on the ironwork. Four of the other horses took courage and followed. They lifted their knees high and half trotted, half leapt over the grid work. The other two watched their braver companions then humbly lowered their heads while Jack and I slipped on their halters. I sent Jack back to the barn, a horse on either side of him.

I jumped in the truck and followed the herd. It was easy enough to keep up even though they were running full out. Two of them skidded and almost fell down going around a curve. I slowed, but they kept going just as fast. A car appeared over the crest of the hill. I hoped the man driving would maneuver across the road, but he drove to the side instead and watched, wild-eyed.

As soon as I made it over the hill, I saw the horses skidding onto Main Street. Stringtown, out in front, tried to put on the brakes before landing on the bank stairs. She lost her balance and fell on her hip. The others stopped, confused now that their leader was down. Two men, wearing sweats and running shoes, ran across the sidewalk and stood with their arms outstretched, blocking the street. Stringtown scrambled back to her feet, snorting and shaking her head. Upset by the fall, she stood still. I climbed out of my truck and called to Lonesome, who waited for me quietly. I slipped a halter over his head, patted the gray muzzle. He sighed. After that it was easy to catch Stringtown. People had come out of their houses dressed in pajamas, wrapped in bathrobes or jeans and no shirt. A few moved towards us, their arms outstretched. The horses let themselves be approached and patted. The adventure was over.

Jack was forking manure out of a stall in quick motions when I walked in the barn. Sweat had soaked his t-shirt, dampened his hair and formed beads on the back of his neck. He stopped when he saw me.

"It's okay," I said. "They've stopped running. We just have to go get them. You go wake up Lydia… no, I'll do that while you hook up the trailer."

Even Rollo decided to come and climbed in the truck ahead of Jack, who wiggled into the back seat. "What on earth," the girl said when I showed her the boards. She sat back in a brief reverie and tapped her lips with a finger. "It's Tony."

When we returned, the crowd was still gathered but it was very hot and the flies made the horses stomp their feet and shake their heads. As soon as we put halters on them, most folks floated away, went indoors out of the heat. I pictured them behind the curtained windows, could imagine the talk. I drove the horses home two by two while Rollo, Lydia, and Jack held the others.

Even Clare up the mountain heard the news. She walked through the living room and into the kitchen. She looked from left to right. "Well, hell, Annie. You moving out?"

"No. I sold off some things to buy hay."

"Right." Clare flicked me a look. "Well, you didn't need that stuff anyway."

"Right."

She pulled out a chair and sat down. "Good. I thought you might be throwing in the towel."

"Now why would I throw in the towel?"

"Oh, I don't know, horses runnin through the village and all."

"Oh, that."

"People comin out of their houses in their underwear."

"Pajamas. You know, Stringtown actually landed on the bank's steps. Fell right on her ass."

"I heard Rollo made an appearance. That's all the people in the feed store was talking about. Six of Annie Walker's horses loose in the village and her black whatever helping to gather them up."

I tipped back in my chair. "Awesome."

"So how did this parade happen?"

"The hand of God, I suppose."

"Now that's righteous. Actually, this has Hozelroad Holler written all over it."

"How so?"

"Crimes against humanity."

"What's that supposed to mean?"

"Maybe crimes against nature is more like it. People in Coleton won't like it either."

"I see." I rose and got two beers out of the refrigerator. I handed one to Clare. "Fuck Coleton," I said.

She drank a long swallow. "Well, at least there ain't any pickaninnies running around."

A week later, three of my boarders had left.

CHAPTER THIRTY-TWO

Ken and Cecil Lowry arrived with their old irrigation system in the back of their truck. They unloaded it next to the woods along Cat Creek, working quickly, tossing the pipe alongside the trees. They said little, and the minute the system was unloaded, they were back in the truck and heading home.

It was a simple apparatus, just a pump connected to a thick black hose with holes in it. I tried to drag the pump along the ground but it just dug itself into the dirt and wouldn't budge. I tugged against the hose, stepping backward and using my leg muscles. It moved a bit before tightening in loops around itself. The harder I pulled, the more it cleaved to the ground. I was staring at it in hopeless fury when Clare rode by on Stringtown. "What in the world?"

"It's the Lowry's old irrigation system."

"It's just a hose."

"With a pump."

"Well, it should work," said Clare after a while. "But you'll never get it to the creek that way." Stringtown stamped her back feet and snorted. "I'll put her away and help you. And you get Lonesome."

Tucked in a back corner of the tack room, there was an old buggy harness that someone had left years ago. I didn't have a clue what pieces went where, but Clare figured it out. The gelding cocked his ears as we buckled the strange leather across his chest and along his back, turned his head and gave me a reproachful look. Clare stood at his shoulder, took hold of a piece of the bridle, and walked a few steps. Lonesome stretched his neck as far as he could without moving his feet. Clare gave a gentle tug to the reins without looking back, and the gelding took one step then another, inching the irrigation system through the trees.

The water still moved though it was so shallow in places you could see through to the amber pebbles on the bottom. Where the creek curved against a bank or was caught in sudden deep holes, algae had started to grow, spreading mossy green filaments through the water. It took us all day and into the next to lay that hose. The morning cool lasted an hour before the sun turned scarlet. At noon, we flopped down on the brittle grass.

"You hungry?" I asked.

Clare shook her head. She had lost weight lately and looked tired. We sat next to the rubber hose, picking at the dried stubble. The sun was strong overhead and the cicada's hum filled the air. My lips were greasy and bitter from fly repellent. I could feel the grit along my cheek and forehead.

"Maybe Ken can help us get it going," I said.

"We can do it." Clare turned her head toward the barn where Stringtown kicked at the sides of her stall.

"Did you ever think of selling her? Buy other horses, make a start."

Clare shrugged. "I've got enough to buy a horse or two. Besides, I like her."

I knew what she would do. She would use the few hundred dollars she kept in her jean pocket to buy a grade horse, or a horse someone couldn't handle. She would work with it using the methods Pap had taught her and sell it for a few hundred more. Her profit would keep her fed for a month if she were careful.

Closing my eyes at the thought, I leaned back on my elbows then lay flat out, using my arm to cover my eyes. I must have dozed, for I don't remember anything until Clare nudged me with her foot. I sat up, feeling sick to my stomach. Clare inclined her head toward the driveway. Three figures stood in front of a low black car, moving their arms like windshield wipers at us.

I realized as I recognized Stewart standing in the wavering sunlight that every time I rose in the mornings to the heat, every time I lay down at night, fixed my meals, wanted to choke Lydia or wondered about Rollo, talked or laughed with Clare, relied on her for help, for company, every time I felt the sweat run down the back of my legs or I breathed in and out, I had been waiting for this moment. The knowledge filled me with despair. It took my breath away, flattened me, filled me with desire and left me empty.

I half sat, half lay where I was, sifting dirt through my fingers.

"Oh, go to them," Clare said. "Maybe Stewart can get this pipe working for you." She rose stiffly, gathered Lonesome's reins, and led him back to the barn.

Darlene's face registered my appearance before she could catch herself. I knew what she saw. Stewart never flinched. He put his arm around me; leaned to kiss my bitter lips.

"Annie," he said, "you look done in." He frowned at the strange taste, wiped his mouth with the back of his hand. The Drakes, dressed in tennis whites, did not move to touch me.

My emotions tumbled, pleasure fighting hard now that Stewart stood beside me. I took the three of them to the house, through the back to the kitchen. They looked surprised but didn't mention the bare room. I opened the freezer. There was a can of orange juice and a can of lemonade. I made the lemonade and filled four glasses. At least there was ice. In the middle of pizza boxes, peanut butter jars, milk cartons, and dirty dishes, they watched me. They did not sit. I handed everyone a glass and led the way to the back room. It was the coolest and darkest room in the house where I sometimes slept in the heavy shade of the elm growing outside the window. I dragged in the two chairs from the kitchen. The Drakes sat straight-backed and uneasy. Darlene glanced around for a place to put her glass, reached toward a windowsill then noticed a handful of dead flies lying in its corner. She rested her glass on her knee. Soon John clapped Stewart on the shoulder, shook his hand while Darlene took the glasses to the sink, which was already piled high with dirty dishes.

Stewart stood next to me on the front porch as we waved the Drakes on their way. I let the screen door bang as we went inside. I plopped on the couch. The springs creaked at my sudden weight. Now that we were alone, I steadied myself for my husband who was not my husband.

"Annie, the house seems a little bare."

"Yeah, well, I had to sell a few things to buy hay. It's been so dry."

Stewart sprawled on one of the chairs. "It seems like a hundred years ago that we bought those things, doesn't it?"

"No."

"Selling off the family heirlooms. I guess business is a little slow."

"It's just that it's been so dry. There's no pasture."

"The racial issue has nothing to do with it, I suppose."

"No. Lydia has more lessons than she can handle. There was an incident, though, that hasn't helped. The horses got out and ran into the village."

Stewart raised an eyebrow. "Into the village? Yes, I can see that might not inspire confidence. And how did they get out? Someone, Lydia maybe, leave the gate open?"

"Some boards were down. They weren't kicked down. They were piled neatly beside the fence." I watched him carefully.

Stewart shook his head. "And you think it has nothing to do with the racial issue."

"No, I don't. I think it is about someone else entirely. One of Clare's exes. Tony. There was a big fuss. His house burned down. Some people think Clare set it on fire. And she took his horse—I mean her horse—she's keeping her here until she can get her place ready."

"Are you kidding me? Houses burning down; horses running through town, getting stolen. I mean, Annie, you've got more going on than we do in LA."

"Stringtown's not stolen. She belongs to Clare. It's just Tony thinks she still belongs to him."

"And she's here? The horse is here?"

"Yeah."

"Once again, you surprise me, Annie."

I stared at him. We watched each other before Stewart slapped his thighs. "You okay for money?"

"Sure."

He rose and sat next to me. "God, Annie, it's hotter than hell here. Hotter than LA even. I'm filthy from my trip. What I really need is a shower."

"You know we don't have a shower."

"What about the horse's shower?"

The wash house consisted of a roofless board box and a hose that ran from the spigot and hot water heater in the barn and was attached to the top of one side. Stewart stripped outside, tossed his clothes onto the grass, and stepped into the wash house. He started by wetting his body thoroughly, wiping the water across his face and chest, ruffling it through his hair. When he was satisfied, he stepped from under the stream and began to cover himself with soapsuds.

"There is room enough for two," he said casually.

I could almost taste the water. I watched it run over him, form rivulets along his legs. I stepped into a corner, peeled off my damp, stained clothing. He paid no attention, was scrubbing himself vigorously with a sponge. I stood under the water; let it dampen my sticky hair; roll the grease off my face, soothe my shoulders and the small of my back. Sudsy from head to foot, Stewart moved into the spray, bumping against me. Eyes closed, he tipped his head back to let the water wash away the soap. Once his face was clean, he turned and took hold of my shoulders and faced me away from him. He put fingers alongside my jaw, told me to close my eyes, and positioned my head so that the water could soak through the dust and sweat in my hair. He massaged the shampoo into my scalp, rinsed and shampooed again until the hair slid through his fingers. He turned me to him, took the sponge, held up my chin with his thumb and squeezed water along my neck, around my ears, rubbed the grime till it broke down, dissolved, washed away with the running water. The pores of my skin opened. My flesh turned pink where the blood moved along its surface. Stewart reached past me, pulled the wash house door closed.

The spray fell on us like fine rain.

That night Stewart filled our glasses with champagne, touched his to mine, and said, "Here's to the future." He had changed into crisp linens, and I wore my sleeveless black dress. We sat in the corner of a restaurant. We had chosen one far from town so we could be alone.

I tasted the champagne, which was light, very dry without being bitter. I tilted my head, took several more swallows. Stewart refilled my glass.

"Come west with me, Annie," he said. "You look so tired."

The waiter brought endive salads followed by veal Oscar. We had chocolate raspberry torte and more champagne for dessert and red wine with our coffee.

Stewart stirred the cream in his cup, carefully placed his spoon in its saucer.

"So what do you say? Will you come to California? This may be your last chance. The company's expanding, thinking of opening an Alaskan division. I've asked for the assignment."

"Alaska?"

"You know I've always wanted to go."

"But Alaska."

"It's the last frontier. It's not at all like LA. You might even like it."

"I don't know anyone in Alaska."

"Just come for a visit. You won't need to know anyone. I'll be there."

"I can't go to Alaska. There is too much to do here."

Stewart leaned back, flapped the napkin in his lap, smiled his easy smile. "There is a fortune to be made in Alaska. You'd love it once you've seen it. I know you would. Like I said, it's the last frontier."

"I don't know what I'd do about the farm."

"Let Lydia handle it. That's why you have her, isn't it? To cover for you from time to time."

"Not exactly."

"It's no life being married to that farm. You should see some of the world, at least. You'll turn into an old woman living out here all by yourself."

"Stop."

He ran the back of his hand across his mouth, said without looking up, "I could sell the place, you know."

Of course I knew. The knowledge was always there, hanging on the edges of my mind. I wondered shamefully if my need for Stewart was a part of my need for the farm. I drank from my coffee, not taking my eyes off him.

He looked up and settled his arm along the back of a chair. "I still like the old place, though. Can see myself using it as a vacation spot during those horrible winters in Alaska. Here or LA Can you imagine my parents if I sold it? Might have to give them the money. And after all the work we did."

"You're never coming back, are you?"

"Not for good, no."

"We did all right together here."

"It was fun for a while. But you have to know when to move on, that's all."

Stewart left the next morning in my truck. He didn't return until afternoon and when he did, two other trucks and several men followed him. Steel piping poked from the beds, caught the sun's glare, winked and rattled as the vehicles bounced up the driveway.

"Where do you want us to start?" He was dressed in white, and his skin was the color of honey.

"State of the art," he said.

The crew climbed down and waited in the driveway. They looked the house up and down as though it were a woman, then went back to watching Stewart. Except for the looking up and down of the house, their faces revealed nothing.

"Speak up, Annie. These men don't have all day. Where do you want this stuff?"

"What is it?"

"Irrigation equipment. State of the art."

"I already have irrigation equipment."

"That antique." His mouth turned up in a bow. "You'd spend days just moving it from one place to another."

"Stewart, this is not a good idea."

"Why not?"

"That stuff cost a fortune."

"It's only money, Annie."

I didn't say anything.

"These men don't have all day."

I thought about the situation. I thought about last night and the ease with which he ordered food and wine, dropped two hundred dollars on the table. I thought of Alaska and the fortune to be made. I thought of California and tall girls with long, white-blonde hair falling combed and sleek beyond their waists. I thought of Jack and me throwing hay to the horses, day in, day out, without a hint of rain. I thought about the farm making an old woman of me.

"How much of that stuff have you got?" I asked.

"Miles," said Stewart.

"Start anywhere you like."

I watched out the window when the first fan of water spurted from the steel. It made a brief rainbow in the red evening light and settled into a steady pulse. I went outside and stood on the porch. Stewart sat at my feet. He smiled into the middle distance; let the apparatus speak for itself. He leaned back on an elbow.

A door slammed. Lydia shot around the corner, small and alert as a squirrel. Jack followed behind her, his face closed and sullen.

Lydia hopped onto the step just below Stewart and waved her hand toward the flying water. "What's this?"

She had paid little attention to Clare and me struggling with the Lowry's equipment, had stopped once during the afternoon as we were laying hose only long enough to shake her head and ask how we planned to get the water from Cat Creek to here. Now her eyes sparkled.

"I thought we'd better do something," said Stewart, "or soon the pastures would blow away." He lifted his eyes to look at Lydia, took in the shape of her along the way. If he leaned forward, he could have placed his head between her hips.

"You mean it's here to stay? It's ours?"

I watched the water make a rainbow as it arced toward the ground. It amazed me to hear the steady swish, swish. I could imagine the new pump, substantial, its moving parts greased and sliding against each other, the heart of the new system. You could see its beat through the water.

"Come inside," I said. "I'll fix us some dinner."

"No, don't cook," said Stewart. He reached into his pocket, tossed Jack the keys to the truck. "Go ahead, take it and pick up a pizza for us."

Jack hesitated, looked at the keys in the palm of his hand. "I only got a learner's permit," he said. His voice was low, sullen, but his fingers played with the keys. "Don't get caught," said Stewart. He handed the boy money. "And get plenty."

CHAPTER THIRTY-THREE

I chose, this time, to say goodbye to Stewart at Dulles International. It had been five months since I'd been to an airport and felt the world's possibilities. It took three hours to get back to the farm. Not even the mountains, dark blue in the distance, could comfort me.

Clare's truck was parked in front of the farmhouse, but she was not inside. I looked in the barn. The horses dozed in their stalls. I walked to the ring where Lydia gave a lesson from under a wide-brimmed straw hat.

"I think I saw her walk down to the creek," she said. Lydia's nose was smeared with zinc oxide.

The path to the creek had turned into a fine dust that rose like smoke around my feet, muffling any noise. When I reached the clearing along the bank, I saw Clare lying naked face down. The sun shone through the trees, making dappled shade on the ground and along her back. Clare's head lay resting on the crook of her arm. A blond man lay next to her. I turned to go but Clare lifted her head, squinted at me.

"We couldn't resist a swim," she said, reaching for her clothes with one hand. "We didn't figure you'd mind."

The blond rolled over, looked at me, and sat up, pulling a corner of the sheet across his lap in one movement. He kept his face turned away.

"Hi, Todd," I said. He and I had gone to school together. He didn't answer.

"We're going to the bluegrass festival at the Gap," said Clare. "Want to come?" She stood, pulled on jeans and a t-shirt. Tony was right. Not a panty in sight.

"No, I don't think so."

"Stewart get off okay?"

"Yeah."

"Sure you don't want to come with us?"

I shook my head.

When we got back to the house, Clare followed me into the kitchen. Todd had refused to come. He stayed seated with the sheet covering his hips, even his shoulders blushing pink.

"I put some beers in your fridge." Clare took two out, offered me one. I shook my head. She twisted off the cap and drank from the bottle in several long, deep swallows. She burped softly. "What are you doing tonight, Annie?"

"Nothing."

"You ought to come with us."

"No. Thanks."

After Clare had gone, I went to the antique gun cabinet and brought out the bottle of scotch. I filled a glass with ice and poured the liquor to the top. I fixed a peanut butter sandwich for supper and took it and my drink to the porch. The liquor had a familiar, welcome taste. I ate and watched Lydia and Jack turning horses out for the night. Lydia was leading Stringtown, while Jack led one of the boarders. Odd. I thought the girl was afraid of the big horse. The mare jigged and tugged at the end of her lead shank. *They should know that you always walk Lonesome and Stringtown out together.* Lydia turned to face the mare. A mistake. Stringtown reared, nearly lifting the girl off the ground then hunkered down on her haunches and scrambled backward, dragging Lydia with her. I ran down the stairs two at a time and across the lawn and nearly ran into Stringtown as she lunged toward Lonesome, throwing Lydia into the barn siding as she did so. To give the girl credit, she hung on. The mare touched her nose to the gelding's and huffed softly.

Lydia was back on her feet in a hurry. She still had hold of the mare's lead shank. "This is insane. That horse is too valuable to be so spoiled," she snapped. "She's being wasted here. Just someone's play thing." She brushed at the scratches on her arms and legs. "And a dangerous one."

"Are you okay?" I reached to take Stringtown's lead shank, but Lydia snatched it away. "I've got her." Jack took Lonesome from his stall, and he and the girl led them out. I helped with the rest of the horses before returning to the house and pouring another scotch.

When I finished my drink, I knocked on Lydia's door. I knocked softly, ready to leave if she didn't answer but the door opened almost immediately. She looked amazed to see me.

"You busy?" I asked.

"Ahhh, no."

"How are your scratches? Did you put something on them?" I looked around. "Where's Jack?"

"I sent him home. I wasn't in the mood for him tonight."

"I've got some ointment, if you need it." I looked past her and noticed an open suitcase filled with clothes on the couch.

"I was going to tell you," Lydia said. "I'm leaving for a few days to look for a horse."

I shook my head. "*Damn it, Lydia.* We agreed you were going to tell me when you were leaving."

"This just came up sudden like. I was going to tell you."

"When?"

"Dock my wages if you want."

God she was cheeky. "I should take all of your lesson money for a week."

The girl rolled her eyes. "Whatever."

"When will you be back?"

"Tuesday, Wednesday at the latest."

"That's five days."

Lydia was silent, her hand stubbornly on the door handle.

"Have you told your students?"

She looked at me, exasperated. "Well, of course."

I went home and settled on the couch with the lights off and listened to the pulse of my new irrigation system, a faint swish so steady that it soon got inside me, beat along with my heart until I stopped hearing it. Now I forced myself to pay attention to its rhythm. Perhaps the sound would lull me to sleep. I counted the beats, lost interest and heard instead the house creaking, settling for the night. To hell with Stewart and his state-of-the-art equipment. To hell with him flying off to Alaska. You had to be crazy to go from LA to Alaska. To hell with him. And to hell with Lydia leaving for another five days. And to hell with Clare and her alley cat ways.

I fell asleep shortly before dawn, woke just in time to see Lydia's low white sports car going down the road.

I took care of the bare necessities then drove up the mountain to Clare's. I left the truck windows open so it wouldn't turn into an oven even though it was cooler up here. Several yards from the cabin, I noticed wire strung among the trees forming a fence. I would not be sorry to see Stringtown go.

"Clare," I hollered through the screen door.

A pot clanged and she appeared, wiping her hands on the back of her jeans. She pushed open the screen door, motioned me in. She had furnished her place with a couch, table, two straight chairs, and a stove in one room, a four poster in the other. She noticed me looking at the bed. It was an antique rope bed made of cherry in simple elegant lines.

"Grandma's," she said. "Pap's been saving it for me. Come on in, I was just fixing something to eat."

I watched while Clare put salt and pepper on two venison steaks then opened the wood stove. A red glow filled the inside. Clare closed the door on it and poured milk into a pot of potatoes sitting on the burner. She added butter and mashed everything with a metal masher, punching it down into the pan. When she was finished, she slid the pan with the steaks into the oven. Next, she scooped big mounds of potatoes onto plates and added fresh sliced tomatoes. Even through the thick iron walls you could hear the steaks snap and hiss. Clare opened the door, snatched the steaks out with a long fork, and dropped them next to the potatoes. She didn't make conversation, and I let her presence ease over me. The steaks were tender and juicy. We pushed the back of our spoons into the mounds of potatoes, forming a pool, and filled it with butter. The silence continued as we ate. When we were done, I took my dish to the metal bucket she used as a sink.

I sat across from her. "Clare?" I began.

"Go on."

"I might go to LA for a bit."

Clare watched me steadily. "You could move back there, you know."

"No way. Anyway, I told you, he's moving to Alaska."

"You might like Alaska."

"Are you kidding me? Why are you even saying that? I live here now."

Clare shrugged. "Yeah, I guess."

"What do you mean you guess? Haven't I made that completely obvious? I sold my furniture to buy hay, for God's sake."

Clare hesitated then gave me a brief nod. "Right. Of course. Anyway, lots of people have long-distance relationships. Even marriages. Tell you the truth, I think it might be nice. Me? I'd love to see Alaska."

I sat up from the back of my chair. "I'll be gone a week. At the most two. I just need a break, that's all. Can you watch the farm? I'll pay you."

"No need to pay me."

"I'll be back."

"Course you will."

I was at the airport by noon. I caught sight of myself in one of the ornamental mirrors on the way to the concourse—simple dress, hair contained by a bow at the nape of my neck, tanned face and arms. You couldn't tell my skin had been darkened by days laboring in the sun. I looked like many others waiting to board. But handing in my ticket, I noticed the tendons standing out like ropes along my wrist and arms and the knobby rough knuckles.

It was dusk when I hailed a cab and gave the driver the address. Lights came on as we drove… all kinds of lights, everything you could imagine displayed against the night sky. After the bareness of the farm it seemed a child's toy, a huge amusement park or carnival. People hustled along as though on holiday, busy to see it all, do it all, except their faces were blank. It had always been hard for me to imagine that people worked, actually held jobs, while all this was going on around them.

Stewart's apartment was in a tall steel and glass building. My heart pounded so hard I was afraid I wouldn't be able to give the doorman my name. He opened the door, stepped back, and motioned me in. "Mrs. Walker," he said softly.

I remembered the smell of the lobby immediately. I went to the wall with the apartment numbers. Twenty sixty-two—Stewart Walker. Big as life. It hadn't changed.

I pressed the bell. There was no response. I pressed again. Still nothing. I looked around for a place to sit and wait for Stewart's return. I heard his voice over the intercom. "Yes?"

"Hi, Stewart. It's me."

Silence. Long enough that I thought he didn't recognize my voice. "It's me, Annie."

Stewart stepped out of the elevator ten minutes later. He looked less stunning than at the farm. As he walked toward me, I wondered how he would compare in Alaska. He did not kiss me but pulled me to him in a gentle hug. He took my elbow, guided me to a set of overstuffed chairs with one hand, took my suitcase in the other. He sat opposite me.

I didn't ask why we weren't going up to the apartment.

"Annie," he said, "I need to tell you something."

I waited while things shifted, slid, like a kaleidoscope changed shape. I held still.

"Lydia's here. I asked you to come. You didn't so I asked Lydia instead."

"Well, sure."

"I'll ask her to leave if you want me to."

"You can't do that."

"Yes, I can. Just give me some time."

"Does she know I'm here?"

"Well, yes, Annie, she could hear your voice."

"I'll go."

"No. I don't want that. Just stay here for a few minutes and I'll take care of it."

An hour later, Stewart came back downstairs.

"I'm leaving," I said.

"But it's all set. We've got her on a flight out tonight. That's what took so long. She's dressing now. Come up and have a drink while we wait."

"Stewart."

"Seriously, everything is fine."

The apartment looked the same as when I'd left, except Lydia sat on the edge of the king-sized bed buckling her sandals. The bed was unmade.

"Did you find your horse?"

"I couldn't very well tell you I was coming out here to see Stewart, could I?" she said.

Stewart cleared his throat. "Scotch okay? Or would you like champagne? I think there is another bottle in the fridge."

"Nothing... thank you."

"Now don't sulk, Annie. Here, let me get you a scotch." Stewart walked to the kitchen and opened a cupboard. He took down three heavy crystal oldfashioned glasses. They had been a wedding present. Everything looked the same as when I'd left: blue canisters on the counter, the green bowl with the bananas. Crumbs on the toaster. It was a tiny room, hardly more than a closet. A small island was all that separated it from the living room. Stewart reached under the sink and brought out the scotch. He emptied a tray of ice cubes into the glasses and filled them half full.

I looked straight into Stewart's face when he handed me the drink. "I'm not staying," I said. He kissed me on the mouth. "We'll leave for the airport soon. Come with us."

"No."

"I don't want to leave you here by yourself. Come with us."

"I should be the one who is leaving. I'll take her flight."

"Don't be silly. I don't want you to leave."

"Let her take a cab."

Lydia came out of the bedroom and into the kitchen. She hopped up onto the island. Stewart handed her a scotch.

She sipped it, wrinkled her nose, and sipped again, slurping the scotch through the ice cubes. "I think I'm acquiring a taste for this stuff."

"Here's to us," said Stewart. I couldn't tell whom he meant by us. Lydia took another swallow of her drink, looking at me over the glass. "I'll take a cab if you want me to. This is really no big deal. I felt like getting out of those damn mountains for a while, that's all. No need to make such a big thing out of it."

"Does Rollo know you're here?"

"Of course not. But it's still no big deal… he comes and goes… you know."

"Does Jack know?"

Lydia started. "Well… no."

"He'd die if he did."

She burst out laughing. "Wouldn't he though." She swirled the liquid in her glass. Or rather my glass… or it had been. So little seemed to have changed since I had left.

Stewart opened the refrigerator and looked in. It was empty except for a container of milk and a bottle of champagne lying on its side. "Shall we stick with scotch or switch to champagne?"

"This is it for me," I said. "I'm curious Lydia—what's the destination on your new ticket?"

She looked confused.

"I suppose you do have to go back to the farm to pick up the rest of your things."

Stewart straightened from where he'd been leaning against the counter. "Don't be hasty, Annie. Drink your drink. This is really no big deal."

"I'm supposed to continue on just like before? Where will you stay when you come to visit, Stewart? Or will you split the time equally… diplomat that you are?"

"Drink your drink, Annie."

"Getting me drunk won't make a difference."

"When I visit, it's to see you."

Lydia jumped down from the counter and went to sit on the couch in front of the wall-to-wall picture window. Behind her, the lights of LA shone as far as the eye could see, dancing and sparkling like beads on a jeweled dress. How many times had I stared at this view and hated it? Lydia crossed her legs and took a swallow from her drink. "Are you firing me, Annie? Because I would think you'd want me to stay, at least until the season is over. I've got over twenty students, after all."

I didn't say anything.

"That's better." Stewart poured another drink and came into the living room. "Annie gets a little old-fashioned sometimes, but she generally recovers." He leaned against the couch, standing behind Lydia. Even using zinc oxide and a hat, the pale skin on her nose had turned red and peeled.

She tilted her head up to Stewart. "Well, she shouldn't be upset. I just wanted to see LA before you took off for parts unknown in Alaska. You'll never catch me in Alaska."

"Oh you'd love it," said Stewart. "It's the last frontier."

I threw my glass. It just missed Stewart's head. Months of lifting feed sacks and hay bales went into the throw. It shattered the window, turned it into a mosaic of cloudy chunks that hung suspended. Lydia froze. The golden liquor had splattered all over her, leaving sparkling droplets of scotch on her face and a trail from me to the ruined window. Unlike Clare, I had meant to hit my target. The sea went out of Stewart's eyes, and though I had just arrived in LA, I didn't hang around to find out what would happen next. I walked out of that apartment, took the elevator to the lobby, walked past the doorman out into the night, and hailed a cab.

CHAPTER THIRTY-FOUR

When I returned, I dumped my bag in the hall, climbed the stairs, and threw myself on the bed. Saturday and Sunday were a blur of risings and fallings onto this bed. I must be sick, I thought, as I rolled into the sheets, pulled the pillow to my face, and slipped gratefully back into unconsciousness.

Jack kept the barn going. He pestered me ceaselessly about Lydia when I did appear. I told him I was ill, that he'd have to do it all for a day or two, that Lydia was horse shopping for the next few days. I felt like I was crawling through water with a rock in my stomach. I could barely make it up the stairs to flop back into the bed. Day faded into night, and I thought I couldn't possibly sleep anymore. But I did.

By Monday evening, the somnolence deserted me. I couldn't keep my eyes closed. Instead, I found myself staring at the cracks in the ceiling, the patterns in the wallpaper. The wallpaper that Stewart and I had hung. To avoid that kind of thinking, I swung out of bed and went straight to the barn.

"How come Lydia didn't take her trailer with her?" Jack asked the minute I walked through the door.

"If she finds a horse she likes, she'll go back for it."

And where was she looking this time? New Jersey. She was looking in New Jersey. I pulled the place out of the air. Did Rollo go with her? No. He did not. This apparently contented Jack for a while. The questions ceased and I helped him give the horses grain. We emptied and scrubbed and filled water buckets for the morning. We threw hay into the field. We led the horses out two by two. My limbs felt like Jell-O. I'd eaten only toast since my return. I stumbled through the next two days, no longer bedridden, but just. I hated how much I hurt.

Wednesday night as I sat on the porch, the white Corvette slid up the driveway and stopped in front of the apartment. Lydia stepped out and without looking in my direction went straight inside.

I waited. Tonight was Wednesday. She'd been in LA for five days. They had been together for five days. Five nights. I rose from the rocker, walked across the lawn, across the driveway, and knocked on her door. She greeted me with a wary face.

"I'll give you two days to pack your stuff and leave."

"You can't do that."

"Of course I can."

"What about two weeks' notice? Not to mention I live here. You can't just throw someone out of their home. You have to give them sixty days. At least. You have to go to the courthouse and file papers."

I wondered how many times this had happened to her before. I considered bluffing. I knew you had to give people time to find another place to live; I just didn't know how much time.

"It's thirty days."

"It's sixty. And I have to find a new job. It's the middle of the season. It won't be easy. And I have a horse to worry about." Lydia shut the door in my face.

I stared at it a moment. It was a pretty little door. Real wood. I wanted to kick it open and grab its occupant by her shiny blonde hair and bang her head against it. Instead I went to the barn.

Lonesome looked mildly startled when I yanked him in from the pasture and snapped him into cross ties. I grabbed the brushes and brushed him three times, working fast and with a lot of motion. Sweat ran into my eyes, making them sting so badly I had to wash them out with water. When I could see again, I kissed my horse on the neck, sprayed him with fly repellent, and walked him to the pasture gate where Stringtown paced and pawed the ground.

CHAPTER THIRTY-FIVE

Coming back from the courthouse the next afternoon, I passed the VFW, a square building without windows. Clare's truck was parked out front. She was getting an early start on Friday night. I pulled in the driveway. A beer or two wouldn't hurt me either.

The room was airless, smoke filled, but even through the haze I made out Clare. She sat in the back, bone pale. Pap was with her. A plate of chicken sat on the table between them. Clare motioned me to sit down.

"Make her eat something," said Pap. "She hasn't eaten in days. I seen this girl put away three steaks at a sitting and now she sits picking at a biscuit."

Clare stood and gathered her keys. "Annie, come with me to the Red Run. There's a new band startin tonight."

"Oh, don't run off, Clare," said Pap. "You can't blame an old man for worrying."

The angles in Clare's face shifted, her wide mouth softened at the corners. She rested her hand on his shoulder.

"How about coming with us?"

"You girls don't need an old man hanging around."

"What's this old stuff? Annie and I will drive up the mountain so's I can change and come back and pick you up."

Out in the parking lot Clare jingled her keys. "How was California?"

"Lydia was there."

Clare stood still, absorbing the information. "Your own employee," she said after a while. "That Stewart. He sure knows how to push the envelope."

"He asked me to come, but I said no. So he asked Lydia."

"Of course he did." She tossed the keys, caught them, then noticing the look on my face said, "You look so sad, Annie. Sad and sick. Come on, let's go dancing; pick up a couple of guys. Forget about Stewart. Forget about Lydia."

It was the first time I'd known Clare to so badly miss her mark. "I wish I could be like you," I said.

"No. Annie. You don't." She swung open the truck door, climbed in and sat looking out the front window. "I guess that's the end of Lydia," she said finally.

"Ahhh... no. I have to give her thirty days."

"Are you serious? Why?"

"I just came from the courthouse. I filed the papers. The clerk said I had no choice. She has thirty days to find another place to live. And, if she hasn't, she can go to court and who knows how long it will take."

Clare thought for a minute. "How you going to keep from killing her 'till then?"

"Christ, I don't know... maybe I will."

"Let me know if you need any help."

We took Clare's truck. She had no air conditioning and the dust flew in the windows. The valley had turned brindle except for my fields. The pumped-in water had turned them green, not the emerald green of spring but a faded green that stood out from the brown around it. I noticed as we passed that the Lowry's irrigation system lay piled in a shed. I only briefly wondered why.

It was all but dark when we hit the woods. We passed Pap's, drove beyond where the road left off, bumping over the path Clare had made on her trips to the cabin. She had swerved around the bigger trees, simply ran over the smaller ones. We twisted and turned, doubled back on ourselves. That is how we approached unnoticed. Trees and the lay of the land blocked our headlights. Clare shut them off, put her finger to her lips to keep me silent, then pointed out the window. Even in the dark I could make out the silhouette of a truck parked near Clare's cabin. As my eyes adjusted, I saw three men walking backwards around the little building, shaking something from a can. They tossed what was left on the sides of the building and threw the cans in the pickup bed. Two of the men climbed in the truck while the third lit a match.

"Christ, Clare," I said, opening my door. She reached across me, pulled the door shut and as she did the man bent over and touched the match to the ground. The flame sparked, lit the grass, made its purposeful way toward the two-room structure. It hesitated for a moment when it touched the bottom of the wall, but only a moment, then climbed the boards, spread in brilliant tendrils, crimson ivy, clinging, reaching with hungry fingers around the old wood.

The third man jumped in the truck, started the engine with more force than necessary, racing the motor above the crackling sounds of burning wood. As he spun around, I fully expected Clare to floor it, charge toward him, smash into the vehicle—roll right over top of them. Instead she backed up and parked sedately beneath a tree while the other truck pitched past.

"We should notify the police," I said.

"What for?"

Clare leaned forward, tilted her head, and looked skyward. "It's been so dry," she said. "We should fetch the fire department."

We had only gone a few yards when we heard the sirens. The glow from the little fire had shone into the valley, a beacon of alarm.

Clare deftly turned her truck around, pulled close to the burning building. The heat hit us in waves and the smell up close was sharp, bitter. We watched the fire truck's headlights wink in and out of the trees, twisting up the mountain. They paused, clustered, formed a wary, watching half-circle where the road stopped.

"Shit," said Clare in disgust. She jerked the truck forward and bounced down the mountain to the stalled firefighters. A man sweating in a black rubber suit approached. Clare leaned out the window and motioned him to follow her.

"I don't know, Clare. We might get stuck."

"No you won't. Just follow me."

"Follow," he called to the others.

"There's no road," cried someone.

Another called, "We'll never make it."

Clare pretended not to hear and drove back toward her burning cabin. She was careful not to get out of sight of the men.

Once at the scene they swarmed over their trucks like black bugs. One of them, the leader I assumed, came up to Clare. He rubbed his chin, gazed at her, back at the fire and shook his head. "Nope, no way," he said. "Sorry, Clare, no way we can save it."

"I know that. I just don't want to see the mountain catch fire."

"Right. Right." He hitched his black rubber pants.

Clare and I watched in silence while they spent several minutes running back and forth unraveling the heavy hoses. A motor started with a solid hum and the hoses jerked, stiffened, jumped skyward. Five streams of water shot at the cabin. It took three men to hold each hose.

"The trees, the trees," shouted the leader, and the firefighters pointed the hoses higher, wetting us with their spray. It was a relief after the smoky heat and, heads back, we watched by the firelight. The tree leaves bowed and danced under the weight of the water. Suddenly there was a hideous choking sound and two of the streams died out. Before we could react, the other three hoses gurgled and went limp.

The leader trotted over to the nearest truck.

"They run out of water," said Clare.

"But that's ridiculous."

"Even so, they have."

In a few seconds the leader was at our side.

"Bad news," he said. "We're out of water. It's the damn drought," he went on, yanking at his pants. "The men didn't think they should waste the water filling the tanks. Cat Creek runs by here, don't it?"

Clare pointed over a rise to the left. The leader sighed. "We got all them trees in the way. Never be able to get near the creek."

"You have axes?"

"Take forever."

Clare stared at him, refused to let her eyes wander. By now most of the men were standing around us. Under their yellow hats, their faces, lit by the fire, were shiny with sweat.

"Start with that one," the leader cried, flinging his arm at the nearest oak.

A broad man stepped up to it and began swinging on the near side. He found a steady rhythm and seemed to gather strength as he worked. He never raised his gaze from the base of the tree. The oak began to moan, to creak. It swayed.

"Jesus, watch out," someone shouted. The solidly built man jerked his head up, jumped back. The oak teetered, hung in the air, then tipped gracefully and smashed onto the hood of the nearest fire truck.

"Holy shit," someone shouted.

Clare laughed.

A tall man approached the edge of the fire's light. He was not in a firefighter's uniform. By now the smoke had burned my eyes so that they were teary and his figure was wavy, indistinct. He tapped a firefighter on the shoulder, held out his hand for the axe. I sensed Clare stir next to me and when I looked, her face showed a mixture of concern, irritation, and relief. Sweat mixed with the tears and I wiped my eyes with my shirttail. My vision cleared enough to recognize Pap as he approached the next tree back. Among the firefighters with their bulky rubber suits he looked insubstantial, wispy, almost frail. I half expected Clare to call out for him, to stop him. Pap's shoulders lifted and he hit the tree with an unimpressive thump. He swung again with no more power than the first time, but he found his rhythm and kept going.

"Here, Jim," someone called, "you don't need to be doing that."

"Is that Jim Raffienne?" came another voice.

Pap changed position. Started a new notch.

I looked at Clare but she had on her inscrutable face. The leader stepped from one foot to the other. "Jim," he said feebly, then gave it up. Eventually Pap stopped, reached forward and pressed lightly on the trunk. The tree resisted, didn't move at first, then it wobbled, arced slowly, faster and faster 'till it smacked the ground safely away from the men and the trucks.

"Timber," said Clare.

Pap joined us; he put an arm along Clare's back while the firefighters began working on the other trees.

Clare looked straight ahead. "I'm just glad Stringtown wasn't here."

"She'd have jumped the fence and run down the mountain to Lonesome as soon as the fire started," I said.

"That's not what I mean. I don't think they would have even started the fire if she were here."

Possibilities formed in my mind. A bucket of grain would have made her easy to catch. A sharp knife along the jugular. At least a merciful death. Or not so merciful, a quick slice through a tendon. Over in seconds but Stringtown crippled for life.

"Your Gram's bed?" Pap dropped his arm from Clare but leaned close enough to touch shoulders.

"Inside."

"Ah, Granddaughter, all this for a horse." He shook his head. The creases around his mouth and eyes were deeper than I remembered. He wiped his eyes with a red handkerchief. Was it the smoke? "It's really time you settled down."

Clare shifted her weight, her arms folded across her chest. She looked at the ground. Pap watched the men drag a hose from one of the trucks. "There's hardly any water in the creek," he said. "They'll run out practically before they start."

The roof of the little cabin was all but gone by now and while we watched, it collapsed, making a shower of tiny sparks. "If the trees haven't caught by now," said Pap, "I don't think they will. Granddaughter, come home with me... we can return in the morning."

Clare didn't argue, didn't mock him or use smart words; she didn't say as I'd thought she might that she wouldn't leave until the last embers died. The two of them turned away, tall and sapling thin.

CHAPTER THIRTY-SIX

The day after Clare's cabin burned to the ground, the heat settled over us like a bell jar. It held us down, bent our heads and kept a sickly flush in our cheeks while our lips turned white and dry. Only the cicadas thrived. Sometimes you had to shout above their noise.

I never went to the ring. That much I could not do. I did the morning feed. It was so hot the horses were in a frenzy to get out of the sun. They crowded around the gate, bit and kicked one another, fighting to be the first one in. Even Lonesome. The face flies bit with fury at their eyes. At me. The horses shook their heads so violently I could hardly get on their halters. Once I did, they dragged me into the barn. Sometimes they all shoved so at the gate they burst past me and, in a frantic herd, galloped into their stalls.

Actually, I welcomed the heat. It gave me a reason for lying on my bed for hours, face down, arms widespread. It pressed against my back; a weight I hoped would suffocate me. On good days I lay on the couch staring at the ceiling. Outside, not even the weeds grew anymore. Their leaves curled and crisped against the stems. The steady swish-swish of Stewart's state-of-the-art system kept my pastures a bizarre green in contrast to the rest of the valley.

I returned to the barn in the evening even though Lydia was there. We developed a ritual. I walked in and said, "Have you found a new position yet?" and she said "No." That was it. At first I could not look at her, my face and body tight. It was difficult to move, and I bumped around filling water buckets, throwing hay, putting on halters, leading horses out. Occasionally, we crossed paths. I kept my eyes down and moved around her. Eventually I found my gaze wandering to her flaxen hair or tawny legs when she wasn't looking. I watched her carefully. She moved slowly, avoiding contact with anything dirty. Her limbs appeared heavy though they were so small. She seemed to dream as she watched the water filling buckets. Had she always been so slow? I could turn out three horses to her one, unless Jack was helping her. The boy kept the momentum going, taking the horses out two by two, Lydia getting better and better with the big mare. Five days in LA. Five nights. I watched her with a sick fascination.

Clare began arriving most afternoons. She'd stand at the bottom of the stairs and call "Annie," not sharply, not crossly, but in a way that made it clear she knew where I was and what I was doing. If I said I was sleeping, she'd thump up the stairs and sit at the edge of the bed. If I didn't sit up, she'd lie down, head propped on a hand or she'd lie back and stare at the ceiling. Until one day she sat straight up and gave me a look. "Did you ever hear what they used to say about Stewart in high school?"

I leaned forward on my elbows. "What?"

"That he'd fuck a snake if someone held its head."

I stared at her. "Fuck a snake?"

"If someone held its head."

"No. I didn't hear that."

Clare nodded. "It's true."

After a long pause, I said, "You're saying I should move on."

"Yeah, you could say that."

"I have. I am. You just can't tell because I'm so hot."

"Oh, is that what it is."

"Yeah." I flopped back against the pillow, my arms flung to the side. "I am totally over that dude."

Clare shook her head but had the grace to say no more.

We stayed that way in silence for a while. I rolled onto my side, propped my head on one hand. "Train for me," I said.

Clare looked around the room, out the window and at the middle distance until I thought she wasn't going to answer. "Maybe," she said, finally. "But no lessons."

"Lessons seem to be slowing down. Way down."

"It's probably the heat."

"I don't have any training colts either."

"I'd do the training colts."

"The last one left a week ago. I haven't got any new ones."

"Things slow down this time of year."

"I think it's the horses running into the village."

Clare laughed. "Yeah, but you're under new management now."

"You'll do it?"

"No lessons. No people even. Just training horses."

I could do the lessons. I didn't want to do lessons either, but it was something I could do.

I went to Walmart the next morning for poster board and markers. I sat at a table in the snack shop and started on my ads. With three boarders gone and no training colts, I was not using the hay up as fast as I thought. I could sell some of it or slash my boarding fee, charge just enough to cover expenses plus change. I stared at the blank boards and decided to make two posters. If I sold the hay, then down came the boarding ad. If I got new boarders, I'd keep the hay. I marked the letters as carefully as possible. Hay for eighteen dollars (a small profit) board for two hundred and fifty dollars. Obscenely cheap. Training same as before.

Next, I stopped at the feed store. The place was empty, and the proprietor greeted me as soon as I walked through the door. I smiled briefly and went straight to the bulletin board, which was covered with handmade amateurish scraps of paper and index cards wanting to sell goats, cows, horses, donkeys, mules, and even a pair of alpacas. I rearranged these to make room for mine.

"Hay." The proprietor was standing behind me, studying my signs. "I believe you are the only person in this area with hay to sell. Most farmers are selling off part of their herds. Who is that?"

I had taken twenty pictures of Clare. Only one worked. In the others she looked anything but professional. In the one I now put on the bulletin board, she had wet her hair, and I had pulled it into as tight a French braid as I could. She wore a t-shirt, jeans, and chaps. She would train either English or Western. Pleasure horses or barrel racers. I pushed in the last tack. "That's Clare Raffienne."

"Really? Guess she's not at Silver Storm Farm after what happened. Doesn't look like her, though. But hay for sale. How did you manage that? This has been an awful summer. Ruined men who have farmed all their lives. Bless your heart for sticking it out."

I thought insanely, why couldn't I have married this man?

"Eighteen dollars. That's not a bad price this year for timothy and alfalfa. You'll have no trouble selling it. You must be a hell of a businesswoman to have some left. Is that really Clare Raffienne? I guess she must have gotten all that business about that house burning down cleared up. She and her Pap have been training forever."

"Right."

"Didn't you have someone else working for you? From out of town?"

"She's going back north."

"Well, it's been an awful year here. Maybe things are better up north. You'll have no trouble selling that hay, though."

The glow of the man's praise filled the truck all the way home.

The phone was ringing when I walked into the kitchen. I had four more calls that evening. One person asked about my new trainer. They had seen her run barrels when she was unbeatable. They wanted to know if she was going to jail. I told them no. They might be interested in her working one of their reining horses. Could she come to their farm and do it? I told them I would ask her. The rest of the calls were about the hay. I could have sold every bale in the barn. I took the calculator from my purse and sat at the kitchen table. I added and subtracted and went through the procedure two more times. I didn't want to miscalculate. Even so, it was a risk. Pap said a drought lasted seven years. But he must have meant the kind of droughts when the Sierra Desert turned into the Sierra Desert. Or the Okies went to California. If this was that kind of drought, I was done for no matter how I calculated. I believed instead that the rain would come again, that I would replace the three boarders when the grass grew, and Clare would bring a new kind of business to the farm. That is what I thought about the rest of that day and the following ones. The other images came to me only at night, when I was sleeping. In my dreams they were very clear.

CHAPTER THIRTY-SEVEN

It became so hot even Clare gave in to it. She lay on the love seat, a hand hanging to the floor and her long legs draped over the arm. She wore shorts, a rarity, and her legs, though strongly muscled, looked an unhealthy white. Her bare feet hung straight down. "Maybe we should go to the creek," she said.

I was on the couch staring at the ceiling. No need to respond. I had lost two or three pounds in water weight during morning stables and felt too weak limbed and lightheaded to move. A hot breeze rattled the screen door.

"I think someone is there," said Clare.

"It's probably just the wind." The sound became more definite.

"No, that's someone knocking."

"I don't think so."

"Get up and answer it."

I moaned, pulled myself up, and went to the door.

"There are dead bodies all over the yard." Lydia stood on the other side of the screen. "The cicadas are dropping out of the sky by the dozens."

I glanced past her, and through the waves of heat I saw the dull gray husks peppered across the dusty grass.

"May I come in?" She stepped past me. "Maybe the heat's killed them. They're covering everything. I hope the horses don't eat them." She looked around, avoiding my eyes. She glanced at Clare, who looked back without moving. "But that's not why I'm here... two things." She plopped onto the couch. "Jack has quit. Rollo and I got into a big fight... I'm surprised you didn't hear us, it was a doozy... and, anyway, I told him I went to California. And for some spiteful reason, he told Jack. I think he's sick of having that kid hanging around with his moon face, as Rollo calls it. Jack threw some kind of fit, throwing things around in the barn, swearing. I didn't actually see it, but Rollo did. Said he almost had to flatten the kid. Can you beat that? He told him if he could handle it being my fiancé and all, what the hell was Jack acting like such a fool for. Well, the kid really went berserk. Called Rollo a nigger and me white trash. Rollo had to shove him out of the barn. What did Jack think? That he had some kind of rights to me? I mean, he's just a kid. Can you beat it? Anyway he's gone, and I am not cleaning stalls."

I stared at her. "When did this happen?"

"An hour ago. I'm surprised you didn't hear them."

I should have told him myself. It would have been better than coming from Rollo. I hated losing him. I hated that he was gone. Jesus, Jack.

"And the other thing," Lydia went on. She took a deep breath, exhaled loudly. "It's too hot to go out. I'm down to five, maybe six lessons a week, at night after it has cooled off. It's just too hot. People don't want to come until later. Not that there ever was that many people. I'm barely able to buy groceries. The other day Rollo had to put gas in my car. He wasn't happy." She glanced around. "Don't you have air conditioning in here?"

"Nope."

This slowed her for a moment, then she went on again, "Look, this hasn't worked out the way you said it would. You told me I'd have plenty of lessons not to mention training colts. Well, I didn't. You misrepresented things."

I didn't mention her raising her prices or leaving town when she felt like it. "It's been two weeks since I asked you to leave. You don't need to worry about the stalls. You don't need to worry about lessons. In fact, stop giving lessons right now. Stop going to the barn at all. Just concentrate on finding another place."

"You can fire me all you want to. That's not what I am talking about. This business was never what you said it would be. You misrepresented it. You owe me. Getting me to come all the way from Connecticut. Bringing my horse. How am I supposed to find a new position in the middle of the season?"

"What are you talking about?"

"Two thousand dollars."

Clare sat up.

I rose and faced Lydia. "Get out of my house."

"I have it all figured out. I'll bring you the figures."

"Get up off this couch and go out that door."

Lydia stood, walked to the door, held it open, and turned back to look at me. "You owe me," she said before letting the screen slam behind her.

I sat down. Clare watched me. "You would have thought," I said, "I'd have noticed the cicadas had stopped screeching."

"Or Rollo and Lydia getting into it."

"Or Jack and Rollo having at it."

"It's been too hot to hear."

I laughed.

"You going to pay her?"

"Hell no."

"Might get her to leave sooner."

"Where in the world would I get two thousand dollars?"

"She's bluffing. It's just bargaining numbers. Offer five hundred."

"I don't have five hundred extra dollars. And even if I did, I'm not giving her a dime."

"Well, that's your call. It might be nice to have her gone is all."

"I could sell off more hay, I guess. But if it's a rough winter, we are done for."

"It's your call."

"I could sell my wedding rings."

Clare whistled.

"No. Nope. Not a chance. I'm not giving her a penny."

CHAPTER THIRTY-EIGHT

I told myself it was just curiosity that sent me to Little's Jewelry Store the next day. The place was empty except for Mr. Little, who was doing something behind the counter. His gray suit hung gracefully on his tall, patrician frame. He was the same age as Stewart's and my parents, and their social circles crossed though not by much. I would take my chances. He didn't look up when I stood in front of him. I saw that he was polishing a pair of silver birds. I placed my little jewelry bag on the counter. He glanced at me.

"Annie."

"I was wondering how much these are worth." I pushed the bag toward him. Mr. Little picked it up carefully; he meticulously undid the string that held the pouch closed and eased the wedding rings onto the counter. He picked up the wedding ring, held it to the natural light from the window, put it down, picked up the engagement ring, the one with the big diamonds, held it to the light, and put it down. "Probably not as much as you think."

I stared at the rings. He picked them up again. "I'll take a look at them through the glass." He went into the back room. I looked uneasily out the window onto Main Street. It was unlikely my father would be walking downtown at this hour. But still. My mind flicked on the possibility of the Walkers passing by, then flicked the image off. I stared down at the displays in the glass counter: ruby rings, a painfully exquisite sapphire necklace, and a pair of emeralds in a delicate filigree of gold. I sighed. I glanced out the window, at the door to the back room, at the clock. Ten-fifteen.

At ten-twenty, Mr. Little returned. He handed me the rings. "They are worth more than I thought. Retail about twenty-two to twenty-five thousand. Wholesale around ten. They are very old. Heirlooms," he added in case I missed the point. His face was a mask out of which blue, opaque eyes refused to register my existence. My skin tingled. I gathered the rings into my pouch. Jesus, next thing you knew I would be loading Stringtown on a trailer and taking her to some big sale barn like the one Lydia went to.

I drove my truck onto the highway to the post office across town, where I didn't know the staff. Inside, I considered the display of stationery. Should I include a note? But what could I say that wouldn't keep the connection going? I asked for a box and a quilted envelope. Styrofoam peanuts. I packed the rings over and over, layer after layer. I insured the package for twenty-five thousand and walked out the door. My mouth was dry and my hands were wet.

The ride back to the farm was okay. It was good to have it over. I was glad the rings were on their way to California. Closure, I thought. What a stupid, empty word. I had known Stewart in high school, dated him all through college, and then I married him. How did you get closure on that? You didn't, that's how. You just kept going, day in, day out, and eventually after a very, very long time those other years just faded away. How long will it take, I wondered. I thought about Clare. Things would work out somehow. We would do fine. I would ask her if she wanted to go to other people's barns to train. She probably wouldn't, but things would work out. We would get through the winter and then the spring rains would come.

I pulled into the Lowry yard before going home. Dust billowed around the truck. Hens squatted in the driveway, fluffing and picking at their feathers, using the grit for a bath. They scolded and waddled out of the way at my approach. I knocked on the kitchen door, and as I waited, sweat trickled down the middle of my back. Between the house and the barn, machines of all sizes lay piled in heaps next to tires, cans, car doors, seats, and chassis, a wringer washing machine, a cart with four flat tires, and numerous items too rusty to identify. I was visually sorting through this when I heard a heavy tread behind the door. Mrs. Lowry yanked it open.

"Why, Annie," she said. "What brings you here?"

"Is Mike around?"

Mrs. Lowry pushed open the screen door. She was a big woman, as solid and straight up and down and gnarled as an old tree. Once blonde, her hair had faded to a yellowish white. "Come in away from the flies," she said. "Mike's with his dad, baling hay. Might as well bring it in before it dries up completely, pitiful as it is."

She faced me squarely, wondering why I wanted Mike, but too polite to ask.

"I'm wondering if Mike could do some work for me—clean stalls."

"Well now, you'll have to ask him." She gestured toward a pot on the stove. "Let me get you some coffee."

"No thanks."

A quick look of surprise then hurt crossed her face before she could hide it. "Pepsi," she said, going to the refrigerator. "You're right; it is too hot for coffee." She plopped a piece of blueberry pie in front of me. The crust was thick, sturdy, and the berries hardly sweetened at all. Mrs. Lowry stood over me while I ate. When I was finished, she took my plate and glass to the sink and said, "There they come now." I looked past her out the window. Mike and his dad and grandfather were standing at the pump outside. Cecil Lowry raised the pump handle, cupped his hands under the flow, and splashed water onto his face. He wet his handkerchief and wiped the back of his neck. When he was finished, his son and grandson stepped to the pump and did the same.

Mrs. Lowry sighed. "I hate to see them baling out in this heat, started way before dawn when there's still enough moisture in the hay. Otherwise it's so dry it just shatters. They're probably done baling for the day. Now's a good time to ask."

The men didn't say anything as we approached. My mouth went dry and for some reason I stumbled over the words. Once I told them what I wanted, Mike glanced at his grandfather. The sun had turned his red hair almost as pale as his grandmother's. He was a handsome boy, but unaware of it and kept his face averted, his eyes looking restlessly past me.

Mrs. Lowry had brought the pie with her. She poked the plate at each of the men. They took the pie, ate it from their hands. Mrs. Lowry watched them for a moment and strode off.

"I'll be bringing your irrigation system back," I offered. "It works fine but Stewart got me one so I won't have to borrow yours. I appreciate your loaning it to me, though. What a difference. Maybe Mike can help me load it up." I paused, then in the silence, babbled on. "Your new one is broken, I guess. Maybe you could use some parts from this one. I hope that isn't why you're not using yours. Sorry I haven't gotten it back sooner. Has yours been down long? Mike, you think you could load the old one on the truck for me?"

"No use for it now," said Mr. Lowry.

"What?"

"That one Stewart got you. It really sucks the water."

I didn't know what to say.

Mr. Lowry finished the pie, raised the pump handle, cupped his hands underneath, bent and drank. He straightened up and wiped his chin. "You been to the creek lately, Annie?"

"No."

"Sometime when you've got the time, walk on over there." He paused. When I didn't say anything, he helped me out. "Down there at the bend you can see the creek from the road."

I'd noticed a creek bed full of rocks from the road.

"If we run out of water all together, it will be more than grass that's dying. I've got livestock to think about. They can get by with next to no hay for a while. We can bide our time. Water's different."

Mrs. Lowry returned with a bag full of tomatoes, sweet corn, zucchini, beets, and green beans. "You didn't put in a garden," she said, handing me the bag. She was right, of course, but how she knew I couldn't imagine. I could imagine what the men were thinking, though... what they had been thinking for some time.

"Well, have you decided if you can help her out with the stalls? She'd pay five dollars an hour, Cecil," said Mrs. Lowry. "And that's tax free, I imagine."

Mike continued watching his grandfather, who said, "Does tomorrow morning suit? The boy has some work to do this afternoon."

Tomorrow morning suited just fine.

As soon as I got back to the farm, I went to the generator for the state-of-the-art irrigation system and turned off the power. Let the place burn up. The green fields were an aberration anyway when the rest of the valley shattered under your feet. I went to the barn to count exactly how many bales of hay were left. Lydia was sitting on the stairs, bouncing her foot up and down.

"Annie, I've got those figures. I hope after sleeping on it you might reconsider. Rollo and I think they are very reasonable. But maybe we could negotiate just a little."

"I told you, I don't need any figures." I started up the rungs of the ladder to the loft, but the girl came over and held on to its side. She looked up at me.

"Well, anyway, I've got them. We figured it out very carefully. We think they are fair and you should too. I've been looking for you. We need to get this settled. Hopefully, without another scene. Anyway, I wanted to talk to you about the settlement because I've found a new position and will be leaving in a few days."

"Really? Well, that's good."

"I'll give you what I've figured out." She put her hand into her shorts and pulled out a folded piece of notebook paper and handed it to me. I reached down and took it and put it into my jeans without looking at it.

"Actually, I'll be leaving in two days. Very early in the morning. Rollo has gone ahead, but he will be back to pick me up."

"I've got to do my own figuring."

Lydia didn't move. "But I'll be leaving in two days." She stood as though she could stand there forever.

"I'll figure it out tonight."

"It's all figured out. It's on that piece of paper."

"Lydia, I'm not going to give you two thousand dollars. Not even close. If I give you anything, it's a gift. Now I've got to get some work done." If she doesn't leave, I'm going to smack her, I thought.

"There's something else. I thought I ought to tell you. I ran into Tony

Raffino in town. We got to talking and he brought up Stringtown. He says she's really his. He was saying how valuable she is now. He wanted to know if she was still here." She watched my face closely.

"She belongs to Clare."

"Tony says he has the papers."

I stepped down off the ladder. "I don't care what Raffino says, the horse belongs to Clare. It's none of your business, anyway."

"I just wanted to warn you."

"Well, you have."

She must have seen something in my face because she said, "I'll come by tomorrow. But you owe me," she added before she walked out of the barn and up the driveway.

That night Clare banged into the kitchen looking as scrawny and unkempt as a wild cat. "You know I love Pap," she said, "but I can't spend another evening with him."

I'd been sitting in the dark at the kitchen table sipping gin—the only liquor left in the house. I was dressed for bed.

"Go change," she directed. "Let's go for a ride."

"Lydia saw Tony in town. They had quite the little chat."

Clare pulled out a chair and sat down.

"He told her Stringtown belonged to him. He even told her that he had the papers."

"She's probably lying. Tryin to scare you. But I could sleep in the barn for a few days, just in case. Or do you want me to take Stringtown up the mountain? It's just, well..."

"Definitely not."

"I could put her in with Pap's horses."

"She'd just cause trouble. Lots of trouble."

Clare ran the flat of her hand over the kitchen table. "How much does this worry you?"

"What can he do? Besides, it's only you and Stringtown that he's after. And frankly, I think it's really just you. I don't think he cares about Stringtown."

"He cares about Stringtown, all right. I'll stay the night if you want me to. Sleep in the barn. But he ain't going to do anything out here."

"What do you mean 'out here'?"

"This isn't your fight. He's not going to drive onto your property and take a horse out of your field, even in the dark."

I wasn't so sure about that but let it drop.

"Anyway, let's get those horses and ride up the mountain where it's a shade cooler."

I doubted it was cooler anywhere in these hills, but I didn't know if I could stand another evening with my own four walls, so I obeyed.

The moon was full. Stringtown whinnied at Clare's approach—the first sign of affection for a living creature other than Lonesome I had ever seen the mare display. And for once, she didn't kick out when Clare saddled her, didn't swing her head around to bite, didn't jig and dance as Clare led her out of the barn or even as we started down the driveway. She kept pace with Lonesome, who stretched his neck and shook his head, happy to be out on the trail again.

Once we crossed the abandoned tracks and entered the woods, it was utterly dark. I followed Clare's lead by sound until my eyes adjusted. The dry husks of dead cicadas rustled like corn shucks under the horse's feet. The night was alive with the sound. Down the valley a whippoorwill began its insistent, lilting cry and along Cat Creek a few stubborn tree frogs trilled as though it might rain.

As we climbed, the air really did cool, and through the branches the stars were sharp, absurdly clear against the black sky. The sweat along my neck and back cooled and a slight breeze lifted wisps of hair from my face.

I was riding blind. I did not know these woods the way Clare did, and she followed no discernable path. I could tell by the labored movements of Lonesome's muscles underneath me that the climb was steep; we were riding straight up, not zigzagging to make it easier. Even so, Lonesome stepped smartly, stirred by the breeze and the night scents. It had been so dry there were no mosquitoes, just gnats, and they were asleep. A ground hog whistled and though her head went up, Stringtown's feet stayed on the ground. She stopped and looked back at Lonesome, who walked quietly on. His breathing was deep and regular. I watched the mare's powerful haunches move in rhythm as she pushed up the mountain. Her head bobbed with the motion. In the steeper places, I grabbed Lonesome's mane to keep from slipping off the back. I patted his neck and felt the sweat. "Let's rest the horses," I called to Clare.

She pulled up and stood amongst the trees. Stringtown wasn't even breathing hard. We stood until Lonesome's breathing returned to normal and then we climbed for another half hour. I recognized the lay of the land, the fencing among the trees, the still sharp smell of smoke. In the clearing around the ashes, the moon shone almost like daylight. We rode to the edge of the burned ground. Stringtown lowered her head, snorted suspiciously at the ashes. Cinders flew. She jumped backwards and stood with her legs apart, snorting and rolling her eyes, tamed but only half. Clare laughed and patted her neck. We sat on the horses in silence while Stringtown settled. Way down the mountain we heard a cry, not a scream, not a cough, but both and more. Clare and I turned our heads to listen. It came again and again, echoing along the hills, moving toward us, the sound carrying in the night air. It was the cry of a bobcat. He was moving, and with each unhurried step, he called a warning. He undoubtedly had a kill hidden somewhere and was returning to feast for the night. Abruptly the sound stopped, startling us with the silence. Clare sighed.

"After supper Pap likes to sit in his rocker and talk," she said. "I guess he's been alone too long. He just rocks and talks, talks and rocks. You know I love him, wouldn't hurt him for the world, but his voice just fills my head sometimes. I can't hear nothin but words." She stared at the ashes.

"Lydia is leaving in two days," I said.

"Sweet Jesus, there is a God."

"She still wants money."

"Well, give her some. Just enough to get her gone. We got enough to worry about without her hanging around."

"I sent my wedding rings to California. I had them appraised and was tempted to sell them, so I sent them to Stewart. Cat Creek is running really low. Because of that irrigation system Stewart bought. I should have figured it would do that. Anyway, I've turned it off. If it doesn't rain, the pastures will die for sure. I might have to sell more hay. How many bales do you think we'll need for winter?"

"I don't know. Eight, nine hundred." Clare paused. "Wedding rings. Lydia. Looks like you're cleanin house. I'd have sold the rings though."

I stared at the spot where the shack had been.

"Things always work out, Annie. I can work a horse or two for Pap and get them sold. I might even timber race S.T. again. Who knows, it might be fun without Tony getting on my nerves. And there's hell's own kind of money to be made timber racing."

"That would be your money."

"If we're goin to be partners, it's our money."

"Clare."

"You helped me when I needed it."

"We'll see." I couldn't remember a time when Clare had needed help. We dropped the reins, let the horses graze. They moved at will, prissily selected one patch of grass over another. For a moment I forgot that I had spent the summer sweating from the heat and loss. I felt the giddy relief one experiences when the worst of a serious illness passes.

Back at the barn, Stringtown stood quietly while Clare took a rag and wiped around her eyes and nose. When she picked up her feet to clean them, the mare did not try to chuck her into the wall, but when I went by, she bared her teeth and flattened her ears against her head. Same old Stringtown.

The next morning, I wandered through the house picking up clothes dropped where I had stepped out of them and threw them in the machine to wash. I gathered dishes from every room, ran them through the dishwasher. I went through the mail. I dusted. The empty house felt airy, unburdened. In the late afternoon I returned to the barn to do some cleaning there. I stripped Stringtown's and Lonesome's stalls and put five loads of clean bedding in each. I scrubbed water buckets, let the water splash across the front of me; patted it onto my face.

I sat head down on the steps to catch my breath and did not hear Lydia's approach. A pair of childish, brown legs crossed my vision. I looked up and she hesitated. "I'm leaving tomorrow. Can I have my check now? Rollo will be here in the morning."

"I have to go to the bank first."

"Can't you just write me a check?"

"I can't write you a check if I don't know my balance."

"Can't you just call them? Besides, I gave you the figures."

"You're crazy if you think I'm going to give you two thousand dollars."

"Rollo figured it out."

"I don't give a rat's ass what Rollo did. I'll give you something just to shut you up and get you out of here."

"You owe me. You got me here under false—"

"You might just as well shut up about how much I owe you and everything else." I stood up.

Lydia didn't miss a beat. "I'll come over as soon as you get back."

The unfortunate truth was she was right. The business hadn't turned into what she or I had thought it would be. She was lazy, it was true, but it was the heat and the drought that had killed off most of the business. And the horses running into the village. If you took Stewart out of the equation, she was relatively innocent.

You couldn't take Stewart out of the equation. But she was leaving and it would be over.

I turned the horses out early and went to the cool hushed atmosphere of Coleton's Citizens and Farmers. It was five minutes to closing and the bank was empty except for the tellers. I went to the window where a huge woman sat. I handed her my checkbook and asked if I could have my balance. She consulted her computer, punching in several numbers. Eventually, she wrote something on a bank receipt and handed it to me. The figures were a little higher than I expected.

I walked back out into the heat, which was like walking into a door. Feeling well off with the little extra, I stopped and bought a small pizza and a bottle of red wine.

Clare was in the kitchen when I got home. I showed her the pizza and held out the wine bottle by the neck. "Let's go for a swim. Have a picnic at the eddy."

She shook her head. "I feel like dancing tonight. I think I'll go to the Red Run. Just wanted to let you know I heard some guys talkin at the feed store. Tony isn't going to rebuild his house; he decided to go back to the city instead. Guess he's sick of the country. Not enough action." She looked at me and smiled.

"He's leaving?"

"Yup."

"Just like that?" He had been here all summer. He had been here when I came back. He and his men in black suits. He and his money. His threat of violence. "What about Stringtown?"

Clare shrugged. "I don't know. He could always send someone to get her. I think the whole thing's over and done with, though. Stringtown is good, but she ain't so great he'd spend time on her once he cooled off and moved on."

"What about the other horses? The business?"

"He's going to hire someone, put in a trailer. Some dude from out west."

"They said all that in the feed store?"

"Annie, you know Silver Storm's the biggest news around here."

"So that's that? He's just going to leave. Never come back."

Clare looked at me, her smile quizzical. "Well, sure. He don't belong here. This was always small time for him."

"It just seems strange. Tony Raffino gone for good."

"He was never one of us."

We watched each other. Finally, she said "I wish you'd come to the Red Run with me."

"I have to take care of business with Lydia. Anyway, I'd like to be at the eddy for a while. Take a swim."

"How come you never want to go dancing?"

"I will. Just give me some time."

I changed into my swimsuit and slipped out the side door to go to the creek. I didn't want Lydia coming around and spoiling my evening off. I would give her a check, but I suddenly wanted very much to be alone with the water and the silence.

The sun barely penetrated the woods on the path to the eddy and the air was breathless. The cicada skeletons were thick here. I could not keep from stepping on them and they made a curious popping crunch under my feet. How had I missed their passing?

I had brought a blanket and spread it on the coarse sand. It was old, but still had enough pile to protect me from the small stones. I took off my shoes and walked on it to be sure. I scrunched some of the rougher places under my feet, smoothing them out. The beach had widened since I'd been here last. I put the pizza in its box on the blanket and walked to the creek to put in the wine to keep it cool. I walked across the wide, pebbled beach and stopped when I came to the dark, thick muck. Beyond the muck Crab's Eddy was black… so black and thick I couldn't make out the bottom. There was a strong earthy smell and along the surface fuzzy circles of algae floated, a bright, cheerful green. Crab's Eddy lay still, paralyzed by lack of rain and in its motionless depths reproduction flourished.

I stared at the water. I thought of my state-of-the-art irrigation system built with the strength of a dinosaur. I saw again the Lowrys as we stood around their pump and my whole body flushed with shame.

I had sucked the creek dry—or almost.

I went back with the wine and sat on the blanket. I stared at the rocky bank across the creek. It really was a very steep climb to the top and over the other side to the Holler. I uncorked the wine and took a piece of pizza out of the box. It was still warm. I took a cup from the package of plastic ones I had brought and poured in some wine. I drank and ate a little and settled onto my back and watched as the sun lowered toward the back of the mountain. I adjusted my shoulders to find a more comfortable spot and closed my eyes. No good. I sat up, poured more wine, and drank it. I lay down again and wiggled my shoulders into the indentation I had made. Chocolate would be good with this red wine. Or some of that coffee I made this morning. Chocolate and red wine. Coffee and red wine. I ought to kill her, I thought. And with that thought, despair hit my chest with so much weight I lost my breath. I thought

I would die if I could not get away from the pain.

But I had learned to wait, to breathe slower. I held each breath carefully before letting it go. My hands fell to my sides and I lay motionless, emptied my mind of everything but a lone fly that buzzed around my head.

I fell into a half sleep and dreamt not of Stewart but the Lowrys. In the dream, the men were harnessed to my irrigation system, trying to pull it from my fields. They strained against the straps and as they did so, the leather made indentations in their shoulders. Mrs. Lowry and I waited in the shade at the edge of the woods, the boundary between their place and mine. We waited in silence while the sweat ran off the men and their faces turned red. Cecil Lowry's lips began to swell and his cheeks trembled. Still he would not stop pulling against the harness. I realized he was about to die. I closed my fingers around Mrs. Lowry's wrist. Her expression did not change. I waited and watched. All three men kept on tugging. I looked again at Mrs. Lowry, and she stood still as granite. I ran, staggering over the rough terrain. When I reached Cecil, I put my arms around him to hold him up. He was slick with sweat and slid through my grasp. I held on and on and on, my tears mingling with the sweat until Cecil turned into Stewart and I jerked awake. I was soaked and it was dark.

Nothing. Or maybe a crunching pop.

I realized it was the sound of crunching that had woken me. I turned around and Lydia stepped into the light the moon made on the beach. "Listen, hiding out here by the creek won't help. I'm not leaving until you give me some money."

"Well, obviously I don't have any money with me here."

"Then I'll just have to stay here until you decide to go back to the house and get it." Lydia plunked herself down on the blanket next to me and I burst out laughing. "You really are something else."

Lydia drew her knees up to her chest and wrapped her arms around her legs. "Yeah, I know. How about some of that wine. Do you mind?" She reached for a plastic cup and poured in some of the red wine.

"Do you want pizza to go with that?"

"Don't mind if I do." She took a piece from the box.

God she was cheeky. Give her just enough to get her gone, Clare had said. I sipped the wine, which was becoming unpleasantly warm. "I'll give you five hundred dollars. That should cover your moving expenses. I really can't afford anymore. I'm sorry it didn't work out any better than this, but you didn't need to go to California or raise your prices. And while we're at it, you could have been more enthusiastic. And spent more time in the barn. Or at the shows. Or with the training colts. You could at least have been nice to your students." Shut up, I told myself.

Lydia drank some more wine. "Anything else?"

"I think that covers it."

"I'll talk to Rollo, but five hundred will probably do just fine."

My cheeks burned. I could have gotten rid of her for a hundred bucks.

Lydia helped herself to more pizza.

Stung with the foolishness of my offer, I finished the wine in my cup, reached for the pizza box, paused, hand in mid-air, listening. I slowed my movements, picked up the plastic cups carefully so the paper didn't rattle, once again stopped, motionless. Nothing, just the night sounds. I quieted my breathing, carefully folded my towel. The night sounds became more distinct. But for some reason their familiar noise was no comfort. I looked around, turned and peered into the woods. They lay dark and untouched by the moonlight. Lydia and I on the other hand cast shadows in the clearing's milky light.

"What?" she said, looking from side to side.

I pulled on my socks, slowly tied my sneakers. I stood, was about to tell Lydia to get up, when a figure stepped from the woods.

Jack.

I jumped, though I was less surprised than I might have been.

"Hi, Jack," I said and at the sound of my voice, Lydia looked over her shoulder and stood. As she did so, three more figures stepped from the darkness of the trees.

"What are you guys doing here?" I asked as off-handedly as I could, but my voice rang false even to me.

"What're you doin here with her, more like it?" said Jack.

I didn't answer.

"You're sicker than she is for lettin her stay. White trash will sleep with anything: niggers, other people's husbands. Here she fucks your husband and you act like nothing happened. You deserve what you get."

"How much have you had to drink, Jack?"

Jack raised the beer can to his lips never taking his eyes from my face. "Enough."

Lydia crushed her plastic cup. "Go on home, Jack, you don't understand."

She didn't look at him. She was merely annoyed at this point, had misread the situation entirely. I picked up a corner of the blanket, started to fold it.

"You can leave that here," said Jack.

I continued folding the blanket. I even picked up the trash, stuffed the dirty cups and leftover pizza into a bag. At the same time I glanced past Jack at the other boys. I didn't recognize any of them.

None of them moved while I put the empty wine bottle in the sack. They just drank from their beer cans and watched.

I held the blanket against my chest and stepped toward the path. The four boys moved together and blocked my way.

"Don't be funny, Jack."

"You think it's funny she went and stayed with your husband, been porkin a nigger all summer, right under your own roof?"

"Oh, for God's sake," snapped Lydia. She was starting to be afraid. She crossed in front of me and tried to bluff her way out. She pushed against Jack. He grabbed her roughly by the arms and shoved her back. Lydia stumbled but kept her balance. All four boys came forward, formed a quarter moon around us. The tallest boy reached for Lydia. I threw the sack with the wine bottle at him. The range was too close and I got no momentum. He laughed an ugly laugh for it caught him on the hip. He picked it up, took out the bottle and looked inside, turned it upside down, shaking it. I dropped the blanket and stepped farther back, grabbing Lydia's elbow and pulling her with me as I backed toward the water. She jerked her arm free.

"How did you like them horses running through town?" said the boy with the wine bottle. "We shoulda burned the barn down."

I reached for Lydia's hand, tried to pull her into the creek with me. But, stupid girl, she struggled away, more afraid of those dark waters than what waited for her on the shore. I stepped backwards into Crab's Eddy. Algae clung to my legs and thick muck pulled at my sneakers. "It's impossible to swim with shoes on," my mother had always said.

"Get her," commanded Jack.

One of the boys threw a beer can at me—too far to the left. He staggered a little as he threw.

"Jesus, not like that," cried Jack. "Go after her."

"Are you nuts? That creek is prob'ly crawling with snakes."

Jack clasped Lydia by the shoulders, pushed her toward the other boys, and waded into the water. He did this in one fluid motion, so graceful I didn't realize what was happening before he grabbed my wrist. His grasp was like iron. I pictured him swinging the manure into the cart, day in day out, growing stronger with each toss. I only halfheartedly tried to break loose. I knew I was caught. He jerked me against his chest so hard all I could think of was walking into a door. I considered, for an instant, giving up. Then an image of a girl popped into my mind: the supple arc of her neck, her hair hiding her face as she darted, leaned over that other boy's hand so many years ago. Jack held me against him so closely it was like a lover's embrace. I bent my head and sunk my teeth into his shoulder. He shouted, jumped back, and struck at me with a fist. Too late. I was already in the water struggling through the silky filaments that closed around me. They hung in my eyelashes, around my arms and in my hair. The smell was sharp, alive. I held my breath, ducked under and swam as long as I could then surfaced, my lungs bursting. I needn't have worried. No one else ventured into the creek. Two boys held Lydia. Her skin was luminescent, fragile in the moonlight. Jack sat pulling off his wet shoes while the fourth boy carefully spread the blanket on the beach.

I ducked under again, but did not go far before my feet touched bottom. I paddled as quietly as I could downstream 'till I was out of the eddy and bumping into rocks. I half swam and half stumbled over them until the water was so shallow I was barking my shins more than swimming. I crawled to the bank opposite the one where I'd left Lydia. The algae matted my hair; I had to spit it out of my mouth. The Lowry farm was no more than a mile from here.

The porch light was on, but all the windows were dark. Two cats lay curled together on a rug next to a bowl of milk. I didn't hesitate, walked right up the steps, waking the cats. They blinked, stretched to their feet then caught a whiff of me. They hissed, arched their backs and fled. I knocked on the door. No one came so I knocked again louder. I heard muffled sounds and a light went on. To my relief it was Mrs. Lowry who opened the door. She had rollers in her hair and a man's bathrobe on.

"Good God girl," was all she said. She stepped back, motioning me to come in. "Cecil," she hollered over her shoulder. "Come quick."

I told them about Lydia, about Jack and the other boys. I said they'd been drinking and Lydia was still there—she wouldn't cross the creek with me. Mr. Lowry went to the bottom of the stairs and called, "Ken you'd better come on." Mike followed his father down the stairs. They were both buttoning their shirts and carrying their shoes, heavy ankle-high work boots.

Mr. Lowry fetched two rifles out of the hall closet. He handed one to his son. "Some boys from the Holler have that horse trainer of Annie's at the eddy. They've been drinking."

Ken rested the gun against the kitchen table and sat down to pull on his socks and boots. "You can't go, Mike," he said without looking up.

"Aw Dad."

"No." He straightened, nodded toward where I stood green streaked and dripping on the floor. "You'd better come though. She'll need someone she knows."

I apologized for soaking the seat of the truck, but all Mr. Lowry said was, "Is that path to Crab's Eddy wide enough to drive through?" I told him no and he parked at the edge of the woods and we walked in. The men swung wide flashlight beams ahead of us, their rifles resting on their shoulders. I heard crashing through the woods. Any other night I would have thought it the sound of a startled deer. In the clearing, Lydia sat wrapped in my blanket. She did not move at our approach, just stared into the light, her eyes dark caves in her white face. The Lowry's swung their flashlights into the trees. The cones of light picked out the trunks and patches of ground. The men swung the beams slowly, first through the woods then over Crab's Eddy, back into the trees on the left. It all looked as it should on a summer's night. Except for Lydia.

I knelt in front of her. "Are you okay?"

"I want Rollo."

"We'll go to the house and call him."

Mr. Lowry took Lydia's elbow, steadied her while she uncurled, straightened, and rose to her feet. They were both very careful not to dislodge the blanket. He walked her down the path toward the truck. She walked like someone who has been very sick for a very long time. She shuffled through the dead cicadas as though they weren't there. Mr. Lowry eased her into the truck, gathered the trailing blanket around her.

"I'm going to stay a while," said Ken Lowry. "Check a few things."

I climbed in beside Lydia. She tightened the blanket around her and stared straight ahead. No one said anything until we got to my door. Mr. Lowry helped Lydia out of the truck. "You ought to see a doctor," he said. I opened the front door for her. Cecil watched her go through with the end of the blanket dragging behind her. She was barefoot.

"Call my wife if you need anything," he said to me, "and you may want to call the police."

Lydia went straight to the phone. She dialed, waited, then hung up. She dialed again and asked for Rollo. After a second or two, she put down the receiver and, holding the blanket very carefully, wrote some things on my notepad. She dialed again, reading the number from the pad. She asked for Rollo and again wrote something on the pad. She repeated this—calling, writing, calling again—three times. She punched in numbers with one hand, clutching the blanket with the other. When I finally heard her say, "Rollo come and get me *now*," I left the room. I sat on the hallway stairs. I could hear Lydia's voice but not the words and when it stopped, I went back into the living room and found her sitting in the rocker still wrapped in the blanket.

"Rollo will be here in four hours," she said.

I went to the gun cabinet and retrieved the gin bottle. I poured two glasses. "Do you want me to call the police?"

"*No!*" Lydia swallowed some gin, shuddered, closed her eyes and took three rapid gulps.

I refilled her glass and waited. At length, she put the drink down. "I want a shower."

"There is no shower in the house. How about a hot bath?"

Lydia nodded, pulled the blanket tight, and went upstairs taking short, stilted steps. I heard the tub fill. A few minutes later I heard it drain. The pump came on and I heard water running up the pipes filling the tub again. I sipped the gin but it did not help. I picked at the algae in my hair. The tub drained again. Filled again. I went out to the porch. The algae had dried and though I brushed at it with my hands, it clung to my clothes, my skin, would not let go of my hair. I pulled at it and worked at it while I waited for Lydia. As I pulled at it the strong, disturbing smell came back. I wondered if I would ever be able to go to the creek again. I had gotten most of the algae off my body and was working my fingers through my hair when I heard Lydia come down the stairs. She had on a shirt and a pair of pants I'd thrown in the drier that morning. The pants dragged on the floor. She was still barefoot and her feet were pink and wrinkled from all the water.

I took my turn in the tub. There was no hot water left. I had to shampoo and scrub three times before I got the algae out of my hair. By now I did not care about its smell.

Lydia was still in the living room when I came downstairs.

"What do you want me to do?" I asked.

"I'll stay here until Rollo comes."

I poured her more gin. Lydia looked at her glass; sipped at it methodically until it was gone.

"Would you like to lie down?"

"No, just let me sit here until Rollo comes."

"I'm sorry, Lydia," I said.

She looked at me for the first time since I'd left her on the creek bank. She didn't move for what seemed like forever then leaned her head against the back of the rocker. Eventually, she closed her eyes. I didn't move. Lydia shifted, her head fell forward. Being careful not to wake her, I tiptoed to the front porch where I sat on the steps and waited. The wind had picked up and blew cicada carcasses across the yard into the driveway. It took Rollo less than four hours to get here. I watched his headlights swing down the valley, taking the turns without slowing down. He drove right across the lawn and stopped next to the back door. He went into the house, came out with his arm around Lydia, and they disappeared into the apartment.

CHAPTER THIRTY-NINE

It was mid-morning and still blowing when I woke and went outside. Swirls of dust rose off the driveway and the dry leaves made a racket in the trees. I noticed immediately Lydia's truck and trailer and low white sports car were gone, blown away it seemed by the sharp wind. I felt relief, low and shameful.

I squinted, raised my arm against the blowing dust. Clare's truck stood next to the barn, the only sign of life. The horses were not in the pasture. I didn't see their heads hanging over the Dutch doors or hear them banging against the feeders for breakfast. All I heard was the wind.

Clare leaned over a stall door, her chin resting on her arms, watching Lonesome. The bones on her wrist stood up like marbles and the muscles lay defined along her bones. When she glanced up, the look on her face shocked me as much as anything that had happened in the last twenty-four hours.

To cover up, I asked who had given the horses their breakfast.

"I did."

I walked to where she leaned against a stall. Lonesome was looking past us toward the driveway. I leaned over to pet him but couldn't reach. He took a bit of hay from the floor and chewed, still watching out the door at a spot in the driveway. The other horses all had their heads down, concentrating on their breakfast.

Clare turned to me. "Did you ever find out where Lydia and Rollo are from?"

"She told me Connecticut."

"I mean where in Connecticut. An address? A phone number? Anything?"

"No. I threw all that stuff out not long after she got here."

"No address? Nothing?"

"No." I thought of all those numbers Lydia had called.

"I was curious," said Clare, "because they've gone and taken Stringtown with them."

I looked into Stringtown's stall. I should have noticed right away that she wasn't there, but I hadn't. Now I saw the fresh sawdust piled high and banked around the sides. There were no piles to be picked up and no hay tossed around the stall the way Stringtown always did. I remembered yesterday afternoon as though from a long distance. I remembered cleaning out the manure and walking it in the wheelbarrow to the pile, the weight of the load pulling at my arms. I remembered dumping the loads of fresh bedding into the two stalls. I'd made ten trips and my arms ached after the first load. Even so, I had taken my time and raked the shavings to the sides to protect the horse's legs when they rolled. Stringtown's stall was just the way I'd left it.

Rollo and Lydia must have gotten a very early start. I must have slept like the dead not to have woken when the mare started yelling for Lonesome. I tried to picture Rollo and Lydia coaxing her onto the trailer. I remembered the patience with which Lydia, who had patience for nothing, led the dancing mare in and out of the barn.

I looked at Clare again. I couldn't read her. Her face was a mask and had changed, the edges blurred. She turned away from me.

"Are you sure it was Lydia and Rollo?"

"Yeah."

"Okay," I said. "It was Lydia. She made a lot of phone calls yesterday. Maybe I still have the numbers lying around. It's worth a shot."

"And we'll just call and say, 'We'll be by to pick up Stringtown.'"

"We'll find out from the numbers how to locate her and call the police."

"I don't have a bill of sale."

I didn't say anything.

"That's okay, Annie. It was a stupid idea. I was just ramblin. Without a bill of sale, we can't do anything. She's gone and that's the end of it." Clare straightened. "I gave the horses hay, but I didn't know how much grain to give so I didn't. You'll need to do that." She rubbed her face, pushed the hair away from her eyes. "Man, I'm tired," she said. "I think I'll go home and go back to bed." She started to walk past me.

"I'm so sorry."

"Annie, this ain't your fault. You got to get over thinking you can control everything."

"Clare," I said. "Something else awful happened last night."

She watched me quietly. She looked very tired. "I know what happened last night."

How? How did she and Pap and the Lowrys always know?

"I brought Lydia here," I said.

Clare put her hand on my shoulder. I would have told her the whole story then. I wanted to go into every detail. I wanted to tell her everything. I wanted to tell her what I'd seen and what I hadn't seen. I wanted to tell her about Jack. I wanted to tell her he had been coming here all summer and I thought I knew him. I wanted to tell her I thought he was just a kid that Lydia had invited into her shower because he smelled like the barn. I wanted to tell her the stuff I knew and what I didn't know. I wanted to tell her I should have left the farm alone, like she said. But a gust of wind blew some bedding into her eyes. She ducked, shielding them with her arm. She turned away from me, her elbow crooked around her face. "We'd better go," she said. "Before the storm hits."

I looked outside, noticed for the first time the heavy clouds hanging close to the valley. They were dark as the early dawn near the horizon. I paid attention to the wind. It had the flat, cold feel that is a sure sign of a change in the weather. I realized I had goose bumps.

CHAPTER FORTY

The rain began that afternoon. It started with a thunderstorm, not the false promises we'd had all summer but one that moved right on down the valley and cracked and boomed so close to the house I jumped and dropped my glass, shattering it in pieces. The rain pelted down on the roof and against the windows and tore the dry leaves from the trees. Within minutes, rivulets ran across the yard and into the culvert where the frogs had begun to trill so loudly I could hear them above the pounding rain.

The wind blew all night, shoving storms up and down the valley. At times the rain stopped and I thought that was it, but suddenly it turned light as day outside and the thunder cracked so near the windows rattled. It kept up until dawn when suddenly the wind died, leaving only the rain coming straight down in a steady beat.

On the third day, I headed up the mountain toward Pap's. The road was a mess. The rain had dug deep gullies around the rocks and the sides had turned to mud. It was tough going even with the four-wheeled drive. I kept bottoming out, the tires sinking to the axles in the mud, grinding the frame against the rocks. I decided it would be better to walk and jumped down to the road. It was a sizeable jump, and I slid on the mud when I landed. I caught hold of the door handle to keep from falling. When I got my feet back under me, the mud was up over the rubber bottoms of my shoes. It sucked at my soles as I walked away from the truck. I leaned forward to adjust to the uphill climb and within yards the front of my thighs began to ache. The rain wet my hair, my shoulders, and the legs of my jeans. It ran down my face and I blinked it out of my eyes. It was a warm rain, and the dry leaves had uncurled under it, softened and turned green again. The water dripped from them steadily and the tree trunks were dark and glistened. The grass, when I stepped on it, was spongy underfoot and it too had changed color.

I left the road and walked a short way into the woods. The wet leaves slipped under my feet more than the mud. I broke off a branch to use as a walking stick. When I knocked on Pap's door, I was sweating from the climb. He called me to come in.

Clare lay on the couch and Pap sat in the rocker across from her. There was a table between them and they were playing, of all things, Monopoly. The house was filled with the damp, sweet smell of hay, grain, and wet earth. All the windows were open to the rain.

Clare rose up on an elbow. Her face had changed even more. The angles were all gone and her mouth was fuller.

"Annie," said Pap, "you're soaked to the skin." He rose from his rocker. Clare sat up, made room for me on the couch while Pap fetched a blanket and draped it around my shoulders. "How about some nice hot tea?" I waited while he poured the boiling water in a cup and dumped in three teaspoons of sugar. I wrapped the blanket around my bottom so I wouldn't soak the couch.

I had my speech prepared and I commenced to give it. I turned to Clare. "I'm sorry about Stringtown. I'll go to Connecticut. I'll steal her back." I knew, even more than they hated the police, the Raffiennes hated leaving the area.

Clare touched my arm, then ran her fingers through her hair. "I can't ride for a while, anyway."

"But… I mean it's Stringtown. You're crazy about that horse."

"Yeah. Maybe later we'll go looking for her."

"Are you all right?"

"I just need to be careful, that's all. Just for a few months." She smiled at Pap. "Pap's going to have to take care of me." She laughed. "Ain't that a stitch?"

Pap settled himself in the rocker, pleasure spreading from his gray hair to his crossed muddy boots. He tried to hide it, but it was impossible. "Old man like me should be the one being looked after."

I didn't know what to say. My speech vanished. Clare yawned, rubbed her face.

"Maybe she'll settle down now, Annie. I don't like the way it happened but things generally work out for the best. A little one will often settle a female down. Why, I've seen many a mare that was wild as a March hare settle right down once she's had a foal."

"I'm no horse, Pap."

Clare pregnant? That wasn't possible. But, of course it was, actually made sense now that the words were out.

Pap tapped himself back and forth in the rocker. "How's that farm of yours, Annie? This rain ought to do it a world of good."

"I think I'm going to hang it up. That's one of the things I wanted to tell you."

"Tsk, Annie. That's no way to talk."

"I don't know. After all that's happened."

"Them boys won't bother you no more—they done their harm."

I looked away.

"You didn't know it would end this way, Annie."

"I brought her here."

"She come of her own free will. And the way I understand it, she wasn't exactly your best friend."

"That's just it."

Pap hesitated for a moment. "You didn't bring Jack and them boys to Crab's Eddy that night. No matter what your feelings was, Lydia done what she done and them boys done what they done without your help."

"And I got myself involved with Tony. You didn't have nothing to do with that, Annie. Or Stringtown."

"Annie," said Pap. "That land a yours can grow anything. You don't need no fancy horse business to keep it going.

"My marriage is over."

"That don't mean you got to run off."

"I don't think I was meant to be in the horse business, after all. I'm not like

Clare. I can't do the tough ones."

"Still no reason to leave. You got family here."

"Stewart was my family."

"We're your family, Annie."

My eyes stung. I blinked several times.

"Where you gonna go?" asked Clare.

"Back to school, I guess." I mocked myself with a smile. "You know, make something of myself."

Clare turned away, but even so, I could see her eyes were wet, something I'd never seen in my entire life.

Pap cleared his throat. "What about the farm? You going to just let it go wild again?"

"It's not mine."

Pap looked confused.

"It's Stewart's land. It's in Stewart's name."

For once, Pap had nothing to say. He just sat back in his rocker and stared at me, silenced at last by someone who would invest in land they didn't own.

I got rid of everything: the remaining furniture, my tack, the few pieces of farm equipment, the truck, the tractor. And Lonesome. I gave him to Clare once and for all even though she asked me not to.

We were standing in the barn, ill at ease with one another. Once started, the rain had no trouble returning. It rolled off the roof as though it had never deserted us, dropped like a gauze curtain past the windows. Even though she didn't want me to leave, I asked Clare for her blessing. What could she do but give it to me?

I had Lonesome in cross ties. He had aged since Stringtown had gone. For the first time, the weight was dropping from his back and his lower lip hung thick and wrinkled. His dark eyes were still bright though and held no reproach for me.

I told Clare to use the barn as long as she wanted, handed her Lonesome's bridle. Before she could answer, I stepped into her with an awkward hug.

"Come back some day," she said in a voice I didn't recognize.

I merely nodded against her thick hair, for I couldn't speak at all. I turned and walked into the shelter of the rain. Clare might easily have followed. Getting wet meant nothing to her, but she helped me as much as she could and let me walk away.

When I looked back, her truck was gone.

I didn't even bother to sweep the debris from the farmhouse floor. I opened the refrigerator door and tossed the few remaining bits of food into the yard for the birds. I threw clothes into suitcases. My father and I heaved them and the made-over gun cabinet into his station wagon. It was the only thing I took with me that was a reminder of what I had tried.

E. Compton Lee began her writing career as a freelance writer of nature and human-interest articles for magazines such as *Mother Earth News, Practical Horseman, American Country and Horseman.*

She is the author of the trilogy *Native, My Name Is Sloan,* and *2026,* as well as the standalone novel *The Heartbreak of Josie Whitt.*

Born and raised in the Hudson River Valley, she left that region at the age of eighteen and embarked upon a journey which immersed her in a multitude of cultures. The knowledge gained from those experiences is what is used when she writes her novels.

E. Compton Lee lived in the Allegheny Mountains of Pennsylvania and western Maryland for fifteen years, where she worked as a therapist and ran a horse business. She currently lives in Williamsburg, Virginia, where she writes full time.